Anubis Reborn
Copyright © Scott R Lean, 2020

1st Edition

ISBN 978-0-6489410-0-2

Anubis Reborn © 2020

Published by Scott R Lean

Author: Scott R Lean

Editor: Nadia van der Merwe

Formatting: Scott R Lean

Interior artwork: Scott R Lean

Special font Zombified: Created by Chad Savage

Cover art and photography: Scott R Lean

Cover models: Adam Grace • Thea Dobbins • Scott R Lean

Back cover wall art created by: Jordan Bruce (Jay Beez) and the crew from Brightsiders (www.brightsiders.com.au) In association with Mackay Laneway Project. Visit them at: www.facebook.com/MackayLanewayProject.

ANUBIS REBORN

SCOTT R LEAN

Dedication.

This book is dedicated to Jessica, Brandon and Oliver.
With special thanks to my wonderful wife; Nilza, my
family and friends who have been my rock and my
inspiration.
To my amazing editor Nadia, thank you for your hard
work, diligence, ongoing belief and support.

This book is also dedicated to the memory of mi
hermano; Rony Coro Rosales.

For the hearts that love and have been loved.
For the minds that dream and have dared to create.
For the eyes that see below the surface of reality and fish the
depths of the unlimited sea that is life.

This story is for you

CONTENTS

CHAPTER ONE

The Death of Death

THE HARSH HEAT OF the day lingered until, like the changing of guards, the cold, sharp air of the night rushed into the chamber caressing the beast's face like an eager lover.

The body lay still, ready for the final preparations. All the internal organs had been dutifully removed, as the sacred rites demand, and the priests were now safe and warm in the sanctity of their houses. The god had often thought of those priests, going about their castrated lives, tending to all the trivial tasks required of them to guarantee safe passage into the next life. For those who cannot afford the elaborate and expensive funerary rites needed to obtain entrance to the

Underworld and all its splendour, such access can only be accomplished by living a life of servitude to the gods.

He often wondered if these priests truly believed in the sacred knowledge that had been divulged unto them. Did they really believe in the afterlife? In the Underworld? The gods themselves? Did they believe in him? They do all the dirty work and the preparations are performed according to his strict written instructions, but do they even believe that he exists?

It matters not, he thought, for on the day that these men expire and if they have paid their due, they would lay eyes upon him and know that their faith had not misguided them.

Indeed, it was of the utmost importance that he not be seen by human eyes until the time comes when man casts off his mortal shell. For the sight of the beast would surely drive a mortal to abrupt insanity, or worse. There are of course illustrations, hieroglyphs and statues of him – the god of the dead, but the true horror of his appearance would cause the body's excretive orifices to surrender their contents simultaneously and at great speed, perhaps even still the heart.

That is why he only comes when the tomb has been vacated. It is a solitary vocation to be sure, but he was never one who took pleasure in the company of anyone except the dead. He shook his head to lose such thoughts, *must concentrate*, the work comes first, always first.

The god looked down upon the corpse of the recently deceased. In life, he was a nobleman of the royal court, well respected within his community. Ehren Bahl was husband to Ariaten, father of two boys and one girl, and lover to many women (as well as a few men). Now he was just a dead man, a body, but not yet an empty vessel, for the soul still resides inside, waiting for the god to release it, to protect and guide it along the treacherous journey through the Underworld.

The soul would have to pass the trials of the five gates, before arriving at the Hall of Final Judgement. It is there that the person's heart would be weighed against the Feather of Truth. If their heart were proven heavier than the feather, they would be judged as a wicked person. For those unfortunate souls, swift punishment would be afoot, as their essence would be devoured by the monstrous Ammit. The god of punishment was a terrifying sight to behold, with the head of a crocodile, the torso of a leopard and the arse of a hippopotamus.

As with most situations in the physical life, the wealthy could buy their way into heaven via the purchase of a book of the dead. The book contained all the incantations needed to pass through each of the five trials, even the final judgement. Each scroll was customised according to the budget of the prospective purchaser. Even the most basic book was well beyond the reach of common folk. Luckily for Ehren Bahl, he had the wherewithal to purchase such a book and very soon he would be freed of his corpse and be on his way.

The blade of Osir was the tool for the job. The legendary blade was created by the father god Osiris, for the express purpose of extracting spirit from flesh. Even a small cut from the blade would be sufficient to begin bleeding the soul, the larger the cut, the quicker the process of extraction. A direct strike to the so-called third eye, or to be more specific, the pineal gland that resides behind the area, would release the soul instantly, as this is the physical location of the spirit of man.

The beast drew Osir from its sheath with loving reverence, and recited the sacred prayer. The blade began to vibrate gently, harmoniously, as if humming along to the prayer. A soft, violet glow emanated from the blade as the vibration intensified, signalling that Osir was primed for its divine purpose.

Suddenly, a putrid scent reached the sensitive nose of the god – sweat and poor hygiene. It was then overcome with the unmistakable smell of mortal fear – the pungent stench of urine and excrement which wafted into the beast's nostrils, followed by a gasp of pure horror.

Word of nobleman Bahl's death had spread rapidly throughout the city, and for some, the allure of gaining vast and immediate wealth was far too appealing to ignore. Jalel knew that there would be a very small window of opportunity to sneak into the tomb of Ehren Bahl and relieve him of his wealth before it was sealed in with him for good. Little good such wealth would do a dead man. Besides, Jalel did not believe in the Underworld and the only god that he revered was himself. All that he needed to do was gather a handful of like-minded individuals and pay a handsome fee to the sentries posted at the entrance of the tomb. A risky gamble, but Jalel was convinced that the payout would be enough for all involved, to live a life of elegant excess.

'You will not have much time,' mumbled the head sentry. 'Maybe you will have forty minutes, maybe if the gods are at your back you will have one hour. I cannot know for sure.' He looked down the main entrance to the lamp glow from deep within, then the sentry continued, 'We have orders to seal this tomb as soon as the lamps inside burn no longer.'

Jalel grunted appreciatively and pushed a heavy purse into the hands of the anxious guard.

The thief's crew were well experienced at silently sneaking into homes and stealing anything of value, leaving the premises without waking its sleeping occupants. However, not even the worst nightmares, conjured by the twisted minds of the criminally insane, could have prepared the group of four men for the sight they were about to behold.

As they turned the final corner into the main burial chamber, Jalel loosed his bowels and his bladder as the beast came into view. A cold wave of fear flooded over him as he tried to scream, instead the sound came as a deep guttural howl. The hieroglyphs he had seen painted on walls and the many statues of the god, were not even close to describing the beast looming ahead.

The beast stood upright at over eight feet tall. It was covered from head to toe with fine, short, silky black hair, which shone with a blueish hue when kissed by the light. The creature had a strong, muscular physique, like that of an endurance athlete. Its loin was covered with a modestly sized cloth that appeared to be a cross between leather and silk, with brilliant gold emblems embroidered into it. These symbols glowed a bright florescent green, as did an amulet around the beast's neck. A bright red glow filled the eye sockets, as no pupils were set there. Its long, pointed muzzle terminated in a small angular nose, beneath which came a deep roaring growl that revealed rows of sharp canine teeth of a brilliant white, each one carved with intricate symbols and housed in blood-red gums, dripping with clear viscous saliva. Large, sharp, angular ears sat permanently in an upright position. Each were pierced with a long gold piece that followed the full contour of the outer edge of the ear, with five thin bars pointing inward.

A terrified Jalel spewed forth another sound, a word, a name, 'Anubis?'

'Humans and their greed,' Anubis growled under his breath. 'How dare you disrespect this sacred place!'

Jalel fell to his knees, unable to muster the strength and courage to move due to utter terror. The god started toward the awestruck men. 'You will pay for this intrusion with your pathetic, miserable lives,' he howled, spraying a jet of saliva, reminiscent of a rabid mongrel being worked into a frenzy.

One of the many perks of being a god, was the ability to perceive all that was occurring in one's presence at the same time. In fact, time itself could be slowed, almost to the point of ceasing, and whilst this was in effect, a god would have almost all the time in the world to consider carefully the situation at hand.

He could easily move at speed among the group, slicing them open with the aid of Osir, allowing their souls to leak out of them, leaving them to wander eternity among the living as mere shadows, unable to experience all the things that make human life so fulfilling. Or, he could reap their souls and drag them to Durat to spend eternity in excruciating agony, where their souls would be torn apart in the most painful and inventive ways of torture imaginable, only to be remade in the very next instant. The whole gruesome process would be unrelenting, repeating over and over for all of time. Lastly, he could make an example of them – rip flesh from the bone and leave their mutilated bodies at the entrance of the tomb as an example to others with similar aspirations, their souls left to rot along with the flesh.

The god mused over these thoughts with pleasure. The first option appealed little to Anubis as it would let them off too lightly. Sending them to Durat was very tempting, but sentencing them to eternity in hell could be considered a little too severe. Besides, he was not a vengeful god, like some. That led Anubis to his decision: let them rot in their shell to putrefy and simply cease to exist.

Anubis considered the blade Osir, still humming in his

hand. He would not use this as a weapon for he did not want to bleed their souls, he wanted to trap the spirit in the flesh. So, the beast dropped the blade to the floor and rushed toward the scattering humans, releasing a blood-curdling howl as he did so. He rushed directly through the gang and up along the long passageway, out to the entrance of the tomb so that none could escape.

Anubis paused to savour the moment. He could feel the cold desert air at his back, titillating the fine hairs of his nape, urging him to spring forth and take the lives of the four despicable cowards that were staring fearfully into their coming fate.

He was not a vengeful god, yet it was not often that Anubis had the opportunity to exercise his physical prowess. Although he was always faithful to his divine work – after thousands, upon thousands of earth years spent dutifully escorting the dead across the threshold – he always cherished the chance to punish the wicked. The first kill was always the most thrilling, and the last was the most precious, worth taking his time as he couldn't be sure of how many hundreds of years away the next kill would be.

Sharp claws caught the first man by the throat and eased in like a blade into hot desert sand. He ripped downward, opening the chest and abdomen, spilling the bulging intestines outward. Taking full advantage, Anubis took a hold of the writhing gut and swung the flailing body into the next target a little further on down the passage. The blow knocked the next man facedown and then the beast was upon him. He grabbed the back of the man's head and, lifting it rapidly back, slammed it down to the earthen floor, smashing his face into a bloody pulp. Just to be sure, he then twisted the head around one hundred and eighty degrees, and the eyes swung wildly from the crushed skull.

Seeing the horrific carnage, the third thief turned, desperately scrambling back into the lamplit burial chamber, howling and whimpering like a dog that had been run over by a camel. Anubis lunged and caught him by the arm, which he tore down upon to rip from its socket. A fountain of blood sprayed out of the gaping wound, and fine tendrils of flesh, sinew and long tentacle-like veins writhed in the stream of blood, which was now rapidly painting the floor. Anubis raised the severed limb high above his head, then brought it down upon the thief's skull, producing the sickening crunch of cranium fracturing as it caved in. The man's tongue had been extended from his mouth in the beginnings of a scream when the makeshift weapon was brought down hard upon his head, teeth smashed together, and the tongue was cleanly cut off. A surge of bright red blood and shattered teeth came gushing forward when he fell to the ground, dead.

A new wave of primal savagery came over Anubis, filling every part of his being with ecstasy.

Jalel was still on his knees when the horrifying beast dropped the glowing blade to the floor and ran past him and his men, up toward the main entrance. It seemed like an eternity kneeling there, waiting for death to strike him down. He could hear the screams of horror behind him, and as Jalel knelt frozen by fear, his eyes did not move away from the glowing blade. He was going to die here tonight, of that he was sure, but panic-fuelled desperation sought his options of defence. Surely if there were any weapon that could wound a god, it would be one that glows mysteriously, perhaps by magic?

Jalel was familiar with the sweet rush of adrenaline. The thrill of thieving, the muffled screams of a well-raped woman or the last whisper of a murdered man. All had given him the utmost satisfaction. That same rush had wrought new purpose: survival. Jalel's heartbeat quickened, beating so hard that he could hear it pounding in his head. With lightning speed, he reached out to grab the blade Osir. To his shock the weapon was vibrating powerfully, so much that it was extremely difficult to hold on to. Jalel turned, getting to his feet to face the beast, who had just liberated Khaled of his left arm and was now busy re-arranging the man's skull with bloody enthusiasm. It was now or never.

The pungent, sweet smell of blood and brain made the god's head swim with unbearable pleasure. However, his ecstasy suddenly came to an abrupt halt, interrupted by indescribable, blinding pain. Anubis howled in agony, thrashing around before realising the cause of his distress. Looking down, his eyes fell upon Osir protruding from his right-hand side.

Osir, his accomplice, his old colleague, his only true friend, the only one who bore witness to his sacred work. Anubis turned to see Jalel running up the passageway on his way to freedom.

Anubis grunted with pain as he pulled Osir from his body. 'Old friend, it is fitting that you would be the end of me,' the god croaked, before letting out a wry laugh. The sad irony was not lost on the beast, for his closest companion, the deadly instrument that he had used countless times to harvest the souls of others, had been turned upon its master.

He could see his essence oozing from him; yes, even gods bleed, even gods have a soul, and now it was slipping away slowly, very slowly. The great god of the dead was doing just that ... dying.

CHAPTER TWO

A Blaze of Glory

THE ALARM CHIRPED incessantly at Sam, in a desperate attempt to rouse him from his deep slumber. With a heavy groan, he shot out his hand, fumbling to retrieve his mobile phone and silence the enthusiastic, yet unwelcome, tone that had so rudely awoken him. The sorry sight of his bruised knuckles greeted him as his eyes opened.

'Ugh,' he moaned, his head pounding as the memory of yesterday's training session came rolling into his mind like a wave into shore, crashing with the sand, then dragging back out to sea, only to return again and again.

Just six more weeks until the National Mixed Style Martial Arts Championship, but already he felt battered and bruised. Oftentimes, the preparation was more brutal than the fight itself.

Sam had performed exceedingly well at the state Kung Fu titles a few months ago. He won his bouts convincingly, with no broken bones or loose teeth. Indeed, he still had a straight nose, no breaks there either, a rarity in his sport. His build was tall and streamlined, his musculature was well-defined, yet not overly engorged. Sam was fast and he hit well above his weight, often taking his opponents down with relative ease, and so, at the age of twenty-four, the title of state champion now hung around his neck.

He shook his head as a new thought entered his mind, *work, got a big week ahead.*

He groaned again, rising out of bed, rubbing the still sleeping palm of his hand over his short brown hair, *better get up and get your ass into the shower*, he coached his unwilling body into action.

'Morning, Sam,' chimed Arthur, Sam's boss. 'Big weekend?' he asked, noticing Sam hobble through the back door with a gentle limp.

'Morning, Arty, just pulling up a little sore from yesterday's training,' Sam smiled, winking at Arthur. 'You know what they say, no pain, no gain.'

The ritual pleasantries were interrupted by the piercing shrill of the shop's front door buzzer.

Wincing at the sound, Arthur said, 'I better go tend to that, early customer, good start to the week.' He then turned from Sam, 'You know what they say, no pain …' He didn't finish the sentence as he scuttled away with surprising agility for an older gent.

The front of the shop served as an art gallery, no Renoirs hung in its showroom, but it boasted some noteworthy pieces to be sure. At the back of the gallery there was a custom picture-framing section, the true money-maker of the business. Whilst the occasional sale of a nice landscape oil painting certainly plumped the ledger, it was the mum and dad customer looking to hang their little darlings on the wall that really paid the bills. It was there that Arthur greeted the customer, a distinguished-looking gentleman who was clutching a large portfolio under his arm.

'Good morning, sir, how can I assist you?' Arthur addressed the customer as he crossed the showroom floor, his walk keen, yet graceful.

The customer turned with a slight startle at the shrill tone of Arthur's voice. However, he quickly regained his composure, displaying a wry smile. 'Oh, yes, hello there, I'm hoping that you may be able to advise on repairing this piece of artwork?'

Arthur extended an inviting gesture for the customer to set down his precious cargo. 'Certainly, sir, let's see what you have there.'

The stately man placed the portfolio gently onto the carpeted bench that Arthur had gestured to. He then proceeded to remove his fine trilby hat, which revealed his balding head, lined along each side with dark, yet greying hair. He turned to Arthur and a generous smile cracked through his salt-and-pepper beard before he cleared his throat, 'Yes well, I have an extremely rare and valuable family heirloom here, that has suffered some damage at the hands of a removalist,' the customer said with a tone of dismay.

'Oh, I see. That is unfortunate,' Arthur huffed. 'Careless! I suppose it's quite hard to get reliable help these days,' Arthur remarked with slightly exaggerated disgust.

'Uh, yes, indeed. Anyway, allow me to introduce myself. Donovan is my name, Donovan Banks,' he said extending his broad hand.

'Arthur!' the storekeeper replied, taking Donovan's hand firmly.

The piece of art was clearly a valuable hand-painted papyrus, very old and intricately detailed. The painting depicted some sort of funerary scene, with beautifully scripted hieroglyphs across the top. There was something unusual about the colours, however, being somewhat monotone, rusty brown except for some fine gold detail. The frame had suffered damage to the bottom right-hand corner and the glass had cracked and run diagonally across the piece.

'You mentioned that this is a family heirloom? Any idea how old this may be?' Arthur enquired.

'Old … very old,' Donovan replied, bringing his face close to the broken glass lovingly, admiring the papyrus as if viewing it for the first time. 'I would appreciate you doing your utmost to ensure that this is handled with premium care – money is no concern.'

'Certainly, Mr Banks,' Arthur replied respectfully. 'We will have to make a new frame as this existing frame is beyond repair, I'm afraid. Obviously, the glass will be replaced, as should the mountings and backing – with new acid-free materials.'

Donovan nodded, accepting the recommendations. 'I will trust your fine judgement, Arthur. I cannot stress enough how valuable this item is to me, both the sentimental and monetary value is beyond disclosure. Please proceed with the necessary repairs and if you would be kind enough to forward me an invoice, I will arrange for your prompt payment.'

The dollar signs started spinning in Arthur's mind. *Oh, what a wonderful customer! Why can't every customer be like Donovan Banks?*

Sam was concentrating hard on his work as Arthur waddled up toward him, whistling some old tune that Sam was not familiar with, and neither was Arthur he suspected, as the key and pitch produced a dreadful noise that made Sam cringe.

'We have an interesting one for you, Samuel,' Arthur called out as he ambled over to his young framer. Sam winced at the sound of his own name. Oh, how he hated being called Samuel.

'An ancient Egyptian papyrus,' Arthur purred as he set the piece down next to Sam.

Raising himself from his bench, Sam removed his reading glasses, pressing the inside corners of his eyes in a half-hearted effort to manually adjust his focus. For what seemed like an extraordinarily long period of time, he stood and stared at the piece, then as a pilgrim prostrates himself before a holy shrine, he bowed down to better inspect the beauty before him. 'Wow, this is …'

'Amazing?' Arthur offered.

'Stunning,' Sam replied. 'This looks very old, the papyrus is extremely dry, but the ink is still in incredible condition. Is this a full reframe?'

'Yup, the works!' Arthur chimed, his smile forming a large toothy grin. 'We'll go all the way with this one, new matting, backing and re-hinge. Let's do preservation-grade glass and choose a nice ornate moulding from stock.'

'Cool, sounds like a plan,' Sam said as he put his readers back on for a closer inspection. 'I think we should treat it for mould too.'

'Excellent, I'll leave it in your capable hands,' Arthur replied as he left Sam to the job.

The papyrus was even more vibrant once Sam had carefully removed it from its damaged prison, and like a newly freed inmate, it almost seemed to be breathing in the fresh air of the open world. He found himself unable to glance away from the images before him. The scene depicted some sort of casket with the head of a dog, which lay upon an ornate gold table with intricate carvings on the legs. At the head of the table was a man who was wearing a mask which was also of a dog, much like the head of the casket. The man in the mask held a staff in one hand and a bloody dagger in the other. At the foot of the table there were two other men, one of which was very tall and strange looking, with an elongated head. Floating ethereally above the scene were hieroglyphs, intricately scripted with obvious loving care. The bulk of the piece was crafted with a rusty brown ink, which had bled very slightly into the papyrus. Sam felt an urge to run his bare fingers over the pigment but refrained from doing so.

Sam opened the lid to the gas box and lowered the work into the cabinet, then he added some powder into a tray which was positioned above a heating lamp. Once heated sufficiently, the powder created a potent gas that would kill any mould spores present on the papyrus. He lowered the lid and secured the locking clamps.

'Now, time for lunch,' he mumbled to himself, then he walked away saying back to the papyrus, 'don't you go anywhere. I'll be back soon.'

Sam had eaten entirely too much food for lunch, but then again consuming extra calories was necessary as far as his martial arts training was concerned. Nevertheless, he felt bloated and sluggish as he returned to the workshop. The memory of his lunch lingered on his senses. He could still taste the unusual combination of bananas, potatoes, rice and barbecued chicken, especially the chicken. He could almost smell the juicy bird cooking over the coals, delicious barbecued smoke – burning? His stomach turned and he felt a sudden rush of panic at the thought now stabbing him in the head, *the papyrus!*

The gas box was designed to gently heat the powder and never exceed the preset temperature, even when operating for days at a time. However, it was obvious that something had malfunctioned. Sam's worst thoughts were confirmed as he hurried to reach the box. The papyrus had indeed started to burn at the edges. Panic seized Sam as he fumbled at the locking latches and lifted the lid. The smouldering papyrus was ecstatic to greet the oxygen-rich air as it combusted into flame and a small, yet comically looking mushroom cloud of dark smoke and gas punched Sam in the face, sending him reeling back against an adjacent bench. The air became trapped inside the young framer's lungs by the toxic smoke that had made its way down through his windpipe, sealing it like a cork in a wine bottle. Flailing about in the now smoke-filled room, Sam desperately tried to make his way to fresh air and safety, but his oxygen-deprived brain refused to cooperate. A sickening dizziness overcame him, and he stumbled and fell hard to the floor. He collected the edge of a bench on the way down, opening a deep gash in his forehead and allowing his blood to do what his body could not – escape. As his lungs began to burn from lack of oxygen, he could feel the dense smoke gently envelop him like a mother covers her child lovingly with a soft blanket.

So, this is it. Really, this is how it happens? Defeated by smoke and fire? The fight in him was failing fast. The seemingly inevitable onslaught of death gripped the young man with fear and his pants filled with urine, his bowels verging on expulsion.

As his eyes began to grow dim, he fancied that he could see something shifting in the smoke, something or someone stirring there, moving toward him. A man? No, more like a dog, yet impossibly tall and dark, difficult to discern, moving slowly toward him. As his vision finally left him, he could hear a whisper in his ear, a whisper? No, it was a low growl. Then darkness, silence, cold and then nothing.

CHAPTER THREE

The Usual Questions

ERICA MURPHY WAS A bright, well-educated young lady. She had worked very hard throughout her school life, as she was not about to settle for the type of life that her parents had. She had been told on many occasions that she was also rather beautiful. Her almost flawless skin was lightly spattered with faint freckles, and her dazzling green eyes could capture the vaguest of glances and warm the coldest of stares. Indeed, Erica Murphy was the type of woman who could choose any path that she may desire to traverse in her life.

Her mother had wanted her to be a school teacher. 'Lead the little children,' she would say, her accent thick with Irish moss. 'You should teach the little ones, for they are the future and knowledge be worth more than all the king's gold.'

'Be a doctor!' her father would say. 'Thieving bastards, the lot of 'em! Cost me a darn arm and a leg to go see that witch doctor down the valley!' he would complain as he sipped at his pint of ale. 'Yup, be a doctor lass, then the money will be rollin' in.'

Erica had eventually decided to become a newspaper reporter. She had a natural curiosity – she needed to know what was happening in the world, what was happening in her city, her street, even her apartment building. She knew most of her fellow tenants by name and occupation, the state of their relationships and the little scandals that rippled throughout their lives.

She had long considered the newspaper business to be somewhat nostalgic, the last remnant of a romantic, bygone era. A time past, where her father would sit at the breakfast table and deliver the daily headlines to the family from the morning paper as they busied themselves with the start of the day.

The reality of the job, however, was considerably less romantic. These days, people could see all the latest news with a swipe of a finger across their mobile phone screens. As such, it was becoming increasingly difficult for newspapers to find enough exclusive content to get to print.

Therefore, being a newspaper reporter was a demanding, time-consuming job. Erica would be lucky to be home by eight o'clock most nights, as she often stayed back at the office to finalise her daily reports for the following morning's press deadlines.

Erica was an only child, born to aging parents, who were in their early forties when she was conceived. Her family had migrated to Australia from Ireland in the mid-nineties, when she was an infant, and as such she had no living memory of her birth country. Australia was the only home that she had known. She grew up in the outer suburbs of Brisbane, before moving into the city as a late teen to attend university.

She had experienced a relatively pleasant childhood, despite that her parents were both alcoholics. She would struggle to recall any day when her parents were not to be found with a drink in their hands of an afternoon. Her father would often say, 'Damn hot today! Get me another cold one, Mother.' Her mother would amble out of her chair and into the kitchen, complaining under her breath as she went, her cigarette hanging precariously from her lip as she did so.

Despite the drinking, her parents were never violent and only had kind words for their daughter; however, a young Erica Murphy often found herself organising her own dinner and if she were to be taken on a night excursion to the local pub, she would have to make do with a pack of potato crisps for a meal.

As a little girl, Erica liked to sing and dance, often staging impromptu performances to her delighted, yet inebriated, parents in the family living room. It was the later hobby dancing that she pursued into her teens. She discovered that she had an intense passion for Irish dance, as she felt somehow connected to her heritage. The music would pulse through her veins and each step felt etched into her soul, as if she had danced them before. She often pondered if perhaps she had lived in some little Irish village in a previous lifetime. It was her natural talent at the craft that provided Erica an invitation to become a professional dancer. She may have been able to travel the world, dancing her way into the hearts of many. However, she decided to follow her sense of destiny and studied to become a reporter. Eventually she applied for a job at The Open Eye, a well-respected newspaper based in Melbourne, and it was there that she became the paper's community-interest reporter.

An impromptu afternoon meeting was about to begin, and Erica fidgeted about in her chair, uncomfortable with the flirtatious stare from her co-worker Kurt. *What a creep!* she thought. She had been warned from day one by the ladies at The Open Eye that Kurt was somewhat of a womaniser who liked to wear shirts and pants that were one size too small.

'Alright, people, listen up. We have had a huge day,' said Tom, the chief and editor of The Open Eye. 'As you all know, we had a murder take place in the early hours of this morning. A pregnant woman was killed downtown. The story is priority, going to print asap. Kurt has the lead on the story, no one else is to touch it. Is that clear?'

There was the nodding of heads about the room in agreeance with Tom's request. Erica may have nodded along; however, she was not agreeing within her mind, nor her heart. She had been waiting for an opportunity to advance her career and she knew that she would not hesitate to get the jump on Kurt if Jessica, her police contact, found any new information for her.

Although she had enjoyed working at The Open Eye for the past seven months, she was already growing weary of being stuck on community interest stories. The only highlight so far had been the gallery fire story that Tom gave to her.

Cunningly, Erica decided to wait and sit by Sam's side for a doctor to come by, pretending that she was his girlfriend, so as to avoid being denied any useful information as a reporter. A few rival reporters had already been turned away, as they tried to get the hot scoop.

As she waited that first day, to maintain her cover, she would take Sam's hand into hers if a nurse called by to check the patient's vitals. As she held his hand, she felt warmth and life desperately hanging on inside the unconscious framer. She also found a subtle strength lingering below his skin, a presence of energy. Was Sam somehow trying to reach out to her? Was the framer trying to hold onto something, anything in the physical world? Like a tether to reality for his unconscious mind? Was she to be his anchor to life? Erica decided that she could be that anchor. She would come again tomorrow and the day after that and for as many days as necessary until the young man regained consciousness.

A second murder had occurred the previous evening, the brutal and senseless killing of a woman in the back seat of her car. Erica's frustration grew as she reflected on the details while heading to the hospital that morning. Apart from wishing to advance her career, Erica just wanted the killer caught and she wanted to help make that happen. Her only real sense of usefulness at that time had been achieved by pretending to be Sam's girlfriend. Such role-play had filled her with a small sense of purpose, that she could somehow help the young man. In the ruse, she found some compassion toward the framer and it caught her off guard. She was currently not in a relationship anyway, so what was the harm in pretending to be in love with him? There was a chance that he may not wake up at all, that he may not live. In any case, she needed the story – she had to get something for Tom. The framer's story had to be told, and she wanted to be the one to tell it.

The doctor finally arrived and explained the situation to Sam's pretend girlfriend. With nothing more to be done for the day, Erica smiled at the doctor and stood from her chair, leaned over and placed a kiss upon Sam's forehead, then she whispered, 'See you tomorrow, my love.'

'Welcome back, Samuel.'

A bright torch light shone into Sam's eyes as he regained consciousness. Sam had no idea what was happening, or where he was. He was confused and scared. Was this heaven? Hell?

'My name is Doctor Campbell. You're here at Excelsior General Hospital.'

'Huh, hospital? Wait, what?' Sam asked groggily. He had a massive headache and his brain felt heavy, very heavy, as if it were full of water-soaked cotton wool, and his body felt numb and sluggish.

'You're quite the lucky man, Mr Baker. It really is a miracle that you are still alive. Do you remember what happened to you? The fire?' Dr Campbell inquired.

Yes, the fire! Sam's memory came upon him with sudden ferocity. 'I remember, but what happened? How did I escape?'

The doctor did not look up from his chart as he answered, 'From what I understand, you were found just outside the rear exit of your workplace, unconscious and suffering from toxic smoke inhalation.'

The last thing Sam remembered was laying on the floor of the workshop, desperately trying to breathe. How did he get out? 'Did somebody rescue me?'

'That I don't know, I'm afraid. I'm sure that your girlfriend or employer will have more information for you. Oh, I should also give you a warning that the police will want to talk with you, to close their investigation,' Dr Campbell stated dryly.

A look of confusion alit Sam's face, 'My girlfriend? I don't have a girlfriend … Do I?'

Dr Campbell offered the warmest smile that he could muster, then he added, 'All of your vitals are stable. You have been in a coma, so it would not be uncommon if you did have some loss of memory. But if I were you, I would not forget that I had a girlfriend like yours. Devoted, quite pretty, she was here every day by your side. Mr Baker, I'd like to keep you here for a few days yet. We also want to run a few more tests now that you have regained consciousness. I'll check back with you in the morning, until then please do your best to eat some solid food. If there is anything you need, the ward nurses will assist you. Goodnight.'

The doctor left Sam to his thoughts, oh so many thoughts bouncing about his mind. The usual who, what, how and why would not leave him with a sense of ease, nor satisfaction. Nonetheless, most of the answers came during the following day. His parents, his Kung Fu master and the police came to visit Sam; yet, his supposed girlfriend was nowhere to be seen. Even a local newspaper reporter came sniffing for a sensational survival story and as always, the inevitable question arose.

'So, how did you escape from the workshop?' asked the overly pushy reporter, her pretty face doing its best to show a display of sincere curiosity, although Sam had considered that for her this story was less than exciting. He also noticed that she seemed a little on edge, as if she were worried that someone else may come into the room, maybe a nurse or doctor.

Nonetheless, Sam did his best to answer the reporter honestly. 'Look, it's like I've told every other visitor that has come to see me, I don't know how I escaped. I blacked out inside the workshop, then I was found on the ground outside the building. My boss has no idea, the police have no clues and I have no memory of what happened after I passed out, nothing except maybe for the dog. I think there was a dog.'

'A dog?' the reporter raised an eyebrow as a small smile appeared, 'What breed of dog was it?'

'I'm not really sure,' Sam replied, suspicious that she thought him mad. 'It was big I think, big and black, tall, but like I said, I'm not really sure. The room was full of smoke and it was dark.'

'Uh-huh, okay, well I think we are done here. I'll leave you to rest.' Standing from her chair, the reporter handed Sam her business card, 'Just in case you remember anything else, please give me a call.' Then, smiling, she added, 'It was very nice to meet you, Sam. I hope you are fully recovered soon.'

Sam watched her as she walked away with a certain confidence that having a figure like hers provides. Sam was a sucker for exotic, mysterious women and Erica certainly was both, a little shorter than him, with a slightly athletic build and yet she had all the right curves where they needed to be, but for Sam it was her beautiful face framed sharply by her long, straight, jet-black hair that captivated him. Her pale skin and slight accent hinted that she may be of Irish descent, and a quick glance at her card seemed to prove that fact. He took a deep breath and released a sigh as he realised that a woman like her would probably never be interested in the likes of him, *too smart* he surmised. The reporter's direct questioning led Sam to believe that she was strong-willed and far too beautiful to be interested in a simple picture framer. Even though she had no engagement, or wedding, ring on her finger, Sam was sure that there must be a long line of successful, handsome suitors chasing after her. Then glancing down at the business card, he replied softly to himself, 'Thank you, Erica Murphy. It was very nice to meet you too.'

It was getting late by the time Erica made her way across town on her way to her small apartment. Her bus had run behind schedule as the police cordoned off an area of the city, due to a third murder that had taken place downtown. Whoever was committing these horrific crimes was becoming more brazen. This time, the killing had taken place in the afternoon. It was the first kill during daylight hours, where before they had all occurred under the cover of darkness.

The victims so far were all women, their bodies found fully or partially clothed, with no signs of sexual assault and various savage wounds, as if someone had ripped them open with their bare hands. No prints had been found. Erica found it difficult to conjure an image of the monstrous fiend responsible for these horrendous murders.

Erica shuddered as she rounded the corner of her block, the poor victims deserved justice and she wanted to play her part. Too bad she was not put on to report this story from the beginning – that honour went to Kurt, the so-called 'ace' reporter. He was only successful because of his father's wealth, influence and contacts. *Nevermind*, she thought, she had a contact within the police force who agreed to give her any new leads on the story. Perhaps if she got lucky, she may be able to promote her way out of doing community interest stories, such as the one she covered yesterday morning.

Oh, her poor fake boyfriend Samuel, or Sam, as he insisted on being called. She felt a pang of sympathy for the poor guy – he almost lost his life in that fire and he did lose his job, for a while at least. The business suffered some damage and it could take a long time for the police investigation and insurance payout to be finalised before the place reopened again. *Nice guy*, she thought. Erica didn't mind playing the role of his girlfriend as he slept. Although she was rather nervous that her ruse may be discovered, she had escaped the deception flawlessly. Besides, she had gotten the story and that was what mattered. She did feel bad for the framer, however. Maybe she might catch up with him sometime later, perhaps offer to take him for coffee or to dinner, maybe a change of scene and some good company could help speed up his recovery. Erica realised that it must be awful for Sam not to remember all the details of what happened to him, and what of the dog he spoke of? She had debated with herself whether to include the dog part in the story, then she decided that any little detail could garner some new information about the fire.

Erica opened her apartment door and stopped as she entered the hall. A shiver ran up her spine and settled at the base of her skull, tingling and prickling like an extra sense, a warning that something was wrong. Was there someone in her apartment? The fear grew as she found the light switch and turned on the lights. No one and nothing out of the ordinary presented itself to the harsh light that now drowned the room with a warm yellow glow. She ran to the kitchen bench and seized the largest knife she could find, then as quietly as possible, she moved down the hall and looked in her bedroom, closet and finally the bathroom – only to find that everything was okay. The buzzing sensation at her nape would not let up, however, and she felt that someone was watching her. With caution, she crept to the windows that looked down from the third floor of the apartment complex. Slowly she parted the blinds and peered down onto the darkened sidewalk at the front of the building. Again, there was no one. A sudden movement shifted in her peripheral vision to the right. There! Across the street moving into the shadows under the tree line a figure stood in the dark looking back at her.

'Damn it!' she mumbled to herself. She could not make out any definite detail about this person, except for guessing that it was a man and not a woman due to their height and solid build. A sickening feeling punched her in the gut, what if he was the killer? Why was he stalking her? Had he been here in her apartment? She startled at the sudden chirping of her mobile phone. She hurriedly reached into her back pocket to retrieve it and glanced at the caller ID – it was her police contact. Erica quickly looked back to the street; however, the mysterious figure was no longer there. It was gone.

'Erica here.'

'Hi, Erica, it's Jessica. You asked me to give you a call if I discovered anything new with the murder investigations.'

'Yes, Jessica, what have you got for me?'

'Maybe a potential witness, but she's scared stiff, won't talk to us. Thought you might be able to use your charm on her to get some info, but remember our deal, no one can know that I am helping you. They will have my head for it, but I want this bastard caught,' the officer replied.

Again, Erica scanned the sidewalk below, and the unease that she had felt waned somewhat. She briefly considered telling Jessica about the mysterious watcher, but she decided that perhaps her imagination and nerves had gotten the best of her. 'Yes, no problem, Jessica. You have my word, thank you,' Erica said reassuringly. 'Have you got a name and address for me?'

Since leaving the hospital, Sam was struggling with various ailments, but perhaps the most disconcerting of these were the mental issues that he seemed to have developed after the fire. He often blacked out, or at least that's what he believed to be happening. He was often abruptly becoming aware of his surroundings and wondering how or what he had been doing, sometimes as much as a few hours had passed while he was unconscious.

After such episodes, his body ached and felt bruised, as he always felt after a fight, and he suffered from horrendous headaches. He also became aware of some sort of presence watching him. Was someone following him? Perhaps the police or a private investigator? Often, he would feel the presence and he would quickly turn to try to catch a glimpse of whoever was responsible for the unease that he felt, but to no avail. Dr Campbell had assured him that these symptoms were not entirely uncommon with people who had been through a traumatic experience and that they would recede over time.

They say that time heals all. Well, Sam was feeling presently unenthusiastic about that saying, as the minutes appeared to tick by at a snail's pace, yet still his ailments continued. He felt heavy and congested in his chest, as if it were still filled with smoke, and at length he tried to cough it up, but to no avail. At times he felt as if his thoughts were somewhat dampened, as if they were a long way from his comprehension. Sometimes Sam struggled to concentrate on whatever task he was trying to accomplish and so, in frustration, he would give up. *Oh well, thinking is overrated,* he conceded.

CHAPTER FOUR

Breaking News

SAM HAD ALWAYS ENJOYED the welcoming fresh air and beauty of the great outdoors, but lately he felt it very difficult to muster the enthusiasm to step out of his small unit. He spent most of his time shuffling back and forth between his bed and the kitchen, when the craving for sustenance forced him to do so. Sam's one-bedroom apartment was basic and modest, but comfortable enough for the young man, besides, it was all he could afford on his wage. Small as it were, Sam found it cumbersome in his present state of mind, and he loathed having to traverse the short hallway which led to the living area and through to the kitchen.

Sam's mother had called in to see him earlier that morning and left him feeling grateful for the barista-made coffee and a copy of The Open Eye that she had brought for him. After his mother left, Sam picked up the paper. He was curious about any new details about the fire that may have come to light. The killer had made the front page again, another murder yesterday, this time in broad daylight. Sam's stomach turned at the thought of the suffering that the victim would have endured while being ripped apart alive, then a rush of adrenaline hit him with a wave of nausea. Why? Why did he feel sick at the thought of the murders? Blood and gore had never bothered him before. He quickly folded the paper and placed it down on the bed next to him.

Needing something to take his mind off the subject, he turned on the television, but the same headlines dominated the local and national broadcasts. Suddenly frustrated, he began flicking through the channels looking for respite when a familiar face appeared. There she was, Erica Murphy, pretty as ever, but Sam's delight quickly soured as the topic being reported became apparent.

Beside Erica stood a Channel 5 News reporter, her stern features displayed a picture of dire seriousness. 'I'm standing here with local newspaper reporter Erica Murphy, who has just spoken with a potential witness to the murder that occurred downtown yesterday afternoon. Good morning, Erica, are you able to provide our viewers with any new information regarding these grisly murders?'

'Yes, good morning to you, Christine. Very early this morning I spoke with a woman who witnessed a potential suspect who may be involved with committing these recent killings.'

'This is huge news, Erica. That is the first and only witness so far, was she able to help with the investigation?'

'Unfortunately, due to the sensitive nature of what I have learned, I can only divulge what the police have allowed me to release to the public.' Erica looked directly into the camera with reluctance, then drawing a deep breath, continued, 'The witness described an individual at the scene in the company of a large black dog. This individual was interfering with the body until they were disturbed by an approaching vehicle. This person had then fled the area on foot. I'm afraid that is all I can mention for the moment, and the police will release a detailed description of all the facts as soon as they are able. They are seeking the public to come forward with any information, and as always, The Open Eye will continue to pursue the story.'

'Thank you, Erica. Well you've heard it here first, folks. Hopefully some important details have emerged.'

Sam switched off the television, his head spinning. A large black dog? Did he hear that correctly? A new wave of nausea accosted him, which was quickly replaced by a sense of panic. It couldn't be a coincidence – exactly how big was this black dog? Could it be the same creature as the vague memory of what he saw emerging from the smoke, and what of its human master? Could they be responsible for his salvation, and if so, how are they connected to the horrible murders? He had so many questions and knew of only one person who might be able to provide some answers.

Sam lunged from his bed and retrieved his wallet and his mobile phone, then after a brief flurry of activity, he found Erica's card and dialled her number. The ringtone repeated several times before her slight Irish accent greeted Sam with a recorded invitation to leave a message. Sam did not want to leave a message, so he hung up and redialled.

'Hi, you've reached Erica Murphy from The Open Eye. I'm unable to take your call right now, but if you would be kind enough to leave your full name and a brief message, I'll return your call as soon as I'm able. Thank you.'

'Hi, Erica, it's Sam Baker here. Uh, we met at the hospital. You did a story on the gallery fire. Anyway, if you could please call me as soon as you can, that would be greatly appreciated, thanks.'

Sam was not always a patient man and he disliked waiting for other people to return his calls. As he paced the living-room floor, he realised that it could be days before he heard back from Erica. No doubt she would be busy with her sudden and important involvement with the murders story, Sam reasoned.

'Screw it!' he blustered as he scrambled to make himself decent. He would just have to try to track her down in person.

Erica felt a great sense of unease as she walked through the town square after her television interview. She had just blatantly lied to the public – live on national television. The whole situation had spiralled out of control. First, there was the entirely unbelievable story which was provided by the so-called witness, who was in so much of a state of shock that her mind conjured such an incredible account – one beyond Erica's comprehension.

Secondly, Erica had to go to the police and attempt to convey the witness account just as it was divulged to her, with as much sincere professionalism as she could muster. The police response was predictable – it was not surprising that the detectives were less than enthusiastic to take the young reporter's story seriously, and even less willing to release an official statement on the matter. So, she threatened to let the public know all the bizarre details herself, but the police had warned her that there would be legal consequences if she chose to do so, and strongly outlined the exact content of the witness account which could be released.

She also had to deal with the occupational risk she had taken to come forward publicly instead of handing off the witness and accompanying testimony to pretty-boy Kurt. She knew that she would be reprimanded by her editor and by Kurt himself, so she had to force her every footfall heading in the direction of The Open Eye. Her mobile phone was safely off in her bag – she had to manage one thing at a time.

As she walked, Erica flicked through her notebook and once again recalled in the story as told to her by the eyewitness and how that information had been stretched to fit the story she spoke of on TV earlier that morning.

The real details were this: yesterday afternoon at approximately one forty-five pm, a woman named Marina was making her way back to work after her lunch break. As usual, she had parked her car in the underground car park below the building where she worked as a bank clerk. As she made her way across the lot, she heard a growling sound like a dog might make when fiercely guarding its favourite bone – so she decided to investigate. Ahead, between some parked cars lay the mutilated body of a woman and crouching over the body was … well as Marina had described it, a werewolf. It was large, with the body of a man and the head of a dog. It was covered from head to toe with fine, short black hair. She had the presence of mind to take cover behind the closest vehicle and continued to observe the bizarre creature, its mouth dripping with fresh blood. Then it began to make a slight crying sound, like a whimper, as it studied the corpse. In its right hand was a long piece of wire, which looked like an opened coat hanger, with the hook still formed. It appeared that the beast had used the crude device to pull the victim's brain out through her nose. As Marina watched in horror, a car came into view. This startled the beast and it stood up sniffing the air. The creature ran off on two legs, like a man, but with amazing speed, and then it was gone. It was only afterward that she cursed herself for not having the presence of mind to record the event on her phone, and Marina stated that she felt frozen by sheer terror and it simply did not occur to her to do so.

It took all of Erica's persuasion and reassurance to convince Marina to open up to her, but once she started talking, it all poured out of her like a burst dam, forcing Erica to scribble down the information as quickly as possible. Even as she continued to stroll along the street, Erica found it a little difficult to read some of her notes. Poor Marina was petrified and too afraid to go to the police for fear that she would be publicly humiliated, or worse yet, the beast that she had claimed to see may track her down and come after her.

Erica didn't know what to make of Marina and her story. Clearly, she was suffering from some type of delusion, perhaps caused by the trauma of witnessing such a horrific murder. One thing stuck with the reporter - the dog part. A large black dog – she'd heard that description before – Sam told her that he thought he had seen a large black dog just before he succumbed to the smoke at the gallery fire. She made a mental note to call him later that evening to see if any more details about the fire had returned to him.

Erica decided it was best to avoid the office until Kurt and most of her co-workers had vacated the building. Yet, she realised that she would have to bite the bullet and call Tom to see if she still had a job to go back to. Erica thought the call went as well as to be expected, mostly a long-winded tirade about professional respect and the official pecking order. To Erica's surprise, Tom actually commended her for having the guts to attempt to give her career a boost into the big league and it was for that very reason that he was not going to fire her. Regardless, Erica was pleased that she had managed to have her name attached to the story, even if it meant that she had to take such drastic steps to do so. Talking to Christine at Channel 5 News was a risky gambit, but it appeared that it had worked.

It was about seven o' clock when, from a distance, Sam spotted Erica entering The Open Eye building. He had spent most of the day out the front of the place, hoping to catch her. He had tried to call her every hour or so, but had no success. The administration clerk at the front desk was also less than helpful. After trying Erica's direct office line, an offer was extended for Sam to wait in the lobby, which he did for more than two hours before hunger drove him to a coffee shop across the street.

Now was his chance. Erica was at the door and Sam called out to her as he rushed forward, but she did not hear him over the noisy street. She swiped her access key and entered the building. By the time Sam reached the door, Erica was gone and the door closed. Sam spotted a cleaner inside, busily polishing the lobby floor. He called out to her, waving his arms wildly so as to draw the woman's attention above the noise of the polisher that she was dancing back and forth. It worked. The cleaning lady turned off her machine and ambled over to the front door, but refrained from opening it.

'What do you want, love? They're closed in here, you know,' she shouted through the thick glass, her smile warm. Yet the woman seemed eager to have Sam be on his way so that she could get back to her work.

'Oh yes, I realise that, but it's very important that I speak to Erica Murphy, the young lady who just entered here a moment ago,' Sam replied calmly.

The cleaner waved her hand about, shooing Sam to move away, 'Oh, love, I'm not allowed to let just anyone into the building. Why don't you try giving her a call?'

'Ah yes, I've been trying to call her all day you see, but I've had no luck. Please, it's extremely important. I may have some information about the murders,' Sam pleaded.

At this the woman's work-worn face turned ashen, her kind tone became deathly serious, 'Well, love, I think maybe you should contact the police department.'

An urgent impulse came over Sam, an opportunity to gain favour, but he would have to lie through his teeth which always discomforted him. Sam prided himself on generally being an honest man, but he felt that this was important enough to warrant a few white lies. 'I will, but I need to talk to Erica first. We have been working on this story together you see. Perhaps you saw us on the news this morning?'

'Yes,' the cleaner replied warily, 'I did see it briefly.'

'My name is Sam and I am a zoologist. I have been working with Erica and I believe that I have identified the breed of dog that was seen at the murder scene. Please, ma'am, you could be of valuable assistance in helping us solve these awful crimes.'

Sam's impassioned plea seemed to have worked, as the cleaner hastily raised her access card to the door panel and with a click, the door opened and Sam slipped inside. 'Oh, thank you … Sorry, what's your name?'

'Sandra is my name,' the cleaner answered tentatively.

'Okay well, Sandra, I will make sure that I let everyone know how very helpful you have been,' Sam said.

'Oh, thank you, love. I just hope that they catch the person responsible,' Sandra replied with a prideful smile.

Sam was about to ask which office Erica worked at, but quickly realised that would blow his cover of working with her. Oh well, how hard could it be? He headed for the elevator.

Erica was happy to find that her office floor was empty, cloaked in darkness, a sure sign that Tom had been on his final round and that everybody had left for the day. The only source of illumination came from the occasional monitor that had been left on, providing ample guidance for Erica as she reached her desk and switched on her computer. In the elevator on the way up, she had decided that the first item of business would be to do a quick check of her emails. Surely there would be at least one from Kurt, expressing his displeasure at Erica for withholding from him such pertinent details about his story. To her delight, there were no emails from Kurt. *That's odd*, she thought. She retrieved her mobile phone and turned it on. There were no missed calls from Kurt either, but Sam Baker had called multiple times and left one message. Sensing Sam's urgency, Erica began to listen to the recording.

'Working late?' came a sudden voice from right behind her. Erica jumped in her seat and swivelled in her chair to see who was speaking. It was Kurt.

'Oh, Kurt! You scared the crap out of me!'

Kurt stood dead still, staring coldly at Erica. His handsome face lit by the unflattering glow of Erica's computer screen, devoid of any sign of emotion, 'Hmm, I wouldn't want to scare you, now would I?'

The steely response sent a chill down Erica's spine, a familiar sensation that she had felt the previous night as she entered her apartment – something felt very wrong. She attempted to lighten the mood with a half-hearted attempt at humour. 'Oh, you know, no rest for the wicked,' she chirped.

'Yes, I know exactly what you mean,' Kurt paused, as if he were measuring his next words with caution, 'and you know, Erica, because you have been very wicked, haven't you?'

'Look, Kurt, I'm really sorry if I've stepped on your toes with the whole witness story. It just all happened so fast.'

'I don't give a damn about your territorial pissings!' he spat out his words with such venom that Erica began to fear the direction that the conversation was heading.

'Please, Kurt, there's no need to be so rude. I've already apologised to you. What more is there for me to say?'

'You're a little bitch!' Kurt snapped savagely. 'You think that you can bat your eyes at me and I will just let this be? You are overstepping your mark, slipping into a dark world from which there is no return and you will have to pay the price for your stupidity.'

Kurt's face shifted into an ugly contortion of rage as he moved toward Erica, and she feared that he may reach out and strike her.

'Hello? Erica Murphy?' came a somewhat familiar voice from the opposite side of the room. Erica's eyes desperately searched through the darkness, to the far side of the office and was delighted to see a familiar face, a face that she gazed upon for days in the hospital.

'Sam? I'm over here!' Erica exclaimed with a huge sense of relief.

Sam spotted the pair and started in their direction. Kurt took a few steps back, away from Erica, as Sam approached. Erica watched her unwitting saviour as he drew nearer, 'Sam, what are you doing here?'

'Hi, Erica, yeah sorry it's kind of important. I've been trying to call you all day,' Sam said with a sense of urgency.

As Sam came close to her, Erica decided now was the opportune time to force Kurt to leave.

'Samuel Baker, this is my colleague Kurt Banks,' Erica turned to face her aggressor as she gestured with her hand toward Kurt.

Erica was stunned to see Kurt's expression change dramatically from anger to fear, his eyes wide in horror as he stared past Erica. Cracking sounds, like the noise of breaking twigs could be discerned over the hum of computers, followed by painful groans and animalistic growls. Erica was afraid to locate the source of the horrible sounds which seemed to come from behind her, the terrible creep of tingles at the base of her skull prickled her with fear. She followed Kurt's gaze, slowly turning her head back toward Sam and upon seeing where he stood, she reeled backward in her chair with fright, falling onto her back, adrenalin shooting up her spine, snatching the coming scream from her throat.

CHAPTER FIVE

So it Shall be Written

ANUBIS SHOULD HAVE CONSIDERED himself grateful for having his soul preserved from an eternity of roaming this god-forsaken world. Instead, what happened to him was surely a punishment and not the salvation that he believed it would be.

After being cut with Osir, as the god lay dying on the tomb floor, word of the ordeal had reached the ears of the sacred priest, who had been alerted by the tomb guards after seeing Jalel flee in terror. Due to his poorly condition, Anubis was unable to crawl away and die in peace and so it was an awestruck, yet fearful, priest who fell to his knees before the dying god.

Not only was Anubis real, he was injured and the priest realised that all that he had learned of his faith had been true. 'Oh, my lord Anubis, what horrible deed has been done unto you? Are you mortally wounded?'

Anubis grunted hoarsely, 'Listen well, priest, I have been cut with the blade Osir,' Anubis motioned with a thrust of his head towards the blade laying a few feet from him. 'I am not long for this existence. My essence is leaking out of me.'

Dread washed over the priest as he considered Anubis's words. 'My lord, surely there is something to be done? What is it that you desire me to do?'

'There is nothing to be done for me. You must take Osir and conceal it. Hear me now, take the utmost care not to be cut by the blade or else your spirit will leave you. Priest, you will need to recite the sacred rites as prescribed in the book of the gods. Such rites will put you into spiritual contact with the Underworld – word of what has happened to me must reach Osiris.'

The beast thought of the father god, Osiris, who had the power of resurrection. Surely his master would be able to restore his soul into another divine body, but Anubis would have to act fast, before his essence leaves his flesh. 'Priest, hasten and fetch some papyrus and a reed nib and bring them to me!' the beast growled urgently.

The priest hurriedly left and returned a short time later with the papyrus and a reed nib with which to write. The god was now very weak, teetering on the verge of demise and with much effort, he gestured for the priest to come closer.

'I do not know the rites of communication, even if I did, they are designed for human spiritual frequency and I no longer possess the strength to open a portal into the Underworld. There is only one choice that will suffice. My essence needs to be kept safe until Osiris comes for me. I shall require a temporary vessel to enter.'

At this, the priest withdrew from his god. Anubis recognised the look of despair etched into the face of the mortal. 'Fear not, priest, I do not desire to reside in your frail frame. You shall take my blood and use it to inscribe a spell upon the papyrus. My soul will be able to reside there in the fibres for as long as it takes Osiris to come for me.'

Hearing this, the priest appeared to relax and returned to his master's side. 'Blood magic? My lord, I am your humble servant, but I'm afraid that I am not skilled with magic.'

'It is well, priest, here,' Anubis drew the required symbols into the earthen floor with his fingernail. 'These are the runes for the magic to work. You must hurry and transcribe them onto the papyrus while my heart still beats, for when it stops I shall be no more.'

The priest began to shake, it was clear that the pressure of the situation was weighing heavily upon him. 'Yes, lord Anubis, I will obey your instructions.'

'Thank you, then you shall be my saviour. There is yet another valuable task that I ask: you must, at any cost, protect the papyrus. In doing so, you will protect me. If the papyrus is destroyed, then so shall I be destroyed. You must pledge your honourable word to me – this will be your duty.'

The priest bowed his head and raised his palms to the sky. 'I pledge upon my mortal soul that I shall do as you have commanded, lord Anubis, protector of the dead. This is my word and this is my bond.'

Once Anubis was satisfied that all would be well, he felt his body grow weaker, 'Hurry now, mortal, I feel myself slipping away.'

The priest wasted no more time. Taking his reed scribe and dipping it into the beast's bloody wound, he began to copy the runes left for him onto the papyrus. After some minutes, Anubis could feel the magic working. He closed his heavy eyelids and saw himself floating above his body. He forced his vision toward the priest and then toward the papyrus. As he drew nearer, he could see that the symbols were almost complete. He scanned over the priest's hasty but clear scribing with elation until he saw one character was incorrect.

A great panic seized the god, but it was too late. The magic was too powerful, and he had nowhere else to go. With his weakened condition, he had limited power and was unable to force himself into the body of the priest instead of the papyrus tomb that was awaiting him.

Slowly the papyrus grew closer, closer until the fibres became clearly visible, closer until the fibres began to part and allow the god into its dull, lifeless matter and soon Anubis was surrounded by it, soon he was one with it. He felt no sensation of body as he settled into his new home, but he could feel the pressure as the priest finished writing the last hieroglyph. Now a new sensation drew Anubis through the fibres to the front, to face outwards to the world, but he could pass no further. The god was trapped inside the papyrus, and he could see the world as if looking through a dirty brown shroud. He could see the worried look upon the priest's face as he peered down at his handiwork, obviously wondering if it had worked, wondering if he had done it correctly. He had not.

One important character of the spell was incorrect. The spell was supposed to say:

Here resides the essence of Anubis, sacred protector of the dead. He shall not perish in this existence, for as long as this vessel is intact. The power of release and of life shall only be granted by Osiris. As the sun shall set, so it shall rise. By the power of Ra, this spell shall be bond.

The priest, however, had drawn an incorrect rune into the spell with disastrous consequence – the spell was changed. Now it read:

Here resides the essence of Anubis, sacred protector of the dead. He shall not perish in this existence, for as long as this vessel is intact. The power of release and of life shall only be granted by fire. As the sun shall set, so it shall rise. By the power of Ra, this spell shall be bond.

By fire? When Osiris does come for him, he can only release Anubis by setting fire to the papyrus. Herein lay a conundrum: he can only be freed from this prison and given life if the papyrus is burned, but if it is burned it would no longer be intact. Therefore, he would no longer be intact; he would be no more, truly dead.

The priest was indeed unsure if the magic had worked. He had rushed against time to complete the spell before Anubis succumbed to his wound, but one thing was very evident, the great god's body was lifeless. The corpse had to be disposed of to preserve the secret of the passing of Anubis from the people, however temporary that passing may be.

He decided that fire would be the fastest, most efficient way to achieve the deed. The priest removed the sacred amulet from around the god's muscular neck and proceeded to liberally douse the body with lamp oil and set it alight. After the flames had taken a hold of the body fats, the fire ate away enough of the physical characteristics that gave Anubis his fearful appearance. The unpleasant smell of burning hair and searing meat hung thick in the air and the priest feared the stench would draw scavenging jackals down into the tomb with the promise of a cooked meal, but he dared not move from his vigil until the corpse was rendered unrecognisable.

It took almost an hour for the flames to run out of sustenance. The body was now reduced to a smouldering mass of charred matter, clinging steadfastly onto the skeletal frame of the corpse, but the protruding muzzle of the beast gave away the fact that it was not human. The priest searched the tomb and discovered a small chest, filled with gold pieces. With some difficulty, the priest lifted the chest high above his head and brought it down hard onto the face of the deceased god with a dull crunch and chimes of clashing coins. The once proud head of the god was nothing but a smashed mess of burned flesh, teeth and broiled brains combined with protruding pieces of skull fragments.

The priest then turned his attention to the corpse of Ehren Bahl, and he looked down upon it with a great sense of sadness. The poor spirit had not been released from its lifeless shell and as such, was destined to reside in the mummified remains for eternity as the mummy would not rot. The priest decided to attempt to release the soul with the aid of Osir so he recited the only funerary prayer that he knew, and to his delight, Osir responded by glowing and vibrating. He plunged the blade deep into the third eye and pierced the pineal gland. A rush of energy ejected from the head of Ehren Bahl as the priest removed the knife. He looked around the tomb, but could see no spirit lingering about, so he gently gathered up the precious papyrus and headed up the passage to the fresh Egyptian air of the dawn.

Once outside, he called out to the head guard who was resting under the sentry canopy a short distance away.

'Your eminence? Is all well?' enquired the weary-eyed brute.

'Yes, all is well. I have finished here. Have the tomb sealed at this time,' the priest replied.

'Yes, my lord, it shall be done.' The guard turned to the nearby slave tent and whistled loudly. An unpleasant-looking, overweight man appeared at the entrance, then with a disgruntled growl he yelled at the occupants to get to work. A steady line of dirty, malnourished men issued forth from the tent, reminiscent of a line of worker ants, going about their business with forced determination to get the work done before the scorching desert sun broke the horizon.

Once the entrance was sealed to the priest's satisfaction, he hurriedly made his way to the outskirts of the city to his humble abode. Once inside, away from prying eyes, he gently spread the papyrus out on his table and studied the spell, not knowing that he had made a mistake with the inscription. He was well pleased with his work and decided that later he would decorate it with some accompanying illustrations.

Not forgetting his promise to Anubis, the priest would attempt to communicate with the father god Osiris to impart unto him the events that had happened in the tomb of Ehren Bahl. To achieve this feat, he must retrieve the tome of the gods from the great Hall of Knowledge in the centre of the city, but for now he needed to rest. It had been an exhausting night and he would need all his mental strength to make the connection with Osiris.

He secreted away Osir, along with the amulet and the papyrus, into a cavity under his cot. Then he lay upon it, closed his eyes, and succumbing to his fatigue, he fell asleep. As he slept the priest dreamt, but his dreams quickly became horror-plagued nightmares. A bloody massacre, body parts writhing in a mass of oozing flesh, all twisted with broken bones protruding, maggot-infested, rotting flesh and with a stench that surely only belonged in Durat. Worst of all were the disembodied souls, wailing, howling with utter despair. Where would they go now that their guide and protector, the great god Anubis, was no longer there to assist them? The screams of the dead grew louder, louder until the priest could bare it no longer, forcing him to consciousness. He sat upright upon his cot, but the screams remained in his ears. They were not of his dreams – they were coming from the street outside.

It was early in the evening as the priest ventured out his door and onto the side of the road. Several of his neighbours had also ventured out of their houses to see what was causing such a commotion. Toward the horizon burned a menacing red glow, a great blaze off in the distance, in the heart of the city. As he had to go in that direction to fetch the book of the gods, the priest decided to join the other citizens who were heading there to witness the spectacle, but not before claiming the sacred items from their hiding place and putting on his robe.

After Jalel had fled in terror from his encounter with Anubis, he hid and rested in the shadow of a large sand dune, which faced the tomb of Ehren Bahl. He could see one of the guards ride off on a camel toward the city at great speed. The sight of Jalel running from the entrance, screaming and covered in blood and brain, was enough to stir them from their corruption and go to the city for assistance. Sometime later, the guard returned with a high priest who entered the tomb alone. The thief sat there in the dark, his skin burning from his urine and shit-soiled clothing. He was in great discomfort and longed to be into fresh garments, but he waited for some minutes longer before he felt it safe enough to head back to his house. He would have to travel the long way around, traversing the outer edge of the desert, as he did not want to be seen by any city authorities. At least the cold night air would keep him moving at a steady pace.

His mind began to wander as he drew near to his destination. He had never truly believed in the gods or the afterlife, for he was a man who only concerned himself with material wealth, but now he knew that at least one of the gods did indeed exist – Anubis, god of the dead. A sickening thought came to his mind: he had wounded the god and no doubt angered him in doing so. Surely the beast would come for revenge. He would most likely come to claim Jalel's life, as the god did with his gang, all dead, murdered with such violence. Jalel was convinced that he would be next. The thought consumed him utterly as he neared his home. The only solution that came to Jalel was to flee as far away as possible, change his appearance and claim a new name. The only means of escape from the city was to take either the north or south road, through the city sentries. The only other option was to take his chances with the scorching, dry and lifeless Egyptian desert. He was convinced that the city guards would have an eye out for him, perhaps Anubis had provided a detailed description to the priests.

Jalel decided that he would create a distraction and slip through the north sentry post while the guards were occupied, but what type of distraction? It had to be big, large enough to draw the attention of the guards. His thoughts then shifted to the priest – he could deal with two issues simultaneously. He would start a fire at the Hall of Knowledge where the priests spend most of their waking hours, studiously scouring the numerous books that reside there. If he started a fire there and barred the doors, the priests would all perish and he would have a mighty distraction to facilitate his getaway. He decided that early in the evening would be the best time to do the deed.

As the sun reached the horizon and darkness began to creep across the land, Jalel readied himself at the rear exit of the temple. He had stolen several small barrels of lamp oil from the city depository, and with the aid of a rickety old cart, he had all that he required for the job. Using his highly honed skills of stealth and silence, he positioned several of the oil barrels just inside the front entrance to the hall, then he retreated outside. Silently, he closed the front double doors and positioned the cart holding the remaining barrels in front of the doors. Lastly, he slipped into the rear of the building while carrying two barrels of oil. He pulled the wooden plug from one of the barrels and let the liquid death slowly flow onto the floor beside him as he made his way to the main hall.

There before him, running along the entire perimeter of the hall, were thousands of tomes and countless rolled papyrus scrolls. Jalel wondered how many eons of mystical knowledge resided here, all that precious knowledge being at his mercy. Is this how it feels to be a god? The fate of these priests and their sacred literature depended on his choice, his desire, and his desire right now was the destruction and death of all that was sacred.

He felt cheated by the gods and the priests that serve them. Why was evidence of the existence of the gods kept from the people, and why did the gods hide themselves behind their human avatars – the priests? Why was it that these men, in servitude of the gods, could use the name of their masters to instil fear and compliance from the populace to force their own twisted desires onto the innocent men, women and children who came asking favour of the gods, asking for gold or occasionally exchanging body fluids for the promise of salvation. Jalel was one of those children, who once came to a priest here, asking for the gods to spare his dying mother from her illness. The priest had offered Jalel some blessed elixir to take to his mother, and in return, the priest had taken Jalel's innocence as a child, not too many feet away from where he now stood.

'How dare they!' the thief blustered under his breath. How could the gods turn a blind eye to the crimes and suffering inflicted by these men of power, and who do the gods answer to? They certainly don't answer to mankind.

Jalel could feel his hatred growing to the point of bursting. Something burned in him, twisting in his blood, like well-rusted wire being dragged through his veins. He could smell the anger now in his nasal cavity, as if the stench of his rushing blood had seeped into his head. He could feel his face contorting, his cheeks afire with rage and at his nape he felt something forcing itself into the base of his skull and squeezing his throat, almost to the point of asphyxiation.

'Enough!' he growled to himself. It was time to get the work done.

The priest had made his way to the heart of the city and stood agape at the devastating sight before him. The great hall of knowledge was well ablaze. Fire raged from every orifice of the building. Agonised screams of pain and terror billowed forth from the interior of the inferno – his brethren all burning alive. A wave of heat blasted toward him, carrying the stench of burning hair and searing flesh. It was horrific confirmation that his fellow priests were indeed inside the hall, being unmade in the heart of the fiery monstrosity, being stripped of their humanity with tortured souls desperate to escape from their excruciating prisons. The priest realised that nothing could be done now, for the priests and the hall were doomed for utter destruction.

He decided it would be wise to move away from the carnage and retreat to the relative safety of his abode. Stopping in his tracks, he realised the devastating situation that had now arisen for Anubis. The book of the gods was surely lost to the fire, and without it he could not contact Osiris, so Anubis would be trapped inside the papyrus, maybe for hundreds of years or more. He carefully brought the scroll out from under his robe and gazed upon it with tears filling his eyes. 'Oh, my lord Anubis, I have failed you. The book of the gods is no more. I have such great sorrow in my heart for you and the souls that will be lost without your guidance. I vow that, for the rest of my days, I shall protect you and pass this sacred duty to my son and the following generations, for as long as it takes for the gods to notice your absence from the Underworld and come to claim you. I pledge this with my blood and the blood of my loins: we shall protect you.'

Jalel was well pleased with the chaotic spectacle he had created and decided to linger among the stunned and frightened onlookers just long enough to be sure that the blaze had taken a stranglehold on the great hall. Once satisfied that it would not easily be extinguished, he decided that now was the time to make haste with his escape from the city.

As he headed along the street which led north, Jalel spotted and recognised the priest from the tomb. He was holding a papyrus, which he appeared to be having an in-depth conversation with.

'No! This can't be!' the thief exclaimed. There could be no survivors, not any priest nor any scriptures and what was he speaking to the papyrus, some spell? Maybe some magic to save the hall and its burning inhabitants? Or worse, is he summoning one of the gods? Anubis? The thief decided that he must destroy the priest and the scroll — there can be nothing sacred left alive this eve.

As he started toward his intended victim, he saw the priest had finished speaking and was leaving the area, heading down a narrow dark lane. *Oh, this is too perfect!* Jalel was delighted. The laneway would provide him the opportunity to do the killing with no witnesses.

The priest felt sick to his stomach at the turn of events that had just transpired and as he walked up the lane that would take him home, his mind raced. How strange that the events of one day could change so many lives at once. A sense of unease took hold, a fear, and as if on cue, he heard hastened footsteps coming from behind him. He turned around in time to see an assailant coming at him. The man appeared almost demonic. His face was somehow distorted, displaying pure hatred. His outstretched hands — although human — were gnarled, fashioned into lethal weapons, desperate, it seemed, to render flesh from bone. The priest flailed backward and the only thought that came to him was to defend himself. He reached into his robe and found Osir eagerly waiting to be brought into service and as he thrust it outward toward his attacker, sacred steel met human flesh once again. The blade slid easily into the chest of the thief, all the way to the hilt, sluicing effortlessly through meat and bone. The internal veins and arteries ruptured, recoiling as they spewed forth rage-filled blood.

Jalel did not see the priest extract the blade from his robe, he was too focused on murder. His fury ceased abruptly as the blade entered his chest, his blind anger replaced with sheer disbelief. The thief stood there incredulously as the holy man promptly removed the blade and ran away up the lane. Viscous blood came gushing from the gaping wound in his chest and his desperate attempt at stemming the flow failed as he felt his strength slipping. He felt the penetrating sensation again at the back of his neck, but this time it seemed to be crawling like a scarab beetle, up his spine, into his skull and arresting at the back of his brain, right between his eyes. A painful shock struck him at the spot and his vision left him for a moment, then he felt as if someone had violently pulled him backward. When his vision returned to him, he was shocked to see that he was looking at himself from behind. He stood there, stunned, as he watched his body fall in front of him, dead.

'Fear not, mortal, for I shall be your saviour,' came a horrible voice from behind the thief.

Jalel turned his new spirit-form around to see who was speaking. An awful-looking being was crouching on its haunches before him. The creature appeared more reptilian than human, its arms and legs were extremely slender, and its skin indeed resembled the scales of a snake. Its long neck, becoming thicker as it reached the base of the head, was like that of the cobra; its mouth was thin and lipless, with a long, slender tongue, which slathered upward and over its pitch-black beady eyes to keep them moistened.

'I am the god Apep. Do you know of me, mortal?' the serpent hissed.

'Indeed, lord, you are known as the god of chaos. Forgive me but I am confused, what has happened to me?' Jalel replied shaking with fear.

Apep snorted as his tongue lathered his eyes, 'Are you such a fool that you do not realise that you are dead?'

'But you did this to me? You pulled me out of my body!' the thief – presently forgetting to whom he was speaking – became angry, and his aggression was not lost on Apep.

'Ah, there it is! Your anger has grown considerably since your little scuffle with lord Anubis. I saw you. I know what you did. You have murdered a god.'

'That is insanity. I merely wounded the beast!' Jalel retorted defensively.

Apep nodded his reptilian head as he spoke, 'Hmm, it is true that you humans have a hard time admitting the existence of magic. The dagger that you used to strike Anubis with is known as Osir. It is an instrument of death, and from the moment that you wounded Anubis with it, he was doomed.'

'I, I didn't mean to …'

'Fool! You have killed a god! Perhaps one of the most important gods to have ever existed, but you have also managed to gain my favour. You see, this situation bodes well for me. I have an opportunity for you, thief, a bargain to be made,' the serpent hissed slyly.

Jalel relaxed his stance as he listened, 'A bargain? Of what do you speak?'

'Your time in the physical realm has been cut short. Your life has been stolen from you. I merely offer you the chance to exact revenge upon those who have wronged you this day,' the reptile smiled broadly as he spoke, his sharp teeth a less than reassuring sight.

Jalel had little choice but to hear of the bargain to be made. 'Yes! I will seek my revenge, but how? I do not understand what you are offering me?'

'You are now a detached spirit with no body, and as such, you are destined to roam this world unable to cross over into the Underworld, for only Anubis knew how the human spirit could gain access and safely navigate through the five trials of the soul and into paradise. Even I do not possess this knowledge. It is true that I can enter the Underworld, but I am forbidden to pass the gate of Final Judgement.' Apep paused briefly before continuing, 'However, with your help, I can. You see, Anubis is not yet truly dead. He is … dormant. His soul is trapped inside a papyrus scroll.'

The thief's eyes flickered with recognition, 'Yes, I believe that I know the scroll of which you speak – the priest carries it on his person.'

Apep slid his tongue over his eyes again and then forced what Jalel saw to be a lipless smile revealing four long pointy fangs set among rows of smaller, sharp teeth. 'Yes, the priest has vowed to protect the scroll with his life. You have destroyed the only means of rescue for Anubis. It was necessary for the priest to contact Osiris to seek help for him. To achieve this, he needed the sacred book of the gods and that has been destroyed in the fire that you started.'

Apep's smile widened as he moistened his eyes once more. 'But again, this bodes well for me. I want you to join my legion of … well some might call them demons; however, I prefer to call them the disenchanted. They are souls who have been wronged by life and are angry, like yourself. Moreover, neither they nor you can pass through final judgement, because of the ill deeds that you have done – you would be promptly devoured by Ammit. So, you see, the disenchanted, like me, want to see a change in the natural order of things. Now that Anubis has gone, there will be many more of the disenchanted who cannot pass into paradise, nor be sent to Durat. I intend to care for these tortured entities until the day comes when I will possess the power of Anubis and send them on to where they deserve to be, in paradise.'

Paradise? The thief needed no further enticement. Jalel had lived a dishonest, self-obsessed life. He had stolen, raped and murdered as he believed it necessary to slake his desires. He was sure to be headed straight to the bowels of Durat for his crimes, but now there was a chance to escape an eternity of torturous agony. 'My lord Apep, it would be an honour to join your cause. Please tell me what you need done.'

'I thank you, Jalel. You will be a worthy addition to my brood. I require you to be my spy, and I need you to watch the priest carefully. You need to be over his shoulder always and if he dies, you must watch the next caretaker of Anubis. You must do this for as long as it takes until he is freed.'

A puzzled look came over Jalel's face, 'Freed? How will he be freed?'

'The priest made an error with his spell. Anubis can only be freed by fire,' at this, the serpent exploded into a fit of laughter, like a wicked child who knew that a sinister prank was afoot. 'Ah that fool priest, little does he know the trap he has set for his master. You see, if the papyrus is destroyed, then so shall the god be destroyed, and he can only be freed by fire! Oh, the irony of it.'

The look of confusion upon Jalel's face became more severe as he tried to understand what the serpent was saying amid the fits of laughter. 'So, you want me to burn the papyrus?'

Apep's smile faded as he slowly shook his head, 'Ugh, so much to learn. Even if I wanted you to burn it, you would not be able to. You are spirit now and without a physical body, you cannot move physical objects anymore.'

The thief was fearful of the reptile, but his curiosity drove him to discover more about his new master, perhaps he may discover some weakness to be exploited. 'I beg your forgiveness, my lord, I am not intimate with this form yet. May I be so bold to ask you a question about yourself?'

Apep stood deathly still, staring at the thief as if giving the thought very serious consideration. Finally, his tongue lashed out over his beady eyes, 'You may ask, thief, but tread carefully. I will not tolerate any unnecessary probing.'

'Oh of course, master. I just wanted to know what you are. I mean, are you a spirit like me?'

The serpent relaxed his stance as he came closer to Jalel, allowing himself to be seen more clearly. 'I am not a spirit like you. I am a god. The humans call me the god of chaos, but I consider this an unfair assessment of my actions. I merely like to test the limits of man's endurance and temperament by creating challenging situations. Like Anubis and the other gods, I am immortal to a point, meaning that I will live indefinitely unless magic intervenes, such as Osir. Mortal time means little to us gods. On the other side, the Underworld, time is of no consequence, not that it matters when you can live forever. Apart from that, I am indeed flesh and bone.'

The thief studied Apep's face intently. His curiosity was apparent to the serpent, who asked the unspoken question, 'You want to know why do we look the way we do? Us gods, why do we have bestial features? I have a reptilian appearance; Anubis was part canine and you would like to know why?'

Jalel quickly diverted his gaze to the ground, 'Sorry for staring, my lord. It's just that well, you are a remarkable being. I am merely curious.'

'Hmm, fear not, human, I will explain. Gods are not born as humans are – we are created. We are from the substance of the stars and as such, this substance is what you may consider to be a soul. Our soul needs a physical form and this body is made by our father Osiris. He infused the essence of a creature with the corpse of a human man. Why use animal essence? Because animals are of nature – they have not the tumultuous emotions associated with mankind – they are loyal to their masters. It is also true that the abilities of particular animals suit the purpose of each god, Anubis for his unquestioning loyalty to his master, Osiris, and his ability to smell when a person is about to die. Horus, like the hawk, is able to fly to the sun, and me? Well, I can exist on the earth undetected. I can pass among people as a serpent or reptile and I can even render myself invisible if I so desire. This, however, is my true form. Only the dead and the gods can see me this way.'

Still not certain exactly what he was to do with the scroll, Jalel hesitated to ask for fear of being seen as stupid by his new master. He decided to steer the conversation to obtain further clarification on his mission. 'So, if you are a physical being, will you be the one to destroy the papyrus?'

Apep snorted and let loose with a hearty guffaw, 'I think not, thief, I cannot be directly implicated in the final demise of my brother god. All of us gods have personalised rules that we cannot disobey, and each set of rules differ from god to god, depending on our vocation. My primary command is that I shall not directly murder or take a life. I can, however, devour a soul once it has left the body. You see, devouring souls is how we can gain that person's strength and knowledge and that is what I intend to do with Anubis's essence once it is freed from the scroll. Now listen carefully, thief, you will watch the scroll. One day it may be destroyed by fire. Once this happens, Anubis will be free for a very brief moment before his soul is obliterated into nothingness. It will be at that very moment when I must devour his essence. You must call my name as soon as you see anything! Do you understand me, thief?'

'Yes, I understand.' Jalel was content with his instructions, even though he did not much look forward to shadowing people for who knows how many years, but the reminder of his possible salvation kept him in steady check.

'All will be well, thief. Once I have the power of Anubis, we can experience the paradise we all deserve and send our enemies directly to Durat. I will leave you now. Remember, if you see anything happen to the scroll, you must call my name immediately. Hurry now, you must catch up with the priest before he attempts to flee the city. He lives directly up this lane, in the red house with the symbol of Ra above the door.'

The thief bowed low in front of the serpent, 'Yes, lord Apep, I will do as you command.'

The serpent seemed satisfied that his new recruit had understood his mission and Apep licked his eyes one last time before vanishing into the cool night air.

CHAPTER SIX

The Great Chase

JALEL FOUND MOVING ABOUT in his spirit-form effortless. It felt indescribably good to be free of the meat sack that used to be his body, all heavy and cumbersome, stinking of blood, shit and snot. He was also acutely aware of his surroundings and had no difficulty locating the priest. As the serpent predicted, the holy man was busying himself with packing his meagre belongings in preparation to leave the city. The priest wasted no time and used the small amount of gold he had to hire a slave to help him with his exodus. Before leaving the city, the priest and his slave visited the burned-out shell of the great hall, stopping to pay his respects to his dead brethren. After some searching, the priest located a well-hidden charity lock box and several small gold idols that had been secreted away. The box contained donations by the wealthy men of Egypt, all hoping to buy their passage into the Underworld. The box was packed till it was bursting with precious gems and solid gold ingots, so it was with great difficulty that the pair managed to carry it to the cart they had hired, and not long after that they were on their way north.

So began the great chase. At first it was easy for Jalel to follow the pair along their arduous journey, but once they had finally made it to Israel, the thief found many exotic distractions and experienced a few anxious moments when he thought he had lost the pair. Eventually the priest made his way through Europe, finally ending in Spain and it was there that he put down his roots. He used the gold to purchase a fine property and passed himself off as a spice trader. He had the foresight to bring with him exotic herbs and spices from the Middle East and soon the priest had a very successful business dealing with rare culinary ingredients. His personal wealth grew rapidly and a year later he got married and went on to raise five children. It was the eldest son whom the priest taught all the knowledge that he possessed pertaining to the truth about the gods, the afterlife, and of course the sacred family mission to protect the scroll of Anubis.

A few short years later the priest passed away from heart failure. Jalel thoroughly enjoyed watching him die, the fear in the priest's eyes as he clutched savagely at his chest, the veins in his neck swelling like large earthworms spreading up to his forehead, his face turning purple before he fell to the floor stone dead. Jalel watched as the spirit of the priest flailed around inside the body, like a drowning cat. He was unable to leave his fleshy prison until his corpse had rotted away.

Hundreds of years became a thousand and a thousand became several more, with each generation of the priest's family continuing to become successful financially, installing the family in good stead within society.

As promised, each following generation continued their vigil over the papyrus, their faith in the legend of the god and their ancient relative, the priest, firmly entrenched in the family's belief system. Each successive protector was unwavering in his duty to protect the scroll and indeed, the papyrus itself had become the family bible. Always looking on was Jalel, who stayed true to his word and dutifully watched over the papyrus.

The scroll and its loyal guardians migrated to England in the mid-seventeenth century and remained there until World War One began. It was at that time that the family fled as far away from Europe as they could, and so they eventually arrived in Australia, a relatively young nation and as far away from their ancestral land of Egypt as one could imagine.

Still, Jalel remained vigilant, making sure that he did not roam too far from the papyrus, which by this time had been professionally framed and as such, it was a taunting sight for the thief as it hung proudly upon the wall, mocking him. If only he could interact with material things. He would destroy the damn abomination and put an end to his torment. In fact, lately there had been a few occasions when the thief briefly considered that Durat would not be as much a punishment as his ongoing vigil. Jalel greatly disliked spending so much time in the presence of the living and the more hours, days and years that passed, the more his humanity was stripped from him. Such was his torment at being unable to interact with the physical world and those which inhabit it, he considered that surely there was no greater punishment awaiting him elsewhere. Yet still, he remained loyal to his master, Apep. The constant fear of having his soul devoured by the serpent kept Jalel in steady check and the hope that his master's plan may succeed retained the thief's servitude.

One hot summer's afternoon, the lady of the house came home after a few days' absence. She had arrived with her husband and now the two were three, as she had given birth to a baby boy. The new mother appeared to be physically tender after the birthing process as she struggled with her mobility, but the family duty to the Anubis scroll would not wait, so she made the effort to lift the child out of its basinet and gently raised the infant up in front of the papyrus. The child's reflection caught upon the glass of the frame. 'Anubis, I'd like to introduce you to your future caretaker. His name is Donovan, Donovan Banks.'

Anubis stirred in the fibres as he looked out into the world. After thousands of years being rolled up and stashed away in one hiding place after another, he now had a room with a view. He could at least see his surroundings and the comings and goings of his protectors. Now the next generation of his protection detail was presented before him, *Donovan aye? Oh well, what's in a name anyway?* He had heard many strange names and languages over the years. In fact, he had learned English hundreds of years ago via the muffled sounds of England's elite who frequented the lavish dinner parties thrown by the Banks family, and over recent years, he learned even more thanks to the small black-and-white television that sat proudly in the middle of the living room. *Ridiculous language*, he thought, *overly complicated*, oh how he missed the loose tongue of the old speak.

Thanks to the family's wealth and social status, Donovan

received the finest education that money could provide. He attended the finest schools and the most prestigious college possible, but the most important education that he received was from his mother and father, as they passed on to him the sacred knowledge and rites of the ancient ways.

As a child, Donovan began talking to Anubis as if he was an imaginary friend, often spending hours sitting in front of the frame, his head turned upward toward the papyrus as he conducted long one-sided conversations with Anubis, whom he saw in his mind as an animated cartoon, due in part to the monotone artwork depicting the dog-headed casket. In the boy's mind, he could imagine the casket lid sliding off and hitting the floor comically, spinning awkwardly like the lid of a tin garbage can rattling noisily as it oscillates to a stop. Then he would see the god leap up out of the casket, just like the black and white animated mouse cartoons that he saw at the cinema of a Saturday morning.

Anubis was surprisingly grateful for the company, even if it was a mere child, at least it was a welcome distraction from his fibrous prison. However, as the years passed and the child grew to adolescence, the daily visits all but ceased, reduced to the occasional nod or wink from Donovan as he passed the papyrus.

Still, the beast watched on as the teenager grew into a young man. He was witness as Donovan's father passed away after choking on a piece of steak one Sunday evening and the sorrowful wake that followed, which was held in the very room that Anubis resided in. With no escape he was forced to endure hysterical wailing, sobbing and unnecessarily prolonged speeches, ambling on about what a great man Mr Banks was. *Great?* the beast mused. He was a good man to be sure, but the god had known of truly great men and old man

Banks was not great. After some years more, the matriarch of the house began to lose her mind due to the insidious creep of dementia and so it was not long before she too became absent from the family home and soon it was just Donovan and the beast.

However, Donovan was far from lonely, as the occasional lady friend called to visit and each one of them fell prey to his sexual advances. Anubis again stirred in the fibres as Donovan had his way with his latest conquest, right there in front of the god on the lounge chair. *Humans and their lustful ways,* the beast lamented. Sex had always disgusted Anubis. Apart from the procreation of their kind, he could not fathom why mortals invested such time and effort into such a gruesome activity. The penetration of the body by another person's body was more than macabre to the god. All the stench and fluids were enough to turn his stomach, and the noises, screams, groans and guttural grunting reminded the god that humans were just animals after all. Little did he know that his future protector was being created before him at that very moment, as Donovan unloaded his seed.

Donovan's lady friend; Alice had become his wife and a baby son was added to the family, once again filling the house with love and noise. Indeed, the child was not as placid as his father had been when he was an infant, and this time there were no imaginary conversations, or black-and-white cartoon dogs. These were replaced by video games and comic books.

The Banks family continued to live harmoniously for years, until the child had reached an age when Donovan believed he was ready to begin his sacred tutorials. Alice did not approve of such nonsensical teachings and what she considered to be generational brain-washing. She had always believed that Donovan was speaking of childhood fairytales when referencing the papyrus that continued to look over them. As Donovan insisted that the learning continue, tensions arose between husband and wife. Eventually, when Alice put forward the old ultimatum of 'either it goes, or I go', the choice was easy for Donovan, so sometime shortly after that, Alice left the marriage and the house.

Two decades passed and the god found himself on the move yet again. Donovan had put his well-funded education and extensive knowledge of ancient Egypt to good use, as he had become a professor of ancient history and archaeology, and so it happened that he was offered a lucrative offer to teach at the Greater Melbourne University. Donovan happily agreed to the new posting, in part because it would give him the opportunity to live in the same city as his now adult son. It was during the change of address that Anubis's sanctuary was damaged by the removal company who were charged with organising the move.

So now Donovan found himself in an art gallery, organising the necessary reparations for the papyrus. The gallery owner assured Donovan that the papyrus would be in the best hands, and he knew that if he threw enough money at the gentleman – Arthur he said his name was – all would be well.

Donovan had spoken with Arthur for a few minutes about the piece when he felt the urge to communicate again the importance of the scroll. 'Now, Arthur, please be reminded that this papyrus is extremely precious to me. If anything untoward were to happen to it, I will hold you solely responsible.'

A nervous smile cracked Arthur's well-worn face as he raised his hands, palms facing outward like a magician would in showing that he is not hiding his trick.

'Oh, please be assured, Mr Banks, my framer, Sam, is one of the best in the industry and we are very blessed to have him in our employ. Your artwork will be in the very best care possible.'

Donovan could do little but to accept Arthur at his word. Still, the thought of parting from Anubis struck him in his throat as if he were choked with grief. The sensation began working on his mind, to the point that he felt it necessary to clear his throat. 'Yes, well I'm very grateful for your reassuring words, however, I would feel more secure if you could complete the repairs at your very earliest convenience.'

Arthur was quick to agree, 'Oh, well we usually have a two-week turnaround for custom framing jobs, but I will personally see to it that your repair is done as fast as our standards of quality allows.'

Donovan seemed satisfied that he had put ample pressure upon the old man and with that, he left Anubis in the hands of the gallery.

Anubis was used to people admiring the workmanship of his prison and as far as prisons go, his was rather beautiful. The priest had taken a lot of love and care in decorating the papyrus. Each stroke of the reed and brush was delicately placed and even the script of the spell, which was scribed so hastily, was now embellished with gold, the precious metal of the gods. Now he was laid on his back, peering upward through the broken glass of his residence, intently returning the appraising eye of the young man who was closely studying the fine detail of the art before him.

What did the old man call him? Samuel? There were times when the beast had to admit that at least hidden here inside the papyrus, people could look at him with admiration, as if he were a thing of beauty instead of the reaction that he would have received if any human were to see his true form. Now again, it was admiration that Anubis received as the young framer looked down upon him. The beast could see into his eyes, through him, into his soul. His essence was strong and honourable, wise beyond his years and his compassion could make him a great man, a leader of people, or it could make him vulnerable, a fool to be taken advantage of. Anubis guessed that he would probably be the fool as the god had seen many great men who had succumbed to the schemers, liars and thieves of this fallible world. In any case, it mattered not to the god, for as soon as Samuel had completed the reparations to his prison, Anubis would not lay eyes upon him again.

Just as Donovan had done, Samuel began talking to Anubis and he found it rather amusing when the human told him to stay where he was, shortly after the papyrus was placed into yet another box. *Ha, as if I could go anywhere anyway.* However, this new prison stank of a strong chemical, which reminded him of the ritual oils that were used in the ancient funerary rites, back in the old times. As he lay there in that stinking box, he noticed that the ambient temperature had steadily begun to rise. The stench of the chemicals increased to an unbearable potency and the beast felt as if what was left of his life essence was being choked out of him. A sudden realisation came to the beast, maybe this would be the end of him?

Is this how it felt to lay rotting in the ground, after the body had ceased to provide a viable vessel for the soul? Panic arose in him and he started to stir in the fibres, moving from one side to the other, from the back to the front, desperately searching for somewhere to shelter from the toxic fumes which now filled the box. The beast began to thrash wildly. If only he could break free from the fibres and escape, but he could not, and his prison held fast, for every time he pushed forward he was held in place and was only released back when he ceased struggling. *This is futile!* Anubis conceded. If this is the end, then so be it. Would it be so bad after all? He had spent what seemed like an eternity in this damned papyrus, an eternity, even through the eyes of a god.

As he let go and relaxed to await his demise, the beast could feel the heat start to warp the fibres and the slight, sweet smell of smouldering reed met his senses as the box started to fill with a hazy smoke. Staring up through the smoke, Anubis could hear muffled sounds from outside and then Samuel's face appeared over the glass lid of the death trap.

Small flames had started to take hold of the papyrus and Anubis could feel himself being pulled slowly through the fibres. He felt as if his blood was beginning to boil as the flames reached the ink, which was not surprising, as the ink was in fact his blood – now returning to its original, liquid state. The spell came vividly into the god's head, *The power of release and of life shall only be granted by act of fire*, and no sooner had the thought appeared than he felt the pulling become intense, like a hungry dog tugging at a dead animal. He felt as if he was being torn from the fibres. Every part of his essence hurt, burned and stretched as the beast struggled furiously to be freed from his entrapment, and just when he felt that he would be rendered into oblivion, his spirit sprung loose from the papyrus.

He felt weak, thin, as if his essence had been diluted in water, then he realised that it was not water, it was smoke. The beast willed himself to condense his spirit. He pulled from every direction, back to a central point of focus and as he did so, the smoke thickened and compressed, almost to the point of being a solid entity. Anubis could feel some of his strength returning, but he realised that he had only one avenue of escape: up and out of this box. He deduced that the human Samuel would shortly open the box and the god could escape, but where to? What would he do once he was out of his coffin? His disembodied spirit had little to no strength, thus he would not exist for long before his essence diluted into nothingness.

There was one other option for Anubis – he could force himself into the body of Samuel. It was not the most pleasant of ideas, but at least he would stay viable and he may be able to take more aggressive measures to seek help from Osiris. Anubis knew that Samuel had a strong constitution and that neither his soul, nor his mind, would allow the god to have full control over his body. In his weakened state, the beast would only be able to ride the mortal for the most part, but perhaps he could plant subliminal thoughts into the human, to enable Samuel to contact Donovan and to finally reach out to Osiris.

As Anubis had predicted, Samuel returned in a flurry and opened the lid of the fumigation box. The god mustered all his strength, which had been tightly compressed like a spring under tension, and focused on the human's face. Whop! The smoke entity leapt forward striking Samuel square in the face, sending him lurching backwards.

'*Anubis!*' came a howl from beside the god. Staring intently at him was another spirit, somewhat familiar to the shocked beast, but he could not recall from where he knew this person.

'*Wha– who are you?*' the beast snarled telepathically to the spirit, as this was the only method of conversation for souls.

The spirit smiled grimly and glided effortlessly around Anubis, coming to a stop between the god and Samuel. '*Who am I? Oh, I don't believe that is important right now. What is important, however, is my master's business with you. You see we have been waiting a very long time for this moment.'*

'Fool! Do you not realise that you are addressing a god?' Anubis growled.

'A god? Ha! You are nothing more than smoke and wind! Oh, it's true that you were once mighty, and I have seen your handiwork in person, but I put an end to all that. Me! A mere mortal who ended the great god Anubis.'

'Ended me? Wait ... you are the thief from the tomb of Ehren Bahl?'

'Ha, yes, dog! You see I feared you once, that night at the tomb you made me piss and shit myself. Oh, the horror of your existence did so terrify me, but then I changed. The years have dulled my humanity and I have come to know the truth of the gods. You are not truly immortal and I no longer fear you dog, I have become strong, brave and vengeful.'

'It's true that I underestimated you, thief. You truly have caused me great sufferance. Now answer me why you are here, or I shall—'

'You shall do what, dog? Destroy me? I think not! As I said you are nothing now. I am just as strong as you are. No, I am stronger and I can see that you grow weaker by the moment.'

It was true, Anubis could feel his hold on the smoke entity shake. It was becoming increasingly difficult to keep this form together. *'Move aside, thief! I shall see to it that Osiris rewards your assistance with great favours.'*

'Ha! You wish to bargain with me, dog? I do not believe that you could offer me a better proposition than my master.'

'Who is this master of yours, thief?'

'Oh, you will meet him soon enough — all I need do is call for him.'

It dawned on Anubis that the thief was toying with the god, and he was enjoying the power of advantage that he held over him. Presently, his strength began to wane, and the god realised that if he did not act now, he would be powerless to prevent whatever the thief had planned for him.

'Do not worry, dog, I'm sure that it will not cause you too much pai–' The words were snatched from the thief as the beast lunged at him, wrapping his smoke-form around him. The thief seemed shocked, taken aback by the attack. In desperation he grabbed at the smoke, but his ghostly fingers passed through the semi-solid substance. Anubis, however, was birthed into the smoke, as it was created by his burning blood. He was one with it, momentarily at least, until his strength fails. The thief thrashed about, shaking his head like a feral cat which was trapped inside a hessian bag, and Anubis used the momentum to turn the pair into a spin, like some deranged waltz. They traversed the room, filling it with smoke. Out of the corner of his vision, the god noticed that Samuel was struggling to breathe, clutching at his throat with his arms flailing about, and the god knew that he must act quickly if he was to save the mortal. With one final swing, the beast released the hapless thief, sending him flying across the room.

Anubis watched as Sam fell to the floor - the last of his oxygen burning out. *'All is well, Samuel, for I shall be your salvation,'* the beast growled softly to the human as he came close to his face.

Summoning all his remaining strength, the god recited the sacred spell that would allow him permission to enter Samuel's body. He could feel himself once again being pulled, gently this time, past the human's lips, over the teeth, sliding across the tongue, and finally he felt himself being dragged down the throat, like storm water spiralling down a drain. As he slid down the throat, the beast heard a name being called out. It came from outside of Samuel's body and he recognised the voice – it was the thief who spoke, *'Apep!'*

The serpent was less than pleased with the events that had transpired before being summoned to the disastrous scene that presently confronted him.

'You imbecile!' Apep hissed at Jalel with such ferocity, that the thief recoiled back with fear.

'My lord, I beg your understanding. I–'

'You beg for my understanding? I have waited for thousands of years for an opportunity to realise my plan and you have squandered it away!' the reptile fumed as he paced about.

'Please, lord, allow me to explain. I am truly your humble and obedient servant, I just–'

'Obedient? Ha! I think not, you are but a fool and I am a bigger fool to have trusted you with such an important task. You did not call for me when you should have and now all is lost!' the serpent was unrelenting with his vicious tirade against Jalel and now began sliding from side to side, his tongue working furiously to keep his eyes moist. When he did stop shouting it was only to draw breath. Every now and then his beady black eyes shot directly at Jalel and each time this happened, the thief shuddered with fear.

'I had the situation well in hand, master. I thought that I could contain the beast myself, to make your consumption of him easier when you arrived. I did not anticipate his strength; he was able to overpower me with ease.'

'Yes, well even I could not anticipate his rebirth in smoke form. By Osiris, the dog truly is blessed! What of him, thief? Tell me what happened to Anubis!'

'As I said, he overpowered me and cast me across this room. I ended away over there,' the thief pointed to the opposite wall of the room, some twenty meters away. 'I was in shock, my lord, and I was unable to see clearly due to the smoke. By the time I had found my way back here, the dog was gone.'

'Anubis cannot survive long without a stable vessel. If he has bonded with the smoke, he will only last as long as he can hold his form together, for once the smoke dissipates, he will cease to exist, and he will be using all of his remaining energy to keep himself in the physical realm. No, he will need a body to occupy.' Apep slowed his pacing as he thought over the possible actions that Anubis might take, then he stopped, motionless, as he stared through the smoke to the faint glow of daylight that could be seen through the thick toxic air – it was the rear exit of the building. Then after a moment, he glided steadily through the smoke to the open door.

Laying just outside was the body of a young man, pale and seemingly lifeless. Jalel had followed the serpent and looked down at the man. 'This is the human who started these events in motion. I saw him struggling to breathe when the fire took hold. It looks like he did not survive.'

Apep drew his reptilian face close to the human, his tongue rapidly flicking the air, sniffing for any sign of life.

'The human is alive, just barely,' the serpent regarded the still body carefully, sniffing the air furiously with his tongue, but all he could smell was smoke and urine. He could not sense any trace of his brother god. 'It appears that this body was too weak for Anubis to occupy; indeed, the human will perish shortly. Hmm, if I were my brother, I would attempt to seek out the only mortal capable of rendering assistance, the priest's descendant, his guardian. I believe that he will go there. He may possibly even inhabit the body of his protector. Either that or he has found another suitable host along the way. There is only one way to be sure.'

The reptile looked directly into Jalel's eyes and spoke a solitary word, the sound of which sent a strong tremor up the spine of the thief, 'Augupte.'

Apep opened his fanged maw wide.

The thief feared that he would be swallowed by the reptile, instead he felt his essence being drawn into the god's mouth. The serpent chewed voraciously upon him and then spat the thief out, spraying his essence across the air. Jalel felt a sensation like racing adrenalin as he concentrated on condensing his spirit back to his former appearance.

'Now listen very carefully, thief, for if you disappoint me again, I shall swallow your soul and shite you into nothingness! Am I understood?'

Jalel began to shake uncontrollably. The sensation of having his essence chewed upon was both disgustingly unpleasant and excruciatingly painful, not to mention the fear he experienced at having his spirit scattered into the air. So, he was under no illusions that being devoured by the reptile would be truly horrifying, his soul slowly being dissolved in the stomach of the god, and he imagined what was left of him would eventually be passed via the rectum, like spiritual diarrhoea. 'Yes, master, I understand. What do you desire me to do?'

'You will go back to the Banks' residence and carefully check for any sign of Anubis's presence. Be especially aware of any changes in the old man, for if my brother is residing inside him then I will have an opportunity to devour his soul. All we will need is to create a circumstance that will end Donovan Bank's life, forcing Anubis to vacate the mortal's body.'

'Yes, my lord, and if Anubis does not live inside of the old man?'

'He will be hiding somewhere, in someone, of this I am certain. I can sense that he has not lost his essence into nothingness, so he must have merged with a living person. However, his energy will remain in a weakened state, unless he devours some souls. You see, he will not be strong enough to gain full and constant control of his host body – he will be far too weakened for that. No, he will have to eat spirit, that is the only way for him to regain his strength, and eventually, he will take full control of the body so he can destroy the consciousness of the body's original occupant.'

'Wait, eating souls? Would he eat me?'

'You? I would imagine not, thief. No, living souls are ... fresher, especially infant souls and particularly the unborn for they are still pure, untainted - the most potent.' The serpent lost interest in attempting to educate Jalel in the fine art of dining on souls and started to become agitated at having to be standing in the blistering hot Australian sun dealing with an incompetent minion, such as the thief. 'I truly hope that for your sake the beast is there. You have caused enough trouble already. If Anubis is not present, then I suggest that you do all in your power to discover what has happened to him. Mark my words, thief, I will feast on a soul soon, if not my brother, then ...'

The serpent did not need to finish his threat, for Jalel understood perfectly well that he would perish if he did not provide Anubis to Apep soon. The thief slowly bowed his head low in front of the reptile, 'I understand fully, lord Apep. I shall not let you down again.'

The god did not bother to reply. His disgust with Jalel was plainly evident as he vanished in front of the thief. Then, as if on cue, the sirens of the emergency services came swiftly to the attention of the thief and without further hesitation, he rapidly drifted up into the air and crawled across the sky, heading back to the apartment of Donovan Banks.

CHAPTER SEVEN

Enter the Demon

DONOVAN BANKS HAD BEEN finishing some paperwork at his university when he received a phone call from the picture framers. The news of the fire had devastated him, to the point that he did not respond to Arthur's sincere apology and simply hung up on the gallery owner. The old man sat in his chair, slumped in a state of shock for a long period of time, staring blankly at the papers sitting on the desk before him. The writing blurred into the paper, as a fitting backdrop for his numbness. Donovan's mind drifted aimlessly, but eventually, the old man felt that he needed to reach out for support and there was only one other human being in the world that could understand the awful situation that had occurred. However, a simple phone call would not be sufficient to pacify Donovan, no – he had to go downtown.

The bright-eyed receptionist greeted Donovan as he crossed the marble tiled lobby, 'Good morning, sir, welcome to The Open Eye. How can I direct your enquiry?'

Donovan frowned and checked his watch to confirm his suspicion that it was in fact afternoon already. 'Hmm, yes good afternoon,' he replied dryly, trying hard not to sound sarcastic. 'I'm here to see my son, Kurt Banks.'

As a child, unlike his father, Kurt did not much care to grow an attachment or bond with Anubis. There had been far too many other exciting things happening in the child's world. Besides, Kurt considered his future responsibilities a chore rather than an honour, and it was this fact that caused the father and son relationship to often be strained. He had even doubted that the legend of Anubis was true. He considered such talk as fairytales, and he rather pitied his father for believing so vehemently, though out of respect to Donovan, he always played along with the impending task of protecting the sacred papyrus.

Because he had been so spoilt by his father, Kurt had developed an attachment and desire for the finest material things in life, from the toys he had, to his clothing, and as he grew older, his cars and even his women. Moreover, the type of women that Kurt enjoyed collecting also had a desire for material things and Kurt was happy to oblige them, at least until he had bedded them and moved on to his next conquest. He was now well into his late twenties, and he did not waste an opportunity to slake his lust, for fear of loss of libido or his sharp, angular good looks. He also went to great lengths to ensure that his physique was immaculately sculpted by spending countless hours working out at the gymnasium.

His father had used his social standing, along with some rather hefty personal donations to the right people in the right position, to secure Kurt his dream job. Kurt had always wanted to be a newspaper reporter and the job certainly had its perks. He was able to access places, people and information that the average Joe could not and so he figured that eventually, when the time came that he would be required to take over the caretaking of the sacred scroll from his father, he would be aware of any news of unusual events that may herald the appearance of Osiris, come looking for his missing son Anubis, as unlikely as such a scenario may be.

Even though his relationship with Donovan was sometimes strained, Kurt loved his father dearly and was secretly very pleased that his father had decided to move to join him in Melbourne. He was equally pleased that his father had called in to see him at The Open Eye, albeit a little surprised that he did not call ahead of time as was the usual etiquette between the two.

'Dad, hey, this is a pleasant surprise. What's up?' Kurt winked at the receptionist as he sauntered past her, sending the naive beauty into a fit of smiles and giggles. *Must remember to keep onto that one*, he made a mental note to talk to her later.

'Kurt, son, we must talk urgently. Is there somewhere a little more private where we may go?' Donovan had a desperate, manic manner about him and Kurt wasted no time in ushering him into an adjacent vacant office.

'What's happening, Dad?'

'Something terrible has happened to the scroll.' Donovan began to tremble, almost uncontrollably and it was clear that he was doing his best to hold back tears.

'Anubis?'

'Yes, there was a fire. He has been destroyed!'

'Destroyed? Wait, is the house okay?'

'The house? Oh, yes it's fine. I had taken Anubis to an art gallery to have his frame repaired – it was damaged in the move down here. Somehow a fire was started at the framing shop and from what I understand, the scroll was destroyed in the blaze.'

Donovan could contain his grief no longer and erupted, sobbing like a child who had lost his dearest toy, the tears rolling steadily down his well-aged cheeks. Kurt did his best to attempt to calm the old man as he put his large arms around his father and embraced him.

'Oh, Dad, I'm so sorry. That's horrible. What would have happened to Anubis himself? Is there anything we can do?'

The old man sniffed hard at his tears, then he took several long deep breaths to regain his composure. His heavily veined hands slid over his balding head – this was one gene that Kurt was desperately hoping would not be passed on from father to son.

'No, all is indeed lost. As you know, the scroll hieroglyphs stated that Anubis could only be freed by fire, but our family tradition has told us that he could only be freed by Osiris himself. We also know that if the scroll was to be destroyed, then so would Anubis. Herein lies a conundrum, which story is accurate? I have come to believe that there is a little truth in all three statements. It is quite possible that there may have been an error within the spell itself, through human fault. However, if the story of Osiris coming to save Anubis is true, then where is he – why has he not come after thousands of years? Then lastly, he may be destroyed if the scroll is destroyed. I believe that this is indeed the case, for I don't think that our ancestors would have handed down through the generations such a dire warning, had they not truly believed in it. No, this must be the truth!'

Kurt watched on with concern as his father began pacing about the small office, staring at the floor as he seemed to be searching for any possible miracle that may have occurred with Anubis, but he could find none.

'No, I just cannot see any way that the god could have survived, for if this were the case, then where is he? Surely somebody would notice a large humanoid dog walking the streets, likely to be causing bloody havoc. No, the best we can hope for is that somehow he has passed over to his father in spirit form.'

Kurt leaned back against the closed door, his head tilted upward, staring at the ceiling. Although he was indeed concerned about the wellbeing of Anubis, he was more worried about the mental and emotional state of his father. There were several times during Kurt's life when he truly doubted the whole Anubis saga. Was it merely just tall-tales, created to fit their own religious beliefs?

His daydreaming came to an abrupt halt as his father let loose a groan. The old man began clutching at his chest, his eyes filled with dread and his body sprung stiff to attention.

'Dad? What's happening? Dad!'

Donovan dropped to the floor and Kurt hurriedly called out to the receptionist to call for an ambulance.

'Dad, stay with me … Dad!'

The paramedics arrived in time to bring the old man back from the brink of death and transported him to the hospital for further attention. Poor old Donovan's heart did not take the news of the destruction of the papyrus well and so it decided to throw a little tantrum. It did not kill him, it merely wanted him to take a brief rest.

Kurt found himself standing in his father's new house, gathering a few personal items to take to the hospital to help make his recovery a little more palatable. Again, his mind turned to the demise of Anubis as he thought, *what now?*

Suddenly his future had a huge open end for him to explore, full of possibilities. Now that the scroll was gone, he would no longer be destined to spend his life in servitude of the god. He could do anything and go anywhere, with whomever he pleased, with no more ties to bind him to the one fate. If he was being honest, he was feeling a huge sense of relief at this thought.

As Kurt rummaged through his father's dresser, his mind drifted back to the cute little receptionist at The Open Eye. Maybe he could whisk her away for a dirty weekend somewhere. She had a nice body, firm, yet shapely. He could already imagine what she was hiding under her clothing, the shape of her breasts, the size and colour of her nipples.

As Kurt began sifting through the clothing, he saw something glint against the light in his father's drawer. It was the sheathed dagger, Osir, hiding among the neatly rolled socks. Bringing it out into the light, he slid the supposedly sacred blade out a few centimetres. The motion of the sliding blade was pleasing, even erotic to Kurt. He slid the blade back into the sheath, before pulling it out again, simulating the copulation that he so very much desired to have with that receptionist.

'Ah!' Kurt exclaimed as his imaginations came to an abrupt halt. He had cut his thumb upon the blade as he slid Osir back into its sheath and he was now bleeding. In shock, Kurt dropped the blade to the floor, before swinging his hand wildly through the air.

'No!' Kurt shouted out as he slammed the drawer closed

with enough force that the dresser rocked backward violently, leaving an indentation in the plaster wall behind it. His father had warned him about the dire consequences of being injured by Osir and if the story was true, then his life would be ending a lot sooner than he had planned.

'No! No! No! No! Why me? Why?' He started up screaming as adrenalin came, flushing his senses with a manic urgency to do something, anything to avoid the supposed curse that was now upon him. Spells? There must be some spell, some antidote. Kurt rushed back to the dresser and furiously began searching each drawer for the family tome of old magic that his father had shown him when he was a child.

The book was written by the very first sacred protector of Anubis, a priest, the very same priest that began the legend of the Anubis scroll. He had filled it with various prescriptions for all types of ailments, and if there was any salvation, surely, he would find it there. Finally, he found the book, drew it out and placed it on the floor in front of him. As he flipped through the pages he could indeed feel himself grow weaker. Was this psychosomatic? Was he imagining himself slowly slipping away, or was his soul truly leaking out of him? Luckily, Kurt found possible salvation within the first quarter of the book. There written in the old language, was a passage which described using the spirits of Mother Earth to heal serious sickness and other potent morbidities.

The prayer called for the summoning of nature spirits to heal the affected individual from within the body. Surely if anything would be able to save him, this must be it. Kurt carefully read the scripture, taking each character into memory and when he felt certain that he had the spell firmly in his mind, he lay down upon the floor, flat on his back with his hands forming the classical prayer position, palms facing together and resting upon his chest, with his fingers pointing toward his chin.

He lay still, staring intently at the ceiling as he began reciting the prayer.

'By the power of Ra, I call upon the free spirits of the earth to come unto me. May they favour me with the blessings of healing and may I be restored to wellness. I open my body to your presence and beseech thee for your compassion, to be thy saviour, and I shall praise thee to the heavens. This I ask by the name of Ra, so it is said, so shall it be.'

Kurt repeated the prayer again to be sure and then he lay still, but inside of him the anxiety grew to an unbearable intensity, to the point that he feared that his heart would fail him at any moment. *Come on Kurt! Relax, breathe*, and this he did, deeply inhaling and exhaling, slowly and deliberately. As he did so, he felt that his energy was bleeding out of him with every breath. For what seemed to be a very long period, nothing happened to Kurt as he lay on the carpeted bedroom floor, but then he became aware of a presence in the room and although he could see nobody, he desperately hoped that one of the earth spirits heeded his call and had come to save him. Then he felt a pressing sensation at his lips, as if something were trying to coerce his mouth to open. His mouth was violently wrenched wide by an unseen force and Kurt felt a thick, dense matter push its way into his mouth and slide toward his gullet. He felt as if he were being choked by the presence in his throat and he attempted to clear the horrid sensation by coughing harshly, but to his surprise, the matter slipped down his throat and he could once again breathe freely.

Was the spell working? Were the earth spirits real? More importantly was one of such entities now inside of him, healing him? He had not expected an earth essence to be so violent with its penetration and he was hoping that he may catch a glimpse of his saviour before it entered his body. Before Kurt could think any further, there was a loud bang inside his head and then blackness as he lost consciousness.

Jalel had dutifully done as his master had instructed. He did indeed return to Donovan's apartment and shadowed the man, watching him closely for any signs of occupation by Anubis, but to his dismay there were none. The only notable highlight of the last few days was watching the old man collapse of a broken heart. The old man had survived his heart attack and was now resting at the hospital.

The thief had become desperate with the whole Anubis situation and as such, he began to look for any means of escaping Apep's wrath after the seemingly inevitable failure of his mission became apparent to the serpent. Without any further leads, Jalel decided to follow Kurt back to Donovan's apartment, in hopes that Anubis may make his presence known to the son.

The thief could hardly believe his luck when Kurt had injured himself upon Ōsir and the ensuing desperate attempt to save his soul was put into motion. Jalel could see a means of escaping the maw of his wretched master Apep. Surely the reptile could not dine on the thief's soul while he was hiding in the body of a mortal being. Did he not say that he could only devour a soul once it had left the body? In any case, the thief had decided that he would take the chance and slip into Kurt Banks as the invitation to do so presented itself. As the dying young man spoke aloud his spell, the thief could see a break in the aura of Kurt's body as a passageway into a mountain may suddenly reveal itself. Jalel looked around the place nervously, checking for said earth spirits to reveal themselves, but to his joy none appeared and so he wasted no time in attempting to enter Kurt. Not having done such a thing before, the thief had tried to push his way into Kurt's mouth, but found once again that he was unable to manipulate the physical world. The disembodied spirit became desperate and furious at the hopelessness of his spirit form. The rage in him grew and grew. His energy became dark and dense with hatred and just when he felt he was about to erupt, the thief forced open the mouth of Kurt Banks, pushing his essence into the human's mouth and, struggling with all his might, managed to wriggle down the back of the man's throat and then into his lungs.

Jalel could feel his energy diluting and spreading throughout Kurt's bloodstream, permeating all parts of the body. The thief felt weak, but at least it appeared that he was now safe from Apep. *What now?*

If Jalel was to have any hope of living once again, he would have to somehow gain permanent control of his host's body and in time, destroy Kurt's consciousness completely. Apep had let slip the secret to the success of the thief's plan - he would have to go forth and devour the souls of living people, children did he say? Especially the unborn? *Then so be it,* he committed. He had waited for thousands of years to be free and what would it matter if he took the souls of the unborn? He'd never murdered an infant before, but he'd be doing them a favour, he justified to himself. They would not have to experience the pain of being born and existing in this terrible world, filled with horrible people and awful experiences. For the moment, he had to rest to regain his strength and when an opportunity presented itself to eat his first soul, he would be ready.

The first few moments of occupying Sam's body were awkward, and an unusual experience for Anubis. He had successfully managed to merge with the human and realised all too soon that if the body continued to lay there on the floor, Sam and the god would both perish from smoke inhalation. The beast had almost depleted his energy in the process of getting to this point, but now he had to find a little more strength to get the both of them outside to fresh air and safety. He concentrated hard on bringing his consciousness forward and taking control of Sam's body. As he did so, Sam's cells began to mutate, changing: his body stretched and his muscle mass increased threefold, his skin darkened to a matte black colour, his head and face stretched and elongated, taking on the form of the great god Anubis. His hair too became misshapen and appeared as the two long pointed ears of the beast, along with his body hair which grew out to cover his skin with the fine, short coat of the dog and in just a few moments, the man had effectively become the beast. Anubis was suitably impressed with this change of form and, feeling like himself for the first time in a thousand years, found a surge in adrenalin as he thrust the body up off the floor and stumbled heavily toward the rear exit. Once outside, the fresh air hit him like a solid wall, painfully forcing the lungs to surge again with glorious oxygen. This made the beast's head swoon and when the god became dizzy, he fell to his knees. He could no longer muster the strength to move and so the transformation reversed itself. So barely in existence was Anubis, that he retreated deeply back into the sanctity of Sam's inner workings, anchoring his consciousness deep in the abyss of spiritual dormancy, losing the ability to sense or be sensed. It was hardly surprising that Apep could not detect his presence in Sam's body, nor could Anubis learn of the serpent's gruesome quest and his subsequent plans for the beast. No, the god could do nothing at this moment and this pleased him greatly, for now was his chance to recuperate and regain his energy levels.

Sam's body was the worse for wear after the whole ordeal and as such, his consciousness had also sunk down into the nether regions of existence, while his body began to repair itself as he lay in his hospital bed. He would not recall any of the time spent floating around in nothingness, a dark and cold place where not even dreams nor nightmares dared to venture. Meanwhile, Anubis was much more active at this time, not physically, but rather he busied himself with getting to learn more about his host by delving into Sam's memories. He learned that Sam had grown up in a poor household, a child who was deprived of many things, but was compensated by the company of good friends and mostly pleasant childhood memories. A sometimes-mischievous child, Sam had his fair share of tomfoolery, which sometimes landed him in hot water with his parents, teachers or friend's mothers, but he was always good at heart and that was his saving grace when trouble came begging. As Sam grew into adolescence, his strength of character hardened and formed the foundation of the man he would become. He often found himself standing up for those who could not stand for themselves and never hesitated to take a punch from a bully to protect the intended victim, and he was equally as fast to counterpunch as he saw fit.

Love did not bloom for Sam until he reached his late teens and it was this first love that broke his virgin seal. Her name was Maya, a dark-haired, brown-skinned musical type and Sam considered her to be the most beautiful girl he had ever known at that point. His affections went as far as to suggest that she would be his first and only love, the one he would marry and spend the rest of his life with. That was until he discovered that she had cheated on him and so Sam was dealt his first broken heart, a pain that he would experience several more times and a pain that he would never get accustomed to. Anubis could see that those early tumbles had taken a toll on Sam's confidence regarding relationships with women, especially ones that he found attractive, as he simply believed that he was not good enough for them. Although Sam lacked confidence with women, he more than made up for it regarding his work and his kung fu.

Anubis was surprised to learn of Sam's martial arts prowess, not the talents that the god would have attributed to the body type that he currently resided in, but Sam's form was quite strong and resilient. His build allowed for great speed and his knowledge of martial combat complimented him superbly. What impressed Anubis the most was Sam's never-give-up attitude regarding his chosen sport. He had the heart and soul of a warrior, devoid of any fear toward his opponent, no matter how big or powerful they may appear. Even big men must fall, and Sam believed that he would be the one to bring them down.

During this time of contemplation, the god had started to formulate a plan of action. He was unable to take full control of Sam's body for more than about an hour. He had tested this by transforming into his bestial-form and sneaking out of the hospital in the small hours of the morning, after the nurse had completed her final rounds. Anubis discovered that human clothing was cumbersome attire. Sam's work clothes were too tight for the god's body and they had also ripped at the seams during the initial transformation at the gallery fire. He found the garments rather constricting and his beastly hairs itched as they caught against the fibres, his movement somewhat restricted and as such, he decided to shed Sam's hospital gown and enjoy the freedom that his nakedness provided him.

Anubis discovered that almost all his divine abilities were serviceable in this form, the downside was that the more he drew on those abilities, the faster he felt his energy drain. This, combined with the focus required to keep his form together and his consciousness on the forefront, resulted in him not being able to maintain full control of his bestial body. There were of course a few options. The first and easiest method was to simply go out and absorb some souls, thus growing in strength and being able to sustain longer periods of control over the host body. That option was against the beast's moral code and such actions would see him lose favour with his father Osiris. That was a fate worse than death, as Anubis was truly a loyal and obedient servant to his master, so the god ruled out that possibility.

Alternatively, the beast could make direct mental contact with Sam and attempt to explain the entire story to the mortal. Anubis could tell that the human did possess an open mind to extrasensory and paranormal realities, but there was the chance that such direct contact could push the human to madness. After all, how does one begin to explain to a mortal man that they have an ancient god living inside them?

The third choice was to plant subliminal messages into Sam's consciousness, attempting to direct him to make contact with Donovan Banks. Once Sam was in close physical proximity to Donovan, the beast could take over the body and reveal himself to his loyal protector and perhaps together they could finally contact Osiris and Anubis could be fully restored. This option would be the longest course of action, as it would take time to subtly guide Sam to Donovan. Already the paths of both men had crossed via the medium of the framing gallery and perhaps they may meet because of the fire. In any case, this would be the most palatable course of action, with no innocents being hurt and what was a few more weeks anyway? So much time had already passed, yes this was the best plan. The beast had made up his mind and retreated deep into Sam's fibres, content that all would be well, but all was not well, for a few miles away evil was awakening and both beast and man would soon be thrown into chaos.

Jalel was quite excited by his new surroundings. Kurt's body was warm and welcoming, a far cry from his exiled existence as a detached spirit who roamed the earth unable to sample its pleasures. The body was also very strong, being well-packed with muscle mass, and the thief was convinced that this strength would come in rather handy when it was time to dispatch his victims. It was with this conviction that he happily rode at the back of Kurt's consciousness, like a jockey rides a horse. He had been in the body for a full day now and felt restored enough to attempt to control the bulking carcass. His first attempt at controlling Kurt resulted in a severe spasm in the right bicep muscle, forcing the unwitting man to violently thrust his arm outward, jarring at the elbow joint and causing him to yell in shock at the outburst from the offending limb. Jalel was frustrated with the result – it was like being inside a vehicle and not knowing how to drive it.

Upon his next attempt, the thief decided to wait until Kurt had fallen into a deep sleep, and it was at this point that he could concentrate to bring his consciousness forward. He found that he was able to open the eyes and sit up. *Yes!* He could move again; he could feel the firm mattress underneath his bare buttocks as Kurt always slept nude; he could smell the air which was thick with expensive aftershave and the light stench of the day's body odour, and he could taste thick, stale saliva upon his tongue. He was ecstatic at these sensations – they may appear as trivial to most, but this was the feeling of life.

Realising that his breathing was laboured and finding difficulty in moving his head to look about his surroundings, Jalel urged the naked body to its feet and stumbled clumsily across the room to the ensuite bathroom, and fumbling at the wall, found the light switch and turned it on.

Instantly the room was drowned in bright iridescent light and the thief caught sight of his appearance in the adjacent mirror. He was horrified to see that he no longer resembled Kurt, nor himself, but rather his appearance was an unpleasant mixture of features and colours. It was as if the host body did not know how to assemble its cells correctly and the resulting appearance was demonic at best. His skin was pale blue, with dark purple and green blotches resembling the deep, dark bruising of rotting fruit. His face and head were covered in unsightly lumps and bumps and there were thick veins pulsating rapidly, writhing under his skin. His hair had flattened and slickened itself to his pasty scalp and forehead, which was now sharply angled back and to a point like a cone.

Perhaps the most unpleasant feature of the abomination was his eyes. They were bright yellow in the white of the eye, with deep red pupils, which closely resembled fresh drops of blood. Several thick black hairs sprouted out from the yellow section of the eye making his vision appear slightly blurred.

Jalel opened his mouth to gasp at his appearance and was sickened to catch sight of his teeth. They were twice as large as normal teeth and appeared to be all broken and twisted, with some roots exposed through the gums, which were also bleeding. Trembling, the thief ran his bony, gnarled and clawed fingers over his teeth and wherever he applied too much pressure, pus issued forth from the bleeding gums. His face and head were just the beginning of the horror, as his body was also severely disproportionate, the formerly well-toned musculature of Kurt's physique was now compressed and elongated in places and swollen to bursting in others.

One side of his chest was collapsed, almost to the thickness of a slice of bread, while the other side was engorged with fluid and wobbled like a water balloon that threatened to explode at any moment. The stomach appeared as if the torso had been completely twisted around three hundred and sixty degrees, with strong muscles that coiled around the mid-section, like thick wire cables. At his groin was his penis, which was impossibly long and twisted, resembling the curve of a ram's horn. It was dark green in colour and appeared like a rotten banana skin. The member seeped a bright orange fluid that hung like the thick drool of a dog and the testicles were nowhere to be seen. His legs were once again mismatched in size and length, and were set upon wide, flat feet that were twice as large as a normal human being.

'What manner of madness is this?' sputtered the abomination with utter disgust. So appalled was the thief that he lashed out violently, sending Kurt's personal hygiene and grooming products flying off the bathroom counter.

Jalel could not have anticipated that his merging with Kurt could cause such an awful configuration of the flesh, but what to do about it? The thief stood under the hideous, stark lighting, just standing there, staring into the mirror. His anger increased. His blood raced as the rage in him grew, and as it grew, he could see his vile flesh move and pulsate. Upon seeing this, he focused on the movement within him and concentrated with all his might, and to his astonishment, the flesh was stilled. The thief pushed the tissues with his mind and was thrilled to see that he could begin to reshape his form. Jalel continued to work on the transformation for several minutes longer, but reached a point when he could move the flesh no further. The result was much closer to the shape of a man, but he could not be rid of his skin colour, nor his large clawed hands – and his overall appearance could not be considered human.

'This will have to suffice,' growled the demon, his jagged and broken teeth jutting outward from his mouth whenever it was opened. Jalel decided that it would not be wise to attempt to leave Kurt's apartment tonight as his energy levels were dropping rapidly, due to the effort required to reshape his body. No, he would wait until tomorrow night and then he would see what dining opportunities arose. Although, he was still uncertain exactly how to harvest a soul – he needed to figure it out. Looking down at his clawed hands, the demon could foresee that despatching his first victim would be a messy job, but at least he would not require a weapon.

It had been two days since the fire and Sam had not yet awoken from his coma. During this time, Anubis continued to peer into the human's consciousness and whenever he did so, he found that he received some of Sam's energy – this nourished the god a little and Anubis was grateful for it. Perhaps he could be active for longer periods of time by using this method. The beast had to be cautious, for if he drained Sam too much, the human may not recover, and they would both be trapped in a useless body until the day Sam dies. At that point, both god and man would be lost.

Delving into Sam's mind and memories kept Anubis thoroughly entertained. The beast found himself wanting more and more time there and all the while Anubis learned not just more about Sam, but he discovered a great deal about humanity in general. The god could experience and feel raw human emotion through Sam. Such fears have mortal men, these fears cause all the faults of humanity: anger, greed, jealousy and lust, not to mention cowardice and the fear of death rules above all. Anubis saw that Sam had seemingly conquered some of these fears; he was not a greedy man – all he wanted was to be content with simple pleasures. He was not a lustful man; he sought the connection of intimate companionship, perhaps to heal from the wounds of past relationships, but he considered sex to be nothing more than a pleasurable bonus. He did not fear death; all men must perish, so Sam chose to look life in the eye and wink back at it, until the day when his eye would be closed for good. As for anger and jealousy? Well, he was still working on those. The god learned that Sam had pain and anger inside of him – the great flaw of his character. His only source of release was his Kung Fu, and he would spend hours venting his frustrations upon his kick-bag.

It was in the early hours of the morning, as the beast began to draw back out of Sam's consciousness, that a scent came to him, an all too familiar smell. It was the stench of death and although it was true that the god had detected the scent several times while in the hospital, the cause of those deaths was natural or illness-related. However, this was different. This impending death would be at the hands of pure evil and it would be an innocent death. Anubis would not sit idle as it happened. The beast stirred in the body, anxious because he had the ability to detect death before it happens, a premonition in the form of smell, and if he acted now, there was a slight chance of preventing the death from occurring. Anubis felt honour-bound to do something. Protecting the dead had been his vocation since his creation and for thousands of years he had been helpless to do that job. Even as his previous sacred protectors concurrently died, and the forewarning of those deaths came to the god, he was physically unable to render assistance. Now he had no excuse. He had a body and there was an innocent mortal who was about to be murdered.

CHAPTER EIGHT

Bon Appétit

THE GOD HAD SENSED impending murder and hesitating no longer, Anubis brought his consciousness forward. No sooner had he done so, than he could feel the physical change begin to take place. Tolerating the immense pain of the transformation, he rolled out of the hospital bed, as he had done over the previous two nights, just in time before his body became too large for the bed and thus making unwanted noise. He extended himself upright as the pain of tearing muscles and cracking bones racked his body. He pulled off the hospital gown before it was ripped apart, while his fine silky hairs sprouted forth from the now blackened skin. As he moved toward the door, his night vision came to him as his deep-set eyes glowed bright red.

Using his hyper-sensitive hearing and smell, the god had no trouble navigating his way through the corridors without being discovered, and soon enough he was through a rear exit and out into the brisk early morning air.

The beast stood erect and motionless as he sniffed at the wind which carried the clinical stench of the hospital, along with the stale smell of cigarette butts that had been discarded nearby. Concentrating harder, Anubis could now smell the various scents of the city wafting lightly upon the cool breeze and it was not long before he had the path of the potential victim. Then, with lightning speed, he rushed through the backstreets of the city heading toward his target.

It was very early in the morning, so the beast found a little comfort in that he may not be noticed if he did his best to stay in the shadows, and move with his god-speed. A few people were wandering the streets of the city, but Anubis sped past them with ease. Only a few of the pedestrians turned their heads, thinking they could see something move in the corner of their vision, but quickly returned their gaze forward upon seeing nothing.

Jalel had been stalking the woman for several blocks and was ready to make his move. He had spotted her as she left an all-night convenience store. She appeared to be heavily pregnant and as she made her way through the quiet neighbourhood, the demon decided that she would be his first victim. A tinge of humanity hit the thief in the pit of the gut; he knew full well what he was about to do and the thought of taking two lives was not pleasant. No, he had to focus – he needed to grow strong enough to destroy Kurt's consciousness and this was the only way. Perhaps he need not take two lives, he thought, as he was only interested in the unborn. Maybe he could simply knock the woman unconscious and then perform the task. Yes, that is what he would do.

The woman was alert as she passed through the empty streets, heading to her apartment a few blocks away. This part of the city had a higher than usual crime rate and so the expectant mother was being especially vigilant of her surroundings. It had rained late last evening and as such, the vacant bitumen streets were wet and glossy with oil, with the orange glow of an overhead street light laying it's lazy cast over the area. The early morning air was pungent with the scent of water drains, which had been aroused by the downpour of rain, their filthy contents stirred into action and a dank smell wafted up through the gutter vents. Somewhere nearby something had died – the sweet, sickening stench of death came to her nostrils, causing her to gag with the threat of vomit beckoning.

A strange sound came to her attention from behind her. She heard what sounded like thick slabs of raw meat being slapped heavily upon the concrete sidewalk, coming toward her. The woman turned toward the incoming sound and screamed in utter terror at the abomination that was suddenly upon her.

Jalel was hoping to attack the woman from behind – without being seen – so the sound of her scream sent the thief into a fit of rage. He swung his large, clawed right hand at his intended victim and struck her heavily on the side of her head, collapsing the skull and dropping her to the ground.

Jalel dragged the woman into the shadows of some nearby foliage and tore at her clothing, ripping her flesh open as he did so. The clawed hands of the creature were merely weapons, and unable to perform delicate tasks such as removing clothing. This further enraged the thief, causing him to slash at the body as he desperately searched for the unborn. He could feel his energy begin to drain already and knew that his time was limited, *where is it?*

He had no time remaining to search for the unborn, so he turned his attention to the mother – her essence would have to suffice. With much frustration, he began to take several mouthfuls of torn flesh from her body in the hope that he could literally eat the soul from her meat, and after several swallowed morsels, the demon decided that this was not the way.

Where is the soul? Jalel thought hard, back to when his soul was taken from him by Apep. He remembered a tingling sensation at the back of his neck, spreading up into his head, just behind the eyes, right before his soul was ripped from him. *Worth a try,* he conceded and so the demon turned the body over onto the stomach and forced his hand into the back of her neck. The creature's claws slid easily into the flesh and grabbing the top of her spine, the demon pulled downward and out of the body, like pulling a hose free from its connection. Blood jetted out of the gaping hole as he came closer to peer into the fleshy cavity.

For a few seconds the thief saw nothing, but then deep in the wound, at the back of the neck, he saw a faint blue glow. Hurriedly, he placed his wretched mouth over the wound and began to suck deeply, but all he could taste was blood. A moment later, a new taste came to him, a sweet taste, with the flavour of roasted lamb. A hot feeling filled his mouth and as he swallowed, he was reminded of the soups that he enjoyed back in Egypt.

The thief had done what he does best, he had stolen. He had stolen two lives, but most importantly he had stolen a soul and he felt a surge of energy as the innocent woman's essence was absorbed. He had no time to celebrate his gruesome victory, however, for no doubt the woman's scream may have alerted someone to come and investigate the cause of her distress. So, the demon decided that he had taken his fill for the night and retreated away into the darkness.

Anubis had been too late to save the woman and as he looked down with sorrow at the ravaged corpse, his heart ached for her loss of life. Her soul had gone from its flesh shell and upon further inspection of the body, the beast could see that it had been extracted from the base at the back of the skull, but why and by whom? As far as Anubis was aware, only the gods possessed the knowledge of soul ingestion. His mind raced through the pantheon of his brother and sister gods to pinpoint a possible culprit for the horrific murder and only one god came to his mind - Apep.

Anubis remembered his encounter with Jalel during the gallery fire, where the fiend had made mention of his master's plan and did he not hear the name 'Apep' being called out as he disappeared down Sam's gullet? At the time Anubis considered that the thief was merely cursing at his current situation, as the name Apep was commonly used as vulgar vernacular in the old times like one might use the word 'shit' today.

However, something did not seem right: Apep is strictly forbidden from taking innocent lives by Osiris. Such an act would leave a spiritual stain on the reptile and would consequently be noticed by Osiris, so the resulting punishment would be severe beyond measure. It was true that Apep could devour any soul guilt-free once it had left the body – perhaps the thief and his brother god were working together. Was the thief doing the killing and the serpent devouring the freed soul? but to what end? Apep was indeed a powerful entity, so his consumption of souls was not necessary. Besides, the method of extraction was crude and far below Apep's standards.

For a moment Anubis considered calling out to his brother god to confront him about the situation, but he realised that if the reptile was indeed involved, the beast would not yet have the strength to fight Apep. No, for now he had to do his best to be vigilant, keeping his senses alert for any more killings and be ready to act in the hope that next time he would be in time to save any innocent souls.

Anubis was just about to leave the grisly scene when he sensed a soft glow deep inside the womb of the body. The poor woman was with child. At realisation of the tragedy, the god howled with anger and sadness, for it was said that children are a direct gift from the father god Osiris, that each child is born pure, a small sample of heaven and truly precious. Anubis kneeled close to the body. He could see the poor, innocent little soul struggling inside the dead flesh. It had to be released.

The beast looked about the place for something that could be used to open the body to gain access to the languishing soul. Not far from the corpse, Anubis found the neck of a broken beer bottle and decided that it would have to suffice. After cutting through the already mangled layers of skin, fat and muscle, the god found the soul hovering above a pool of thick blood that had collected inside the incision. Lovingly, the beast lowered his hand and the small essence of the child playfully climbed onto his palm and glowed brightly at the god. *What to do with the little fellow?* the beast pondered.

He certainly could not escort it to the Underworld and he was not about to let the infant soul wander around aimlessly, lost in the material world. So, there appeared to be only one viable option – Anubis would absorb the child's essence. At least it would live on forever inside of the god, free from the curse of humanity.

Anubis raised the tiny soul to his canid mouth and gently drew it in, inhaling the essence into his lungs, as a smoker might take a long, smooth drag upon a cigarette, and there the soul remained, tingling inside the beast's tissues.

The joy that the god felt at freeing the soul quickly soured, as his attention returned to the despicable monster that had perpetrated such a horrendous murder. The beast decided, at that very moment, to abandon his own quest for restoration, in lieu of bringing this soul-sucker to justice.

Osiris would have to wait for now, because Anubis was protector of the dead and for too long the dead had been left neglected. Although it was true that he could not do his usual job in his present condition, he could at least do his best to protect the innocent from being killed for soul food.

Anubis felt the energy of Sam beginning to stir. The human had been close to returning to full consciousness during the afternoon, but slipped back at the last moment, back into the deep abyss of his subconscious. The god realised that perhaps over the next few days Sam would awaken proper, the situation resulting in Anubis taking a back seat, while his host struggled to regain his faculties.

Taking one last glance at the corpse, the beast turned and with his god-speed, made haste back to the hospital and then to conceal his presence, he washed himself of blood and grime. As his bestial-form receded, he slipped the robe around himself and lay down upon the bed, retreating back into the comfort of Sam's being, and with no further thought, the god slumbered.

Kurt awoke with a start from his nightmare-filled sleep. Images of death and mutilation plagued him throughout the night, dreams so realistic and frighteningly vivid, that he feared that he would be surrounded by bloody mayhem upon awakening. To his relief, all was still in his small, yet well-appointed studio apartment. He had not escaped unscathed from the terrors of the night, though. He was drenched in sweat and felt like he had run a marathon. Every muscle of his body ached. He fancied that he may have some residual health issues after his brush with Osir a few days prior. Now a vile taste came to his attention, the taste of dry blood. As he struggled to rise from his bed, severe cramps accosted his washboard stomach, bringing nausea and subsequent vomit spewing forth across the floor, covering his clothing from yesterday which had been clumsily discarded. Kurt was horrified to discover that he had evacuated several large blood clots and what appeared to be some type of partially digested meat across the floor. He frowned and tried to recall what he had eaten for dinner the previous evening.

Finally, Kurt made it into his shower and sat down on the tiled floor, with the hot water peppering his aching body. His thoughts drifted back and forth between his nightmares and the day ahead, and after several more stomach evacuations, he decided that he was well enough to leave the sanctity of his steamy, wet fortress of comfort.

As he readied himself for a shave, his thoughts turned to his father. The doctor had called the previous afternoon, stating that Donovan was recovering well from his heart flutter and after several tests and scans, it was determined that surgery would not be necessary at this time. To avoid any further stress for his father, Kurt had decided not to tell Donovan of his injury from Osir and his dalliance with ancient magic, such information would be too much for his father in his poorly condition and may put the old man down for good.

The sound of his mobile phone ringing roused him from his thoughts and after a few unsteady steps, he located his phone and answered with a dry, raspy voice.

'Hello?'

'Kurt, it's Tom. Are you okay? You don't sound well.'

'Oh hey, boss, yeah I'm okay. What's up?' Kurt rubbed his face and began dressing himself.

'There's been a murder – it's just come across the police scanners. It happened several blocks from you, near the underpass on Grace Street. I need you to get your ass over there asap. You should easily beat our rivals to the story, hopefully get a few exclusives.'

As Tom was talking, Kurt felt heavy and fuzzy and so it was with some difficulty that he managed to navigate his way about the room. Kurt was half dressed, his shirt unbuttoned, and a designer tie draped over his broad neck and shoulders. He clumsily slipped on his shoes and managed to locate his keys and wallet, but where was his phone? It took a moment for him to realise that he was still on his phone with Tom and hence why he could not locate the device, his confusion dampening Tom's words.

'Hello? Kurt, are you listening to me?'

'Huh? Yes, boss, I've been getting ready, am on my way now.'

'Excellent! I've got the photo crew on their way, but be sure to take some pictures with your phone until they arrive.'

'No problems, boss, I'll be into the office as soon as I'm finished up at Grace Street.'

Tom seemed satisfied and promptly hung up on Kurt, an all too familiar mannerism from his boss. He was a tough, but fair man and rightfully so, as was necessary to oversee a major newspaper. Kurt payed him no mind, he was getting accustomed to Tom's abruptness.

As Kurt arrived at the scene, the usual dance with the police began, denying the reporter access into the cordoned-off area. The pungent smell of spoiling blood met his nostrils, carried on the air by the rising humidity of the rainwater which had evaporated from the warming bitumen. The sickening scent made Kurt gag, but he pushed on with his probing questions and as expected, few answers were surrendered by the officer standing sentry at the tape. Progressively, the police forensic unit finished their documentation and the coroner dutifully removed the covered body, of which Kurt managed a few photographs on his phone.

Kurt noticed that one of the forensic officers had parted from her colleagues and was heading to an equipment van. Perhaps he could try his charm to pry a few precious pieces of information from her. 'Hey there, I haven't had the pleasure of meeting you at one of these scenes before,' Kurt quipped as he followed the woman to her van.

The officer turned and looked Kurt over with suspicion. She was short and a little on the larger size, her unkempt hair sat sluggishly upon the woman's head. Her broad face was devoid of any sign of warmth, with light brown eyes appearing as overly large, thanks to her glasses, which looked rather small set on her large round face. She raised her short, plump fingers to her face and brightly painted fingernails traced her thin dark hair back around her ear, away from her cheek, 'I'm sorry, who are you?'

The sight of the woman made Kurt recoil inwardly, but he had a job to do and the officer was his best chance at getting any details about the murder. 'Kurt, Kurt Banks,' the reporter purred, as he softly took her hand into a gentle, deliberate shake. 'I'm a reporter with The Open Eye.'

Upon learning of Kurt's identity, the woman quickly withdrew her hand from the tender handshake and turned her frame toward the van, busying herself with stowing away the equipment.

'Well sorry, Mr Banks, but you won't get any sensationalism from me. I know your type. Any information you get ends up being overly exaggerated.'

'Oh, you have me all wrong Miss … Sorry, I didn't catch your name.'

'And I didn't give it. I fail to see how I can help you anyway. We both know that all information and evidence gathered will be retained from public knowledge until the police commissioner is ready to release a statement.'

Kurt's frustration grew with ferocity and consequently, he felt something stirring at the back of his mind, making him dizzy and unable to focus. He raised the palm of his hand to his forehead and discovered that it was slick with sweat.

It seemed that the thief was tired of having to witness the pathetic scene playing out between his host and the unpleasant woman and, as such, decided to test out his growing strength to see if he could take control of the body while Kurt was still conscious.

The forensic woman turned back to face Kurt and a look of concern flashed across her broad face, 'Are you okay, Mr Banks? You're looking very pale.'

Kurt's eyes met hers and with a sudden change, his face contorted into a vicious scowl. His cheeks flushed with rage, casting a bright red hue as he erupted with a venomous tirade at the shocked woman, 'Bitch! You are a disgusting lump of filth! You have no idea who you are talking to!'

The demon attempted to reach out for her, but he was unable to raise the heavy arms from his sides, likewise, he could not step forward. His anger surged at his impotence, sending the veins in his neck and face into a network of swollen, pulsating anguish, almost to the point of eruption. The thief became blind with rage as a scarlet haze fell across his vision and feeling his energy begin to wane, his consciousness struggled – like a drowning cat.

As suddenly as the contortion had begun, it disappeared – Kurt's face pacifying as he regained control of his faculties. His vision returned to see the shocked stare of the forensic woman standing with her mouth agape and her eyes wet, almost to the point of tears. Clearly, she must be a strong woman, hardened by the scenes of carnage as her career demanded. However, something had obviously transpired in the last few moments that had shaken her, and Kurt, not knowing what had happened, tendered out his hand as a gesture of concern.

The woman convulsed as she retreated up against the back of the van, desperately attempting to evade the reporter's touch. 'You, keep the hell away from me!'

Kurt withdrew his hand and took several steps back away from her. 'Look, I don't know what has upset you. I was just hoping to get some insight into this terrible crime, but I don't want to distress you. I'll just go now, let you be.'

With that, Kurt turned and started away, but the woman called out after him, 'You're sick! You need to get some professional help and you are so lucky that you did not lay a hand on me, or I would have you arrested for assault!'

The reporter did not look back at her as he hurried away, but a sense of total confusion came over him. What had happened? He had blacked out obviously, as he had several times over the past couple of days. Maybe he did need to see a doctor, but that would have to wait for now. He had to get something for his story. So he decided to just be still and observe, and hopefully he could piece together a report for Tom.

ÇHAPTER NINE

The Angel of Death

JALEL HAD LEARNED HIS lessons from the murder in Grace Street, the first of which was the element of surprise. Last time his presence was detected early into the attack, resulting in the woman screaming. Next time, it may be possible that someone could interfere with the harvest. He was clumsy and awkward in his demon-form and consequently, any hope of sneaking up on his victims was dashed. He thought it best to try to utilise Kurt's appearance, to be able to get closer to his target before changing into the demon. The plan would not be very convenient for Jalel, as he would have to wait until Kurt was close to a pregnant woman and his host would have to be near exhaustion, only then could the thief take over control of the flesh.

Fortune smiled upon Jalel sooner than he had expected. Early that evening, Kurt decided to go to his gymnasium for a workout to combat his sense of sluggishness. The result had the opposite effect, as Jalel could feel the workout left Kurt feeling fatigued and run down.

As Kurt made his way along the street, he decided to call into a chemist in hopes that some vitamins could help him through his fogginess. It was there that he noticed a woman discussing her pregnancy issues with the pharmacist, and the gentleman was pleased to provide her with some herbal supplements to help remedy her morning sickness. Jalel could barely contain his excitement at the opportunity before him, and as his energy surged, he crept forward into Kurt's consciousness and rode just behind the reporter's awareness. This trick appeared to work well for the thief, as from this position he had a command view of the situation and he felt that if he willed it, he may be able to lightly influence Kurt into following the unsuspecting victim. To his utter delight, it worked. He succeeded in urging his host to follow the woman at a distance and the last thought that Kurt had before he blacked out was, *why am I following this lady to her car?*

The sun had just sunk below the horizon as the woman made her way across the avenue and down the street to the open-air carpark, where her vehicle awaited. It was true that she had turned and noticed the handsome young man behind her, but payed him no mind as he appeared to be walking in a daydream state, perhaps thinking of some lucky woman. *Better be careful,* she thought, *or else that couple might be having a baby of their own.* The idea brought a smile to her face as she held her swollen belly.

As she opened her car door, she heard a squelching sound as the strong stench of sour body odour and sewerage met her nostrils. She did not see her assailant approach as he landed a blow to the back of her head, painting it with the creature's foul-smelling sweat as it made contact and sent the woman into unconsciousness.

The fiend bundled the woman into the back seat of the car and rolled her onto her back. Then wasting no further time, he first opened the woman's clothing and then her flesh, more carefully this time. Jalel sliced through the tissue and after a few moments, he succeeded in finding the unborn infant. To be certain, he took the entire fleshy mass into his mouth and slowly chewed down upon it, sending a mixture of blood and fluid oozing out from his busted mouth. The buzzing tang of iron-laced blood and tissue was offensive at best, but after several unpleasant chews, that familiar taste of hot roasted lamb sent a surge of energy into the demonic fibres of his twisted carcass.

The reptile Apep had told the truth, this energy was strong and pure, so it was easily absorbed and remained for some minutes, vibrating intensely before finally resting in the demon's chest.

The thief immediately felt like he had harnessed the power of a god and that he was aware of all around him. It was then that he spotted an ominous figure slinking through the shadows some fifty meters away, heading directly toward his location. Due to his poor vision, he could not see much detail of the figure, nor did he need to – all he knew was that he must flee the scene. Jalel did not want any type of physical confrontation. He had worked entirely too hard for his reward and he did not want to spoil the energy that was still buzzing inside of him, so he moved across the body and the slickened vinyl seat, which was now sticky with copious amounts of blood. The demon fumbled at the opposite door, his malformed digits struggling to find purchase upon the doorhandle, before managing to push it wide open. Slipping out of the car, he hurriedly made his escape across the lot, over a fence and into the darkness beyond.

Anubis had again felt the forewarning of murder and did his godly best to speed to the scene of the inevitable crime. The hospital was not an easy place to escape from undetected, especially during this early time of the evening. Luckily, Sam had a private room, which made the mission somewhat easier. The god now needed his human host to regain full consciousness and recover, so that the beast could operate with greater ease from Sam's home.

As Anubis approached the area where the impending scent of death had led him, he saw a bulking figure clamber away from a parked car, and with a turn of blinding speed, the god surged after it. He fully intended to pursue the assailant, but was stopped in his tracks at the sound of a woman's groan coming from a vehicle ahead of him. The beast desperately wanted to catch the perpetrator, but if his victim was still alive, then her life was far more important.

The woman showed no sign of fear as Anubis approached and gazed sorrowfully upon her. Perhaps she sensed that the beast meant her no harm, and besides, she had lost a massive amount of blood and was far too weak to conjure a scream. The god appraised the woman's injuries and soon realised that she could not be saved, not by any hospital, nor any witch doctor. 'You have been mortally wounded. I'm afraid there is nothing to be done,' the beast spoke calmly to the woman.

'My baby … Is he gone?'

'You were with child?'

The woman slowly nodded and Anubis held his hand over her mutilated belly, but could not feel a presence, nor could he see the glow of a soul there. 'He appears to be gone,' the god replied tenderly.

The woman let out a soft, solitary sob of grief, as if that was all the energy that her failing body could provide her.

Anubis felt great anger welling inside of him, such a primitive human emotion to be sure, nevertheless, an emotion that he felt come naturally to him. He pushed the fury aside as he moved to reassure the dying woman before him. 'You have not much time left on this world, please try to be at peace.'

The woman looked up curiously at Anubis, her breathing had slowed, as had her tears, 'Are you an angel? Perhaps the angel of death?'

A slight smile came to the beast upon hearing her question. He had never considered himself an angel – he was a god, but in the new religions, angels and gods were operating on different levels of hierarchy. Whereas, in reality the gods and angels were one and the same. His brother and sister gods could in fact be called angels in today's world, but he still called himself a god, as the old religion decreed. 'I am a god, the god of the dead. However, you can call me angel if you wish.'

The woman was becoming weaker by the moment, but still her questions came between ragged breaths. 'Wow … a real god? I never really believed … in religion. Tell me, god of the dead … is there a heaven? A hell?'

'Of sorts, yes, but not as you have learned of. All worthy souls have an opportunity to pass into the Underworld. Once at the entrance to the afterlife, a soul is weighed and if your heart is light with good deeds, you may continue to the father god Osiris, where one can spend eternity in what you may consider to be paradise. On the other side of the scale is a place known, in my tongue, as Durat. If your heart is heavy with evil deeds, then you will enter a plane which you may know as hell. Do not worry mortal, I can see that you have lived a good life. However, for the time being you will go to neither realm. I'm afraid that, as protector of the dead and guide to the Underworld, I have been temporarily stripped of my capabilities and my tools.'

A weak look of panic crossed the dying woman's face and noticing her distress, the god reassured her, 'Fear not, time moves quickly in the spirit world. It will seem that time has barely passed before I shall be fully restored, and I will personally take you, by hand, to the afterlife.'

The woman relaxed, her breathing slowing to a soft wheeze. Anubis gently cradled her head in his hands and brought his face close to hers. The woman had one final question and it took all her strength to ask it. 'Will it ... hurt?'

Anubis gave a slight nod of his head as he answered, 'Only for a moment, once the body ceases to function you will feel no more physical pain and I will free your soul. You will be free to roam the spirit world until I return for you. Now, my child, let yourself slip away. Look deeply into my eyes and let go of this body.'

The woman did as she was instructed and with a final, sustained groan of pain and a sudden, violent shudder, her body was still. Anubis could see her soul resting in the pineal gland and wasted no time in dragging her body out of the car.

He rolled her onto her stomach and raised her head back, then he smashed it to the bitumen over and over until the head split open. At this moment the soul was freed, and it lingered there briefly before it took the appearance of the young woman, hovering over her body. As a spirit, all communication was now non-verbal, but the woman found no difficulty in speaking to the god. 'Thank you, I am so grateful to you. Oh my, I never did ask if you have a name.'

'Anubis is my name.'

'Well then, thank you, Anubis.'

The spirit looked down at the mangled mess that was once her body with a look of dismay. 'Oh well, looks like there is no going back now.'

'No, I'm afraid not.'

'Not that I would want to – it feels so wonderful to be free.'

'Well, it is true, you are free and moreover, there are such wonders awaiting you in the afterlife. As I promised, I will return for you, but for now I must be away from here. Farewell–'

'Jennifer, my name is Jennifer.'

'Farewell, Jennifer.'

Anubis was becoming increasingly frustrated at his inability to prevent the killings and his lack of control over the human body which he co-inhabited. It was not long before the thief struck again and Anubis would come close to preventing the murder. He had successfully managed to escape yet again from the hospital, despite it being during the day. Thankfully, Sam had awoken from his coma, so there could be several reasons why he would be missing from his bed. The god had once again followed the stench of death which lingered on the air and arrived on the scene as the assailant was in the process of butchery.

The demon, now busying himself with the soul harvest in broad daylight, was under the cover of an underground car park in the centre of the city. Anubis was grateful for the parked vehicles offering ample coverage for him to close in undetected.

Anubis was aptly appalled with the appearance of the demon. He had never, in his very long life, witnessed such a twisted monstrosity of creation. How and why had this abomination come to exist? Yet, the warped and clumsy form of the entity betrayed the considerable strength that it possessed. Anubis moved to attack without warning and the demon was stunned to see the beast before him. The demon attempted to speak, but the god struck him before any words could be formed.

Anubis could sense that he did not have the strength to overwhelm the hulk of the form with which he now tussled, but the beast had managed to wound the demon. He bit and latched onto the foul flesh of its twisted left arm. The fiend screeched in pain and, with a surge of strength, the murderer broke free from his entrapment before escaping from the carnage with great speed.

With the killer gone, Anubis attended to the third victim, but once again there was nothing to be done to save her – indeed, she was already dead.

The beast had come prepared this time. The previous victim had required her skull to be smashed open to access the pineal gland, thus freeing the trapped soul. The god knew of a better, cleaner way of freeing the trapped essence. He would remove the pineal gland via the nasal cavity. After Jennifer's murder, Anubis had fashioned a hooking implement from a wire coat hanger that he had discovered in a janitor closet at the hospital, along with a long shaft screwdriver.

His mouth still dripping with the demon's blood, Anubis went to work, first cracking through the nasal cavity with the use of the screwdriver and then expertly locating and retrieving the pineal gland from the head. And finally, with a gentle squeeze, the soul was released from the flesh. The freed essence took the form of the woman, as she was in life, and after introducing himself, Anubis reassured the woman that he would also return for her, and that she would not be destined to remain on this plane forever.

The whole process of soul retrieval was so much easier with the aid of Osir, a simple slash of the flesh releasing essence slowly or a plunge into the heart or head resulting in instant release. Oh, how he missed his old colleague. The god was deeply wounded at losing his long-time companion in Osir. As he looked down at the corpse, he was reminded of all the loss of life that was occurring around him and at his ineptitude to prevent such dreadful loss. His emotions welled up inside of him, and for the first time in his life, he felt vulnerable and utterly alone. This feeling caused the beast to let loose a whimper, which became a soft howl of sadness.

At the approach of a car engine heading his way, Anubis was stirred from his moment of sorrow. So, he rose and after seeing the spirit of the murdered woman also retreating into the shadows, he made good on his escape.

Early the next morning, there was a meeting at The Open Eye and all were present as Tom provided details of the third and latest murder, as provided by Kurt. He then went about distributing story tasks to the others.

Tom turned his attention to Erica, who was busy flicking through her notebook. 'Erica, you were working on the art gallery fire … what did you get there?'

Kurt looked the pretty young reporter up and down. Erica Murphy – she'd been struggling to find her way at The Open Eye for over six months now, but had recently found her feet after doing some classy reports on the emerging downtown fashion renaissance, which was currently sweeping the city. *Sexy little piece*, Kurt mused. She had near perfect proportions, long legs, shapely thighs and hips, and she had a flat stomach – above which perched an ample set of breasts, threatening to detract attention from her gorgeous face. Her pallor was too pale for him, but he could forgive that flaw if the mood lighting was dimmed. He chuckled to himself at the thought of her sweet surrender to his charming seduction. He had even gone out of his way to follow Erica to her apartment the previous evening. He had a habit of stalking his prey, always looking for an opportune moment to 'accidentally' run into them away from the office, *want to grab a bite? Fancy a drink or two?* Kurt had stood across the street from Erica's window and watched from the shadows as she peered down into the street. At one point, he feared that she may have seen him, and he moved to retreat further into the shadows before slinking off down the street.

'The police have been far too busy dealing with the prenatal killings, so they have put the gallery fire investigation on the back burner for now,' Erica replied courteously to her boss.

Kurt cringed at the sound of her accent, that was a deal-breaker for him and so she would have to remain as eye candy. Oh well, there were plenty of other women for him to pursue.

'Okay well, any progress with the picture framer in the hospital?' Tom asked Erica with his usual bossy tone.

'I've been visiting with him the past three days. He woke yesterday, but can't remember much about the fire, so I don't have much of a story yet. I'll check in with him later,' Erica replied dutifully.

In truth, Erica had a far more interesting story to follow up on. She had secretly conducted an interview with an eyewitness to the recent third murder and consequently, she had quite the tale to tell police. She had decided not to share any information with her boss, or Kurt, as she knew that she would not be able to take credit for the story. Instead, she'd go to the police directly with her information, then she would contact Channel 5 News. The station was owned by the same media company that ran The Open Eye – that would hopefully lead to her big break. Besides, sometimes only the daring prevail, and if she were to promote her way up the hierarchy ladder, she would have to be bold.

CHAPTER TEN
All Caught Up

KURT WAS BEGINNING TO worry about his state of mind, especially the missing time that he had started to experience with increasing frequency. He felt that his mind had somehow been damaged by his near-death experience, following his wounding by Osir – and speaking of wounds, what had happened to his arm? He had woken to find that his left arm was crudely wrapped with his gym singlet, and upon removing the wrap, he discovered what could only be described as a large bite mark. *How did that happen?* He scratched his head using his other hand. *How did I get home?* He could remember leaving the gymnasium and he could remember going into a chemist for vitamins, but nothing after that.

After rummaging through his bathroom drawers, Kurt found a suitable bandage, and after gently cleaning the throbbing wound with soap and water, he covered his injury.

He also feared that the horrific nightmares that he continued to experience were somehow linked to the recent murders of pregnant women. In such bad dreams, he witnessed things that would later be revealed by the police – things that only the killer would know. Was he psychic? Had his brush with death and his consequent gamble with magic resulted in his gaining of mind powers? He decided that the answer was no, since he could not yet read women's minds. As if to provide proof that he did not possess said abilities, Kurt was astonished and outraged to learn that his fellow reporter Erica had gone behind his back and filed a report with Channel 5 regarding the prenatal murders.

The feeling of betrayal grew inside of Kurt progressively throughout the morning. If he once saw any appeal in Erica, it was well and truly gone now. He tried to confront her at her apartment, only to find that she was not there. Even Tom did not know of her whereabouts, so he decided to wait at the office for her to show up and then he would really let her have it.

He waited, seated in the nearby meeting room of The Open Eye and he watched, peering through the partially opened horizontal blinds the large pane glass window, which provided a command view of the communal workspace. Gradually, all his fellow workers left their work stations for the day and headed off to tend to their own personal business. He watched as Tom made a quick round trip through the work area, stopping occasionally to snoop about his employees' desks, and after some time, Tom left the room and turned off the lights.

An eerie glow was cast about the now vacant area, with vivid hues of white and blue from some of the computer monitors that were still turned on. The hum and buzz of the consoles set an ear numbing soundtrack to the otherwise silent scene.

Just as Kurt was debating to himself if he was wasting his time, wondering if his confrontation with Erica was justified enough to endure such dreadful monotony, he spotted her as she quickly crept through the darkened room to her desk and turned on her computer.

Kurt felt his head spin as he rose to his feet. He had also lost some feeling in his feet and toes, now tingling with the welcome restoration of ample blood flow. As he advanced slowly through the meeting room door and into the work area, he fancied that his vision was beginning to haze over, and little blue points of light sparked in his eyes. *No, must hold on,* he urged himself. After such a long period of time seated, waiting for Erica, he could not lose the chance to confront her now.

Kurt enjoyed seeing Erica startled as she spun around with fright at the sound of his voice. Once again, they were face to face, however, this time Kurt saw no beauty there and no thoughts of sexual adventures entered his mind. Indeed, the only feeling growing inside of him was rage and as the anger grew, he felt his mind start to slip as if a dark, damp blanket was being pulled over his brain. Erica's pleas for Kurt's compassion and understanding did nothing to quell his temper, but he did his best to hold his frustration in check. The horrible sensation of creeping darkness continued to crawl over his mind and lurked at the very edge of his consciousness – much like a cobra standing in strike position, threatening to lash out at any moment. Kurt felt the muscles in his face and neck begin to twitch and contort as he looked coldly upon the frightened young woman. Her fear gave him much satisfaction.

Without warning, a new voice came from the far side of the room and Kurt looked up to see the figure of a man standing there in the doorway, silhouetted by the fluorescent glow from the lights in the hall behind him. The stranger seemed hesitant to interrupt the intense exchange between the two colleagues, his voice tinged with uncertain enquiry, 'Hello? Erica Murphy?'

'Sam? I'm over here!'

Erica's relief was evident upon her face as she looked urgently at the stranger who was now coming over toward them. Kurt decided to put a little space between himself and Erica, just in case she decided to accuse him of violent intent.

As Erica was busy introducing the newcomer to him, Kurt was shocked to see that the young man's face was somehow changing shape. As his eyes disappeared into their sockets, they were replaced by a menacing red glow; his ears stretched up into tall points, perched fully erect at the sides of his head, all while fine black hairs sprouted all over his face as it warped and reshaped into a canine-like head. His body had also rapidly begun to change. The disturbing sounds of cracking bone and tearing tissue could be heard as the stranger's body began growing in muscle mass and once again the fine hairs were sprouting forth from his body as the beast ripped the shirt off its now fully transformed physique.

Erica had seen the look of terror upon Kurt's face – his gaze was not directed at her, but past her. She had heard the horrible sounds and as a look of utter confusion spread across her pretty face, she reluctantly turned her head back to face

Sam. Her rescuer was gone and, in his place, was some type of creature. Its crimson glowing eyes bore past her, and the beast snarled ferociously at Kurt. Erica let out a horrific scream and fell backward into an adjacent office chair.

Unable to pry his disbelieving eyes from the creature which now towered above Erica and himself, Kurt was frozen with fear until he finally recognised the beast before him as the one whom he was sworn to protect. The dark blanket which lingered at the back of his mind now rushed forward, sending an intense numbness through Kurt's body, and before he lost consciousness, he uttered the name of his god.

'Anubis!' Kurt had barely managed to speak the word before he started to convulse, and he was gone, pulled back into unconsciousness as the thief was now in the driver's seat and making his grand appearance. The transformation into his demon-form was steadily becoming easier for Jalel, and as such, in a matter of seconds, his bulky mass of twisted flesh and bone had manifested itself.

Erica turned her attention toward the sickening sound of twisting meat coming from Kurt's direction and again she let loose with a deafening scream of terror. The warped monstrosity before her was surely something drawn directly from the mouth of hell and she doubted that even the Devil himself could ever imagine such a being into existence. Yet, there it was, the sight of the thing turned her gut and then the smell of the abomination accosted her, with the sickening stench of excrement, sulphur and infected pus. She violently gagged, threatening to evacuate the contents of her stomach, yet somehow, perhaps due to the terror that had seized her, she resisted doing so.

Anubis knew the stench of the killer and had sensed the presence hiding inside the shell of his supposed protector Kurt as soon as he had ridden Sam's consciousness into the vicinity. Indeed, he had little time to be surprised to see Kurt, let alone ponder as to why there was such an evil aura about the mortal he seemingly knew so well. Anubis had little choice, he had the killer cornered, the god had to take control of his host's body and take urgent action to confront the murderer.

The beast and the thief were again at an impasse and a newly confident and empowered Jalel considered himself more than capable of dispatching the god for good this time. At their last meeting the thief was taken by surprise at the arrival of Anubis at the murder scene and yet he had managed to stave off the attack, suffering a bite wound from the beast. He felt, however, that he was far stronger than Anubis and he had only retreated from the scuffle because of the shock at seeing the god, but primarily because he feared being caught and he was not yet ready to give up his newly discovered diet of souls.

'Ah, dog! We meet again!' the demon slurred and sputtered his words harshly, as his mouth was so malformed that it was with difficulty that he could form speech.

A look of confusion struck Anubis – there was only one person that had ever dared to call him dog. 'Thief?'

'Yes, it is me, the humble thief. I am remade – now I am a god like you.'

Anubis scowled at the thief upon hearing the blasphemous words. How dare he call himself a god. 'A god? You? I think not, thief! Gods are not born. They are made by Osiris and they certainly do not prey upon the souls of the innocent unborn.'

What may be considered a smile crept across the demon's face, its decayed and broken teeth sprouting forth from the orifice like rotting maggots pushing out of a bloated corpse. 'Oh really, dog? Is that the truth of it? I have been told differently. In fact, it was your brother god who suggested the whole thing in the first place.'

Anubis needed no further clues as to whom the thief was referring. 'You mean to tell me that the serpent was responsible for teaching you such secrets?'

'Hmm, you are a clever beast are you not? You dare not mention his name for fear that he will come. You do realise, of course, that this whole idea is a part of his master plan and I am but a humble minion to his righteous cause.'

The god had no time, nor patience to hear anymore drivel from the thief. If his brother truly was the mastermind behind this situation, then he would have to deal with him later. For now, he knew that the lives of Sam and Erica relied upon his quick action.

Without another word, the beast leaped at the demon and swiped his canine claws across its face, opening a large wound across the nose from which fluorescent green snot, blood and mucus billowed forth, producing a deep, intense howl of pain from the monster. The god savagely bit at the demon's head but was held back by the brute strength of the hulking mass of twisted muscle and sinew. With a violent thrust, the demon pushed Anubis back against Erica's desk, sending the computer monitor crashing to the tiled floor.

As the god righted himself in preparation for another attack, he called out to the terrified woman, 'Erica Murphy, please make haste and run from here!'

'No, wait, where is Sam?' Erica asked, her wits shocked by the insanity that was occurring about her, then turning to the abomination, she continued, 'Kurt? Why are you doing this and how?'

The creature stared intently at the woman, its eyes cold and unresponsive and showing absolutely no trace of humanity.

'Kurt, please! You cannot be the killer of those poor women. I just will not accept that!'

The demon took a step toward Erica, and at her back she could sense that Anubis was prepared to attack again. She could feel his energy radiating near her, sending the fine hairs on her arms and neck erect.

'Stupid bitch!' the demon slurred. 'You will not reach Kurt – he is gone – now there is only me!'

She felt the warm hand of Anubis on her arm as he gently moved her aside and took a defensive stance in front of her. He lowered his body slightly and tensed every muscle, ready for one final offensive against the demon.

The demon remained still and then shuddered violently, his face convulsed and shifted shape until finally familiar eyes appeared in the pulsing mass of broken flesh and bone. It was Kurt. Somehow, he had found enough strength to break the demon-form, albeit momentarily, like a drowning swimmer breaks the surface long enough to draw a final breath before being dragged back down into the dark watery depths.

'Erica, I, I do not understand what is happening to me!' Kurt blustered at her and then he turned his frightened gaze to Anubis. 'My lord Anubis, please kill me! Quickly before it regains full control. I, I ca– I can n–not hol–'

The god could see his would-be protector struggle for control and it appeared that Kurt was rapidly losing his hold on the gnarled body. Anubis rushed forward, and using all his might, he collided heavily with the demon, knocking him off balance long enough for Anubis to regain his composure. Then Anubis bit down into the mound of meat that could be considered the monster's shoulder. Jalel howled with pain, but the god had not finished with him as he grabbed the thief's arm and spun the fowl creature, sending it sprawling down a row of desks and slamming hard against a nearby wall.

Turning quickly, Anubis took Erica's hand and lead her out the door and into the main corridor. Without warning, he scooped Erica up over his shoulder and ran for the stairs. Then, using his god speed, they descended several flights and burst through the door into the lobby of the building. Luckily Sandra, the cleaner who had allowed Sam to enter the building, was no longer there – for if she was, she may well have died of fright at the sight of the beauty and the beast who were now crossing the room.

Once at the door, Erica called out to Anubis to let her down and she promptly swiped her access card across the door lock, and with a beep and a click they were out in the street.

The god retreated into the nearby shadows, with Erica closely in tow. The reporter looked up into the beast's face with astonishment, curiosity and sincere gratitude. 'Anubis, is it? Kurt called you that – is that your name?'

'It is, and you are Erica Murphy.'

Concern came upon Erica's face, 'How do you know my name? Where did you come from and where is Sam? He left so quickly.'

'Questions to be answered another time, Erica Murphy, but for now we must be away from here.' The beast moved to pick up the reporter once again, but she hesitated for a few seconds, stepping away from him. Then, with a flutter of her hands gesturing to Anubis, as if to say she was ready, the beast gently lifted Erica over his broad shoulder and they sped away from the building.

Erica passed out shortly after Anubis had reached his top speed. The human brain was not designed to travel at such a pace and consequently, her mind just switched itself off momentarily. The god had to carry the extra weight of the human as he travelled, and after the scuffle with Jalel, he had barely any energy left by the time the two had arrived at Sam's house. It was with much effort that Anubis made the final steps into the house and gently lay Erica upon Sam's bed. Anubis made his way out to the lounge room, finding a throw rug which was draped lazily over the back of an arm chair and wrapped it around his waist, then without any further ado, he collapsed onto the couch and fell asleep.

Sam woke with a sense of urgency but was immediately captivated by a dazzling pair of green eyes staring intently at him. He was shaken from his dreamlike appreciation by a sudden, rapid barrage of questions and recounts of the fantastical. It was Erica. Her frantic words were dumped upon Sam like a tsunami and the young man was drowning.

'So, you don't remember anything at all?' Erica enquired with a gush of frustration.

Sam suddenly realised that he was naked beneath the itchy rug in which he was wrapped. His shock at the loss of memory, confounded by Erica's mysterious presence, left the young man devoid of answers. 'No, I can't remember any of that, and to be honest, even if it was all true, I'm not sure that I would want to remember.'

'*If* it was all true?' Erica was exasperated. 'Are you calling me a liar now?' she retorted, her Irish accent becoming considerably thicker, which suggested to Sam that perhaps she tried rather hard to suppress it, in favour of a more Australian inclination.

'No, Erica, not at all, but please, for one moment, just put yourself in my shoes. The last thing I remember is approaching you at the newspaper and then bam! Nothing! Next thing I know I'm waking up on my couch, wearing nothing but a throw rug, with a beautiful woman looking down at me and it's nine o'clock in the morning. The only thing that sounds familiar to me is your description of the thing that rescued you. It's a little weird that it had dog-like features – I wonder if it was the same animal that I saw just before I passed out in the fire at work?'

Erica paused to look at Sam, *He just called me beautiful*, she smiled and she sat next to Sam on the couch, then her face turned serious again, 'Okay, I do understand, but I find it so very hard to believe that you did not see either one of those... *things* – they were a little hard to miss. Oh, and the dog creature? It wasn't an animal. It was upright and had arms and legs like a man, but it did have the head of a dog, only human-sized.' The reporter raised one eyebrow as she continued, 'I also do not understand how I ended up on your bed, or why the creature brought me here, or even how he seems to know who you are and where you live, not to mention your current condition and state of dress. The last thing I recall is being carried away from The Open Eye by the big hairy one. What was his name again?'

Erica concentrated hard as she struggled to remember the god's name, her long, fine, black hair resting casually along the sides of her delicate face. 'It started with an "a". It was an "an" sound. Angbo?'

She now rose from the couch and started pacing slowly, back and forth, and Sam took the opportunity to study her as she moved. Sam liked her spirit and her energy. Erica was strong-willed, intelligent, beautiful and had a figure that belonged more to a dancer than a news reporter. Even in her casual state of appearance, Erica looked amazing to Sam. She was still wearing her work clothes from yesterday: her black fitted pants, clinging to her legs and thighs, like a second skin, showed of her shapely form, and her untucked blouse sheathed her curves like a white-sheeted ghost that shimmered every time she moved about. It would be an understatement to say that he was quite attracted to the young reporter the very first time that he had met her at the hospital. It was an instant attraction and, as Sam continued his observations, he wondered how her lips would taste, how her skin would feel to his touch. Would it be as delicate as her porcelain complexion implied?

As the young man lost himself in wishful thinking, Erica continued to try on different names. 'Andal? Anbar? Yes, it had a B sound as well. Anbis?' A sudden look of remembrance alit Erica's face, 'Anubis! That was his name, Anubis!'

Sam snapped out of his daydreaming at the sound of the name. 'Wait, Anubis? Like the Egyptian god Anubis?'

'Yes, that's what he said his name was.'

The colour ran from Sam's face. *What manner of madness is this?* It could not be a coincidence that only several days ago he was admiring the beautiful papyrus which featured the god. He had worked on the antique artwork and unfortunately it had been destroyed while in his care, although he was not to blame. The early investigations into the fire had indicated that the gas box had malfunctioned. However, he blamed himself for the accident nonetheless.

Was there a connection between all the recent mysterious occurrences – and what of the murders? Erica had told Sam that her colleague Kurt was the prenatal killer, only it was not really Kurt, but some type of entity or demon that had taken control of his body.

It was evident that, whatever was happening, neither Sam nor Erica had the answers. Perhaps they needed to find an expert and Sam believed that he may know whom to approach.

'Erica, maybe we need to talk to an expert on Egyptology – maybe we can get some answers that way.'

'Well, I guess that I could do a search online, see what I can find out.'

'Yes, that might work, but I think that I may know someone who may be able to help us directly.'

Erica seemed suitably impressed with Sam's initiative, and nodded her head in agreement. He had recalled the customer's name without difficulty, as if it had just eased into his mind, like someone pushing an envelope through the mail slot of a front door. Sam did have one lingering doubt regarding his choice of expert: would Donovan Banks want to speak with the man who was responsible for destroying possibly his most precious possession? It mattered not, Sam decided, if Donovan Banks did not want to talk to the duo – at least he would have the opportunity to apologise to the gentleman in person. Besides, if any would know of the secrets regarding the origin or mythology of the papyrus, surely the owner would.

Erica was already refreshing herself in the bathroom and Sam had gone into his bedroom to get dressed, satisfied that this avenue of enquiry may garner some answers, the bonus of spending more time with his favourite reporter was more than enough incentive for Sam to reach out to Donovan.

Erica breezed into the bedroom, as if she was quite at home, and her increasing level of comfort around Sam pleased him greatly. She turned to him and took him by both hands, 'Sam, I've been thinking: we have to be very careful from here on out. No doubt there will be people looking for us. The incident last night at The Open Eye would have been captured on CCTV. There was damage there, a mess, and knowing Tom, he will call the police and they will see the footage.' Her grip tightened on Sam's hands as she continued with her concerns, her eyes now glistening with intensity, 'Then there is Kurt, or whatever that horrible thing was. It will probably come after me and, Sam, I am concerned that you might be caught in the middle somewhere. I don't want you to get hurt or worse.'

Sam drew a little closer to Erica and looked her in the eyes with absolute certainty. 'Erica, I know I don't look like the biggest, strongest guy in the world, but trust me, I can handle myself when push comes to shove, and I can push and shove pretty damn hard.'

As an exclamation mark to his statement, he nodded toward his bookshelf where several tall trophies stood proud. He had hoped that the little gold martial artists that perched upon the top of the towers would be adequate proof for Erica that he was capable. She squinted as she followed his direction, and upon seeing the awards, she let out a soft laugh, then returning her gaze to Sam, produced an unsure smile before letting her hands slip free from Sam's. 'Karate? Don't take this the wrong way, but I'd prefer it if you had a gun.'

'Karate? Um, no, not karate. You're looking at the current state Kung Fu champion, and maybe I don't need a gun,' Sam replied with mock bravado.

'Well in that case then, we had better stick together. It appears that we need to look out for each other, at least until we can get some answers. Now, I don't think it wise to go back to my apartment, just in case that thing is waiting for us there, and neither should you stay here.' Erica gazed about the room as she brought her thumbnail up to press it against her plump lips, a habit that she employed when in deep thought. 'We should avoid the police for now. I don't want to be taken off this story and I don't want to be implicated in any of these killings. It probably won't be long before they come looking for us. We should pack some things and get out of here – pronto.'

CHAPTER ELEVEN

Open Minds

DONOVAN HAD TO CATCH a taxi home from the hospital after he was discharged. Kurt had not answered his phone, nor returned any of his father's messages. *He must be busy with his story*, the old man reasoned as he got to work on brewing up a fresh pot of tea, his kitchen sink still bearing the soiled dishes of his breakfast from a few days ago. Cleaning could wait a bit longer. He was in no hurry to busy himself with chores. 'Not too much excitement,' the doctor had warned him. Little did Donovan realise just how exciting his life would soon become – in fact excitement had just come knocking on his front door.

It was with much effort that the old man got to his feet and made his way to the door, and as he approached, he could hear faint voices in the hallway outside.

'Maybe he's not home,' suggested a male voice.

'Let's just wait a moment longer,' came a female reply.

Lately Donovan had been pestered by local real estate agents who had come looking for prospective sales in his area. He peered curiously through the peephole in the door and there he spied a young couple. The pair appeared to be rather innocent looking, and furthermore, it seemed that they were not carrying any cheesy smiles or sales propaganda. He let out a soft groan of relief and then he cracked open the door, keeping the security chain fastened for good measure. 'Yes? What do you want?'

'Mr Banks? My name is Erica Murphy and I'm a reporter with The Open Eye. I am currently writing a feature article about ancient Egyptian mythology and I was hoping to speak to an expert in the field, such as yourself,' the young woman flashed Donovan a warm smile as she finished her pitch to the professor.

'Look, Miss Murphy, I'm flattered that you have chosen me over the endless quantity of information available on the internet, but I'm afraid that I am unable to help you with your story at the moment,' Donovan replied with a tiresome tone. He was not in the mood to give any impromptu history lessons that afternoon.

'Oh, Mr Banks, please I won't keep you long. I just have a few questions tha–'

'Miss Murphy, I'm sorry to interrupt, but I have to rest now, so please leave me be,' with that, the old man closed the door on the pair and started back to his chair only to be interrupted by another gentle knock at the door.

'Mr Banks, my name is Sam and I was the picture framer who worked on your papyrus. I ... Sam's mind raced to find some excuse to talk with Donovan, then suddenly a thought was pushed into his mind, 'I have a message for you, from Anubis.' Sam looked puzzled by his words and shrugged his shoulders as he shot Erica a nervous smile. To Sam's surprise, the front door swung wide open and the frail-looking professor invited them inside with a sweeping gesture of his arm. As he closed the door and turned to face the pair, he pointed to a lounge chair in the middle of the room.

'Please, you better take a seat,' the old man insisted, 'and I had better sit before I fall down.'

The pair did as they were instructed and sat down next to each other.

'Tea? Coffee?'

'Oh, no thank you, Mr Banks,' Erica replied courteously.

'And you, boy?'

Sam was lost in thought, desperately trying to think up the imaginary message from Anubis that he had promised the professor. 'Hmm? I'm fine thank you.'

The old man sat down heavily in the armchair adjacent to where Sam and Erica were seated. Then, with a weary groan, he stared harshly at Sam.

The young man fidgeted on the chair, trying to position himself to face Donovan more directly. Once settled, he placed his hands on his knees and spoke, 'Well, sir, as I mentioned, I have a message from Anubis.'

Sam could feel Erica squirm next to him, she seemed clearly nervous about this approach. Sam tried to clear his mind. What type of message would an imaginary god have for a mortal man who used to hang him on his wall? 'Uh, he ... I mean, Anubis would like me to tell you that he is okay. That he is hap–'

Donovan shot up his hand in a gesture to stop, 'Enough boy! Do you take me for a fool? Surely you do not come into my home and insult me by pretending to somehow be in contact with a god?'

Sam's erect posture quickly deflated as he slumped in defeat. He felt Erica's hand rest on his, in a show of support. Nodding his head, Sam started to speak, 'Mr. Banks, I apolo—'

'Enough! I do not wish to hear any more lies from you. Is it not bad enough that you have destroyed my most valuable possession?' Donovan's frown intensified and as he opened his mouth to speak again, he was quickly silenced as Sam's head began to shake violently.

Sam's eyes turned upward, revealing the whites of his eyes, before they sunk into his skull and were replaced by an intense, red glow. His whole body then began shaking and his facial features darkened as his head began stretching and reshaping itself. The beast's clawed hands ripped the t-shirt from his chest and Sam's jeans ripped at the seams revealing strong, hairy muscular thighs.

Erica quickly raised her mobile phone and began recording the event on video as she scuttled away from the transforming body.

Within several seconds the transformation was complete and a shocked Donovan Banks sat opposite his god once again, just as he had on many occasions sat opposite the papyrus as a child. However, this time the god was a living, breathing being.

'My lord, Anubis? Is that truly you?'

'Hello, my faithful protector, yes – it is I,' Anubis replied hoarsely, shaking off the lingering sting of the change.

The old man began shaking uncontrollably and the god moved to reassure him by reaching out his hair-covered hand toward Donovan, who in turn stretched out his finger tips to touch the beast's extended hand.

'Oh, I thought that you were lost, my lord,' Donovan sighed heavily as he spoke, tears now welling in his eyes.

'Save your tears, Donovan Banks, for we have much to talk of, much to be done and very little time in which to do it.'

The two conversed about all that had transpired, as two old friends may talk after a long absence from each other. The god spoke of his entrapment at the hands of Donovan's ancestor, the temple priest, and of the consequent years that followed. He described the events that led to his freedom, the subsequent rehousing in the body of Samuel and his ongoing battle with the demon, although he refrained from revealing the fact that the old man's son, Kurt, was the living host for the foul thief.

An awestruck Erica watched and listened, exhibiting the skills of a well-trained reporter in an unfathomable situation. That is, until the conversation reached the point where she became a relevant character, her pretty face displaying a fierce expression of concern as her questions came. 'What about Samuel? Where does he go and why doesn't he remember anything about these events?'

Anubis turned and smiled at the reporter, 'Do not worry, Erica Murphy, he is safe. He has been drawn back into the depths of unconsciousness, where he is sleeping. It is necessary for this to happen so that I may bring my consciousness forward and take control of this body.'

At this point Donovan leaned forward to explain, 'Yes, my dear, you see it is a bit like two individuals trying to operate the same car at the same time, it just will not work. Only one can drive. I have read stories of soul coexistence in the book of sacred magics. Fascinating, just fascinating.'

Erica's face flashed deep concern at learning of this cohabitation, 'But, surely Sam should have some say in all of this?'

The beast sat calmly as he considered an appropriate response. 'It has been, at times, difficult to operate in this body. Samuel has a very strong constitution and I have so far had to operate with a high degree of caution. The truth is that it would be advantageous for Samuel and I to share one consciousness, so that I could more easily navigate through the populace at will in his form. Yet I fear that the human mind is not designed for such a purpose – the result would likely be insanity or worse. You see, whenever I take control with my consciousness, I must change into this form to have control of the flesh. Conversely, when Sam is awake, I cannot use his form. I can merely spectate.' Anubis considered Erica warmly before continuing with his reasoning, 'I can tell that Samuel has some attraction toward you. I have seen his thoughts and they have revealed this to be fact. Likewise, you feel some bond with Samuel – it appears that you care about what may happen to him, yes?'

Erica blushed slightly at the suggestion that she may have some attraction to Sam. Despite the time spent by his comatose side, they had only really known each other for a few days. There was some measure of mutual attraction, an unseen bond between the two of them that Erica could not explain, nor deny. Her concern for Sam would not wane. She felt that, because he was unable to speak for himself now, she needed to represent his best interests. Besides, she had promised that the two would look out for each other. 'Sam appears to be a good and kind man and he should know what is happening to him, and what of his body? Presumably if you are hurt – he is hurt?'

The god turned his gaze to the floor, as a scolded child might do, looking to disappear into the ground, 'I cannot lie to you, Erica Murphy. If I perish in this body, so will Samuel. I am of his being now, and I am in every part of him, in his blood and in his mind. I take my true form by disassembling his parts and rearranging them, stretching them to take the form that you now look upon.'

A puzzled expression crossed Erica's face. She did not at all like the sound of what she was hearing, and she guessed that was perhaps why Kurt took on such a monstrous appearance, simply because the thief did not have the finesse to change shape as elegantly as Anubis seemingly could. 'So, you're telling me that you are in his DNA and that you break down and rearrange his molecules to become this shape?'

'Not DNA, my dear,' Donovan interjected, 'Anubis resides in the cells of Sam's body, every single one of them.'

'Well that's not fair on Sam – he needs to know!' Erica started raising her voice, her care for the framer was now evident. 'Surely there must be a way that he can be aware of all of this, to be a part of it, to have some say?'

Anubis raised his canid head and looked at Donovan, 'There is perhaps a way, if you are willing to risk Samuel's sanity. Donovan Banks, did your ancestors preserve any of my personal belongings?'

'Yes, lord Anubis, I shall go and retrieve your belongings.'

Donovan was a little more sprightly as he arose from his chair, renewed with the excitement of having his idol in the living flesh, his life given fresh purpose. Donovan returned shortly after with a cardboard box, but the old man's demeanour was somewhat dampened. His face turned toward his feet, unable to meet Anubis's eyes. 'My lord, I am afraid that I cannot locate the dagger. Unfortunately, it has somehow been misplaced.'

The god's face contorted into a display of great displeasure at hearing of his missing comrade, 'Osir? It has been lost?'

'It appears so, my lord. I must have misplaced it. I believed that I had it stowed away in my dresser, but I cannot find it,' Donovan replied shakily as he stood at his spot.

'Osir may very well be our only means of salvation. It is of the greatest importance that it is located,' the god said with much chagrin, his face not caring to disguise his disappointment with the old man.

Donovan bowed his head low as he responded, 'Yes, my lord, I will turn this house upside down to locate it.'

Deciding that Osir would be found upon further searching, Anubis moved the subject aside, 'And the amulet?'

'Yes, my lord, I have it here.' Donovan placed the item he was holding upon the nearby coffee table and with shaking hands, fumbled to open the box.

'Ah, here it is, my lord,' Donovan said as he raised an exquisite neck piece from the box. The amulet was made entirely of gold, with various runes etched into the surface. It was wide at the front and became gradually thinner as it wrapped toward the back of the piece, where a hook clasp would fasten it together. At the front was a dark green stone, which seemed to be in its raw, natural state and emanated some sort of energy, soft and persistent.

Donovan shot a quick glance at Erica, 'My dear, this is known as the collar of Osiris. It is a sacred artefact, created by the father Osiris to call his children gods to his service.'

At seeing his collar, Anubis smiled widely – revealing rows of sharp teeth, 'Yes, Erica Murphy, this may allow

Samuel and myself to communicate telepathically while we are wearing it.'

Erica felt sceptical about the whole idea and yet, she needed to work toward finding a solution to help Sam be aware of everything that was occurring around him while he was asleep. After all, it was his life at stake if something untoward happened to Anubis. 'Okay, if it's going to be the only way, but first we need to give him an opportunity to have his say in all of this. Anubis can you withdraw your … consciousness? Please let Sam back – I want to show him this video footage as proof of what is happening to him.'

Anubis appeared a little apprehensive about the idea, then after a few seconds of thought he nodded his agreement, before facing Erica's camera to address Sam directly. Once his speech was done, the god began to shake as the transformation rapidly reversed itself, the fine black hairs retracting, as the canine features and strong musculature shrunk back to Sam's human-form.

'Astonishing, simply astonishing,' remarked Donovan as Sam opened his eyes to see the old man staring intently at him.

A wild look of bewilderment struck the young man as he realised that he was currently shirtless and the centre of attention, 'Wha … What the hell is happening? Why am I half naked and why are the two of you looking at me like that?'

Erica smiled and placed her hand on his upper arm, 'Here Sam, you need to see this.' The video played to a stunned Samuel Baker, who started slowly shaking his head in disbelief. The head shaking did not cease until Anubis looked into the lens and addressed his host directly.

'Samuel Baker, my name is Anubis, god of the dead, guide to the underworld and protector of souls. Unforeseen events have necessitated the need for me to temporarily occupy your body. My story is very long and before entering your body, I was trapped inside a papyrus scroll by powerful blood magic – the very scroll that you had handled several days ago. I was released from my imprisonment by the fire that almost claimed your life; indeed, you would have perished if I had not entered into your ...' the beast turned from the camera to look at Donovan, 'cells?'

'Yes, my lord, cells,' the old man replied.

Then turning back to the lens, the god repeated the end of his sentence, 'If I had not entered your cells. Samuel, you must understand that my energy was almost depleted upon my freedom from the papyrus and I would also have perished if I had not sought refuge in yourself. For this I am eternally grateful.'

Anubis continued to explain all the events that were occurring around the shocked young man and how the consciousness shifts worked. At several points along the video, Sam considered asking Erica to pause the footage, so that he may ask a question or to comment on something that Anubis had said. Yet he found it unnecessary to do so, as he was about to say 'stop', the answer to his question or comment was provided by the god, almost as if via some cosmic foresight. Finally, the beast wrapped up his presentation by providing an explanation on how the collar of Osiris worked, and then he left Sam with one final declaration.

'Samuel, I cannot express strongly enough my sincere gratitude to you for providing me an opportunity to continue to live. Without your presence at the workshop, I would have perished in that fire. I would like to also reiterate the importance of what must be done to stop Jalel from taking the lives of innocent women and their unborn children. It is true that I am responsible for the wellbeing of their souls, and this world has been without me for too long. I must restore order to the earth realm and help the countless souls that have been trapped on this plane of existence for thousands of years. Samuel Baker, I cannot do this without your cooperation. I need you to bring your consciousness into collaboration with mine and together we can restore order to the world.'

At this point the recording stopped. Sam continued to stare intensely at the screen, hoping that there was some last-minute solution put forward by the god that would somehow relieve the young man of his impending duty.

'It is never a pleasant feeling to be asked to do something that may very well take one's own life,' Donovan offered, his face a portrait of sincerity.

Sam directed his attention to Erica, who had not moved from his side, her hand still resting on his shoulder.

'This is the point where you tell me that this is an elaborate prank,' Sam said softly, his eyes searching Erica's for some hint of tomfoolery.

Erica's eyes focused on Sam's, her gaze sincere with understanding, 'Okay, Sam, I know that this is a lot to take in. I'm still struggling to believe all of it myself and likewise, you need to try your best to accept what is happening as fact.'

Sam nodded, his eyes focused, and a look of confidence came to him, 'Of course, this whole situation is crazy. If I hadn't seen the footage, I ... well I'm still having a hard time believing it. It seems like I don't have a great deal of options. I have a god living inside of me. He's read my mind and knows my deepest secrets. If I choose not to do this, I can't hide from him.'

Sam's thoughts then turned away from self-preservation as there were some very important reasons to help Anubis – the lives of innocent people were being taken. 'Those poor women and babies, the thought of what happened to them makes me angry. I remember when I first heard about the murders, I felt so sick. That monster must be stopped! You know what? I will do what needs to be done! I mean how hard can it be to walk in a god's shoes?' He let a nervous smile slide across his face as he turned to Donovan, 'Okay, let's get this happening.'

'Brave lad! You have made a wise decision,' the old man chirped as he raised himself out of his chair and shuffled over to Sam with the amulet, placing it around Sam's neck and securing it in place. Then he took a few steps back and leant forward, placing his broad hands on his knees for support. 'How does it feel? Snug?'

A thought came to Sam as he brushed his fingers over the stone at the front of the collar. 'Wait, if this collar is a communication device, then why can't Anubis contact Osiris and put an end to all of this?'

Donovan smiled kindly as he placed a heavy hand on Sam's shoulder, 'The collar will allow you to communicate with Anubis only, as it was created specifically for him. It is not capable of contacting Osiris, as it was not made for that purpose. It will only allow Osiris to call his servant gods back to his side and not the other way around. You see, my lad, the father god answers to no one.'

'Hmm, seems a little arrogant, don't you think?' Sam asked sarcastically.

The old man sat down in his chair before addressing Sam, 'Now, Samuel, I want you to close your eyes and look into the back of your mind. There you will find him, speak to him.'

Sam had practiced meditation as a part of his Kung Fu training, so it was relatively easy for him to close out the world around him and retreat into his mind. He felt as if he was floating inside the blackness behind his eyes, like floating in thick black liquid. It felt warm and safe and at no moment did he fear that he may drown. Sam soon realised that this black liquid was his subconscious and he could move in it freely, in whichever direction he wanted to go. As he looked around the darkness, he fancied that he could make out a shape a little off into the distance and so, it was in that direction that he willed himself to be carried.

As he drew nearer, he noticed that the black fluid in which he was floating had begun to turn deep violet in colour and appeared to be less dense. Ahead he could see a large shape stir in the darkness and Sam realised that the figure was also black, barely noticeable if not for the fact that the dense space of his mind was darker than that of the figure. He did not need to progress much further, as Sam knew who the shape belonged to. *'Anubis?'*

The figure stopped moving at the sound of the name and now stood upright, then it began to move fluidly toward Sam.

'Samuel Baker, it is an honour to officially meet you at last,' the beast said as his features were revealed to Sam. Anubis appeared as he did when he was in his original body: a truly glorious beast, his coat slick and shining with divine beauty, his body packed with muscle – a modesty cloth at his groin and buttocks and his face fiercely stern, yet to the god's surprise, the framer showed no fear, nor repulsion at his appearance.

'Yes, well it seems that you have me at a disadvantage. You seem to know an awful lot about me, snooping around in my head,' Sam replied somewhat irreverently.

The god lowered his eyes to avoid Sam's gaze, his guilt evident, *'I do apologise, it was mere curiosity as I have never had such an opportunity to see how the mortal human mind works before.'*

Sam was satisfied with Anubis's display of sincerity, *'Yes ... well, that's okay, I guess. I can't say that I wouldn't do the same thing if I had the chance.'*

The beast raised his head to look at Sam, his face now beginning to throw a sheen of violet from the increasing luminescence. *'I am grateful for your agreement to cooperate with me,'* Anubis spoke softly now, realising that he was dealing with a mortal and as such, human feelings were a complicated set of issues to deal with. He proceeded gently, *'I have struggled to find adequate strength to face Jalel by myself. My energy levels are still quite low, and your assistance will help me to wander among the people undetected and therefore conserve my strength.'*

Sam edged a little closer to the beast, showing the god that he did not fear him and as a visual reminder that it was his body that they were playing with, *'I am more than willing to work with you, Anubis, but before we continue, there are some conditions that I would like you to agree upon.'*

'Speak, Samuel Baker, and I shall hear it. I will consider what is said and then you will have your answers,' the god said, his face a display of cautious authority.

'Okay ... First condition is that there is to be no more snooping around in my mind – my thoughts are mine and mine alone.'

'Samuel, that will not be easy to achieve. We will need to know each other's thoughts if we are to both operate this body at the same time. However, when we are resting, or if you require some privacy, I will not connect with your consciousness.'

'Hmm, okay good enough. Second condition is that I want to be aware of everything that is happening, no blocking me out. I want to be awake. If I am going to die, then I want to see who or what killed me and how.'

'Fair enough, I must warn you that you will feel great anguish and discomfort during the physical changing of forms. Your entire being will be stretched and contorted, and it will be very painful.'

'Okay, well, all the same, it's what I want. I will just have to learn to deal with the pain.'

The god continued, 'Furthermore, you may witness many unpleasant events and you will see the demise of our enemy, as I intend to kill him viciously.'

Sam raised an eyebrow and a smile followed the same upward trajectory, 'Oh, I don't doubt that, and that will lead us to my final condition. I want to have total dual control of both of our forms. That means, when you are in your form, I want to be able to control your god-body as well.'

The god appeared perplexed by the suggestion, 'To what end? I do not understand?'

'Anubis, I am a fighter – a good one – and I have knowledge of oriental manual combat. Your thief will not know or expect my style of fighting. We can have the element of surprise.'

The befuddled look did not leave the beast's face as his mind raced to find reasons to reject the final condition. 'Samuel, excuse me, I fail to understand your intent. If you are insinuating that you have fighting skills that can defeat the thief, then I'm afraid that you are mistaken. He is a formidable enemy. He is evil and hungry for power. Even I cannot easily defeat him.'

Sam cocked his head slightly to one side as he peered up into the pits of the god's eyes, 'That is precisely my point. He *will expect some measure of failure from you again and then, when he least expects it, I can take control of your powerful form and assault him with my fighting style, which you would have seen peering into my memories. Don't you think that it is something that would catch the thief off guard? You know full well what I am capable of, just give me a chance. Separately we are strong, but together we can be unstoppable against him.'*

Sam let the thought linger in the silence as the look of confusion left the god at last. *'It is true, I have witnessed your abilities and perhaps you are correct to assume our success, and yet there is much work to be done together to bring our two minds into one form whilst in combat.'*

Sam smiled broadly as he relaxed a little. *'You mean training? Anubis, if there's one thing I can literally do in my sleep …'*

'It is training,' the beast finished Sam's sentence for him.

'Exactly, see? We are working well together already. Now, I take it that you will accept all of my conditions?'

Anubis raised his proud head and nodded strongly with his acceptance. *'Samuel, I am a god – my divine purpose is to assist humanity to enter into the underworld and guide them along each of the five trials of the soul. I must defeat Jalel and restore both the earth and spiritual realms to order. I believe that we may have a higher chance of success if we work together as one – god and man together.'* He then put forward his hand and Sam took it in a firm shake. The mortal appeared surprised by the handshake, so Anubis decided to explain some of the finer points of the strange place that is the unconscious mind. *'It feels real does it not?'*

'Well … yes. How can I feel things physically? We're in my mind, aren't we?'

'Yes, Samuel, we are in the dark sea of your subconscious. What you are seeing and feeling is your conscious mind. When

you dream, things appear to be real, this is because your consciousness makes them real in this place. The blackness is merely a canvas – upon which your soul can paint and oh, such beautiful and terrifying art can be made here.'

'Wait, so this is not really happening? I mean you ... are you real, or just my imagination – some sort of dream?'

'Oh, I am very real, Samuel, remember I share your unconscious space. We are both here and this is very real, as was that handshake.'

'Okay, I think that I understand. This is all metaphysical right?'

'Yes, consciousness is the soul – that which lives on after the body is dead. Come, I shall show you how your conscious mind can see out of this body.'

Anubis stepped forward to join Sam by his side, turning the young man around to face back the way he had come. Ahead was a light, indigo in colour, which pulsated slowly.

'Look, there,' said Anubis pointing Sam's attention to the glow, *'that is from where I pilot this body. It is there that we will begin our journey together.'*

The two floated over in the direction of the light, which became steadily brighter as they travelled. Eventually the luminescence was too intense for Sam and he squinted his eyes as he approached the spot.

'It will take some getting used to I'm afraid,' confided the beast. *'Once the physical eyes are open you will be able to see normally once more. I will go into the light first and transform our body into my form. Once that is done, I will call you forward to join me.'*

Sam nodded in agreement and without further ado, the god moved into the bright violet light.

Both Erica and Donovan were watching Sam intently, eagerly awaiting any sign that the framer had successfully bonded with Anubis. Now the answer came as Sam's body shuddered and shifted, once more transforming into the form of Anubis. Something was wrong this time, as the body twitched, spasming violently, a painful howl bellowed out of the beast, but the voice belonged to Sam.

Once the change was completed, the beast sat erect and motionless, staring directly ahead, his red eyes glowing. Erica and Donovan watched on with shock to see those glowing eyes become black pits momentarily, before a pair of familiar eyes emerged in their place.

'Sam?' Erica enquired tentatively as the beast moved its head from side to side, almost robotically surveying the room. Finally, the creature looked at Erica and a cheeky smile appeared on his hairy face.

Sam spoke through the god's mouth, his voice the same gravelly tone that Anubis spoke with, 'Erica, it's me Sam. Wow, Anubis, you were right, that was awful! That was excruciatingly painful, and I felt like I was going to be ripped apart! Man, this feels so weird – I feel so strange. It's like I'm wearing a costume.'

Erica agreed with a slight nod of her head, 'It looks like you're wearing a mask. Can you see normally?'

'Yes and no. I can see everything very clearly, almost too surreal. I can also see into you.'

Erica instinctively covered her chest with her hands, blushing, and Sam couldn't help noticing that her hands were quite full. The thought of seeing her naked briefly drifted into his mind, only to be quickly shut down by Anubis.

'Really, Samuel? At a time like this? We need to stay focused!'

'*Sorry, yes you're right. It's just that she captivates me at times.*'

'*Samuel, there will be time enough for such thoughts later, for now, we must set our minds to the task at hand.*'

Sam reassured Erica, 'No, I didn't mean that I could see through your clothes. What I meant to say is that I can see your spirit, your soul?'

Sam shot a glance to the left-hand side of his face, as if listening to an invisible speaker reply to his question about whether it truly was Erica's soul that he could see. It appeared that he had his answer, as he nodded and turned back to face Erica, 'Yes, your soul, Donovan's too. I can also see things in super slow motion if I please.'

To demonstrate this new god-speed ability, the beast got to his feet and ran over to a coat rack that was positioned next to the front door. There he took Donovan's scarf and draped it over his broad shoulders. He promptly returned to the couch and sat down cross-legged and erect, with his arms out straight and his hands one on top of the other, resting on his knee as if he were a proper gentleman. Sam's sense of humour was shining through the bestial facade of the god, and the completely bizarre sight of the creature casting the image of elegant sophistication, brought raucous laughter from both Erica and Donovan. The whole event took around five seconds to the human eye, yet for Sam it was a leisurely task. Donovan sobered quickly – the old man was clearly concerned that Sam was not taking his role seriously. Donovan crept forward a little closer to the god, 'My lord, are you there also?'

Sam's eyes began to glow red and the beast replied, 'Yes, Donovan Banks, I am here too. Sam and I have reached an accord. We will be attempting to both have control of the one form – we believe that this will give us an advantage over Jalel.'

Sam's eyes returned as the red glow vanished, the framer adding to the conversation, 'We have a lot of training to do if we are to be ready to take down the thief. Donovan, can you help us to find a secluded space where we can practice getting used to working together?'

Donovan thought for a few seconds before he came up with a response. 'Yes, I think that I know a place. There is a small vacant theatre at the university. It has been closed and used for storage ever since they built a new one a few years back.'

At this point Erica sat erect and turned to face the god, 'Sam, what about the incident at The Open Eye last night? We are probably considered persons of interest by the police now, and what about Kurt?'

Donovan sat bolt upright at the mention of his son, 'Kurt? My son? What about him?'

Erica turned to the old man and her face could barely contain the look of apprehension that she felt at having to tell him that his son was possessed by an ancient thief spirit, turning him into some type of murderous demon.

It was Anubis who took it upon himself to explain the situation to his devoted servant. 'Donovan Banks, steel yourself for what will come next. I will tell you what has happened to your son.'

CHAPTER TWELVE

Concerted Effort

JALEL TOOK SEVERAL MOMENTS to recover after being thrown across the writer's room of The Open Eye. By the time that he came back to his senses and had risen off the floor, Anubis and Erica were gone. The thief was shocked to discover that he had reverted to the form of Kurt, but was still conscious as himself. Was he now fully in control of his host's body? Or perhaps Kurt had been knocked unconscious by the impact when he hit the concrete wall. Jalel guessed that it had to be the latter, so he wasted no time in planning that he could utilise Kurt's form to his advantage. *Yes, murder will come easily tonight.*

He was making his way across the room when he noticed that Erica's computer screen had been knocked to the ground, along with various objects and papers that were strewn about the place. Jalel let out a groan of discontentment. He could not leave the area looking like that, for every good thief knows that one must cover his tracks well if he is to make a clean escape, and Jalel was not a good thief – he was an exceptional one.

It did not take him long to straighten up the room to its original condition. Jalel had excellent recall regarding details, and he had taken his time to study every minuscule thing about the room, as his host awaited Erica's arrival that afternoon. The only object that he could not replace was Erica's computer monitor, which was badly damaged. For now, he had to find somewhere to secret it away, so he took it under his arm and left the room.

A few doors down the hallway, the thief found a maintenance room. He opened the door, stepped in, located a spot to hide the broken monitor and was about to leave, when one of Kurt's memories came flooding into Jalel's mind. The memory had occurred in the very room in which Jalel stood. Kurt's vision showed himself looking down at the back of a woman, who was bent over before him as he stood behind her, his eyes moving down to her exposed buttocks as he was penetrating her.

The petite blonde glanced over her shoulder to look at Kurt as he worked feverishly toward climax, her face a mixture of pleasure and guilt. Kurt knew that she had a boyfriend, but he didn't care and, apparently, neither did she. Following several weeks of intense flirtation, lust was too strong of an instinct for the pair to ignore any longer. The smell of the young woman's perfume wafted up to meet Kurt's nostrils – barely distinguishable above the scent of cleaning products and the mouldy mop, which had been left sitting in a bucket of fetid water.

The thief was impressed with the encounter. Kurt had simply taken the young woman by the hand one afternoon, led her to the maintenance room and used her fine body to satiate his carnal appetite. Jalel found himself suddenly aroused as he reflected upon the encounter that had taken place there. He slid his hand down his pants to feel his swollen member. It had been a very long time since he had found sexual gratification, and for the briefest of moments, Jalel considered stroking himself to climax. But when he attempted to focus upon the woman from Kurt's memory, all he could imagine was taking her to the closet to slice her open with his demon claws and devour the sweet taste of her soul. He imagined biting into the side of her neck, the veins rubbery to his teeth, with warm blood gushing into his mouth. His concentration had rapidly changed from erotica to massacre – two concepts that were sometimes indistinguishable to Jalel. However, his dark mission urged him to let go of the erection and get about his business.

It seemed that his brief sexual urge had stirred something in his host's consciousness as he could feel Kurt attempting to climb forward in his mind. Upon consideration, the thief realised that he was now feeling rather exhausted, and conceded that there would be no murders committed tonight. So, it was with much satisfaction that he made his way out of the building, reassured by the knowledge that, after one more murder, he may be able to finally suppress Kurt indefinitely, perhaps forever.

Kurt had no memory of the previous night's events as he woke the next morning. There were several missed calls on his mobile. He had little interest in returning any of them, especially one message from his father, who had called to know why his son was not there to collect him from the hospital after he had been discharged. Kurt became indifferent to his father's wellbeing, in fact, he cared little for anything this morning, as if he were numb to the world.

He spent the next couple of days going about his tasks with a detachment that was palpable. Kurt was indifferent to the events going on around him: he had no smiles for the attractive women he passed in the street, no time was spent self-appreciating in the mirror, grooming himself like he usually did and he spent no time working out at the gym. It was as if he were a ghost, an entity – aimlessly wandering the world around him, yet not caring to interact with the living.

The thief felt that his strength had increased significantly and that he was very close to having full control. Jalel had discovered that he could subtly operate Kurt's body as the host went about his business: he could pick up various items such as a pen or a coffee cup without Kurt's knowledge, often leaving his host pondering why he had picked up the objects in the first place. Menial things to be sure, but nonetheless, he was rather enjoying his new-found puppeteering skills.

It had been three days since his last kill and Jalel knew that tonight he must find another source of nourishment. He was still unable to take full control of Kurt's body as he had been able to do after the fight with the dog, back at The Open Eye. It was clear now that he could only manage such a feat if Kurt had been physically knocked unconscious. The thief decided to be patient for now, and so he continued to ride at the back of Kurt's mind.

As before, Jalel could whisper words of influence to his host, directing him to follow his next victim as she left a women's clinic. On this occasion the thief was able to successfully follow the woman all the way back to her apartment, but he was disappointed to discover that the woman's husband was also there. *What to do?* Jalel pondered, as he watched the pair through their kitchen window. He could try to kill the husband quickly before the man could find a weapon or call for help, or he could wait to see if he would leave the apartment. He decided to wait and see if the husband was going to leave, and after a little over an hour later, the man did just that. Jalel watched from across the street as the husband exited the building and headed down the street, whistling as he went. *Poor fool,* the thief chuckled, little did the man know that he would never see his dear wife alive again.

Across town, there was some bad news for the quartet. They had turned Donovan's apartment upside down searching for Osir, only to find no trace of the blade and so they thought that it had to be in Kurt's possession – the idea of which brought great unease to Anubis.

Erica mentioned that she did not feel secure enough to return to her home and insisted that she and Sam should stick together. Donovan did not want to be parted from Anubis, he still felt honour-bound to be his lord's protector, and so it was decided that they would all stay in a hotel, not far from the disused school theatre that Donovan had secured for their use.

Anubis and Sam had been practicing dual control of their bodies in the old theatre for hours, with varying degrees of success. Each transformation was excruciatingly painful for Sam and more than once he doubted if he could endure the torturous change any further. Yet, after an hour of practice, he found that he could manage the pain a little easier each time the change took place.

Occasionally, one of the two minds would conflict with the other, like when two people try to talk at the same time. The result was a jumbled mess, resulting in trips, falls and random muscle spasms. There was also a heart-stopping moment whilst attempting to change from Sam to Anubis form: poor mental co-operation ended with a mess of flesh, not dissimilar to the demonic form that Jalel took when his transformation was complete. A moment of panic struck Sam as he struggled to focus upon the shape of Anubis, his mind spinning wildly, like a centrifuge, as he felt his consciousness forced away from the indigo light just behind his eyes.

'*Focus, Samuel!*' Anubis shouted mentally, his voice free from any signs of panic or stress, but firm as to direct the framer upon a course of action. '*Do not concentrate on stopping the spinning, rather you must let go of all thought and find your equilibrium.*'

'*Let go of all thought? Easier said than done!*' Sam responded, the mental comment was intercepted by the god and he replied calmly.

'*The mind truly makes us who we are. Your thoughts create your own reality, just as our thoughts allow us to shift between my form and yours. Think of this as a reset for your consciousness. If you quieten your mind, the body will reset into its natural state, which is your body, Samuel.*'

Sam attempted to let go of all his thoughts as the spinning continued. He utilised a meditation technique that he had learned as a part of his Kung Fu training, by imagining a bright white light surrounding his entire being. At first it did not appear to be working, but gradually the spinning slowed and eventually all was still. Sam could feel the warmth of the white light fill him and as it did so, all sight and sound left him, and the young man found himself floating in pure white bliss, with not one single thought in his mind. Ahead of him, the white light pulsed, and the ether began to shift as it formed into a shape, a face. He recognised her immediately – Erica.

Erica's face did not move, nor speak. It was just there, present in the light with him, smiling. Sam found himself in a tranquillity that he had never known, and all his senses slowly returned to him, one by one. He could hear his companions calling to him. Next, he could feel his flesh mould around his essence. He could smell the stale, sweet scent of the paper-filled boxes that took up a good percentage of the theatre stage. The smell reminded him of the old bookstore that his mother would take him to when he was a child. Finally, his vision returned as he opened his eyes.

To Sam's delight he had returned to his original body shape and Anubis was the first one to speak, and he did so through Sam, whose eyes started to glow red as the god came forward.

'Congratulations, Samuel, it is not easy to do what you have done.'

Sam's eyes returned as he spoke, followed by the red glow every time Anubis responded.

'What the hell happened? Why did we lose control?'

'You must remember what I told you, Samuel. We have the ability to create our image using the power of our minds. We can change into each other's form without too much difficulty. However, if the mind starts to stray as the change occurs, the flesh will be as chaotic as the mind that has conjured it. Hence why the thief has such a horrendous appearance; his mind has not had sufficient training to hold the thought of the desired outcome. Through your martial arts training, you have gained the ability to focus your energy.'

'Well, okay I get it now. But why did I lose control?

Why did I become that … thing?'

'Because your mind started to wander. You may have focused on something other than the moment of now, and when you started to lose control, you panicked, and the flesh did not know what to do.'

'I was focused on the change, but I guess that I was already thinking three steps ahead, what I was going to do after the change had finished.'

'Well, Samuel, herein lies the lesson: always be focused on the change and do not let your mind wander. I could easily have taken control of the situation and restored either one of our forms, but I foresaw an opportunity for you to learn how to correct it yourself and you did just that. However, there is still much practice to be done.'

Anubis then took his own form and Samuel came forward to control the body. He ran through his Kata forms and practised some dynamic power techniques. Sam was highly impressed with how much strength he could generate in the god's body, sending a heavy box of documents flying clear across to the front of the theatre from the stage on which he stood. His companions were also in awe of the display.

'Oh man, Jalel does not stand a chance!' Erica quipped, her delight evident as she beamed an astonished smile.

Donovan, who had been watching in awe, sitting on a chair off to the side, stood up at the mention of Jalel. 'Yes, this is all very good, but what about Kurt? He could suffer because of the destructive power that the pair of you have.'

Anubis now came forward and spoke – to somehow try to reassure his loyal servant, 'Donovan Banks, still your fears for now. You must realise that I would never purposely allow harm to come to your son. It is my intention to confront the thief and, once we locate Osir, I intend to use the blade to wound him. Doing this will release the last soul that was consumed. One by one, the souls of the innocent will be set free, working backward to the point that the thief took possession of your son. Once the foul soul is gone, Kurt should survive, as Osir will only claim the soul that it has touched, and the wound shall remain but a wound. However, you must also prepare yourself for the worst. I cannot guarantee that Kurt will survive the battle that is to come, but if we are successful and Kurt does indeed perish, then be assured that I will personally escort him into the underworld. Whatever the case, the thief must be stopped.'

Donovan wiped a tear from his eye and, with a hard sniff, the old man straightened himself and nodded vehemently, 'Yes, my lord, I understand. Please forgive my moment of weakness.'

Erica placed her arm around Donovan's shoulders to reassure him, 'You never have to apologise for being a good father. If you consider your concerns to be weakness, then you are no weaker than the rest of us.'

'Yes, Donovan. There is no fault with compassion for your child,' Anubis said warmly.

'And I have no desire to hurt your son either,' Sam added, 'I am only interested in helping to end this madness.'

Donovan stiffened his lip and snorted dramatically as he waved a hand as if to swipe away the matter, 'Yes, well, thank you all. Come what may, I guess that the fates will decide his destiny, and please know that I am your most loyal ally. If the worst appears to happen, I will not interfere with what needs to be done.'

The training continued well into the evening and the next morning brought more rigorous activity. Erica joined Sam as the pair jogged laps around the perimeter of the auditorium, talking as they did so. She enjoyed her early evening jogs when her schedule allowed, it was her way of keeping in shape and unwinding after work. Erica smiled and waved at Donovan, who had settled into an old chair upon the stage as he watched the duo make their way around another lap.

'Erica, I'm grateful for you coming into my life,' Sam said as he moved a little closer to Erica, his breathing steady and his words sure. 'I would have been a bit lost in all of this if you hadn't stuck around to help me.'

'Oh, that's okay, Sam,' Erica's words were less stable as her lungs had started to tingle over the previous lap, her breathing coming a little harder now. 'Besides, you are an interesting guy, if not a great story.'

A smile appeared on Sam's face, 'Gee, thanks for that. I'm flattered.'

'Yes, well you should be. A gal like me has a lot on her plate you know, what with trying to juggle a demanding career with an almost non-existent personal life,' Erica laughed as she spoke.

'Non-existent personal life? Oh, come on, you must be fighting guys off with a stick.'

'Yup, a very big stick!' Erica laughed again, more breathily this time. 'Most guys are only interested in one thing … as I'm sure you know, Mr Baker.'

'Most guys huh?' Sam grunted, his eyes meeting hers briefly before moving down her body, the display designed to make light of her comment. 'Not sure what you mean, and I don't see why you would think that. I mean you look okay,' his eyes sparkled with mischief, 'but most guys?'

Erica stopped in her tracks and Sam turned, jogging backward as he smiled at her. Erica placed her hands on her hips dramatising her incredulousness. Upon his next backward stride, Sam slipped on some papers on the floor, falling hard on his back.

'See? That is what you get for being a smart-ass!' Erica chided playfully as she stood over Sam.

Sam laughed as he stared up at Erica, 'You didn't let me finish – I was just going to say that maybe you hadn't met the right guy yet.'

As she looked down at Sam, Erica was reminded of the days she visited him while he was in a coma. He was helpless then and she rather enjoyed just being in his presence, without the need for any words between the two of them. The past few days had further strengthened her opinion of the young man: he was thoughtful of others, a fierce and loyal friend, and although she could not know for sure, he did seem to be genuinely interested in her as a person. The two had long conversations, some well into the early hours of the morning, and they had quite a few things in common, apart from the current dire situation that they found themselves in. They liked different types of music, but they did share fondness for songs from the eighties and they often found themselves breaking out with impromptu vocal performances, much to Anubis's disdain. Erica ate healthy foods, while Sam consumed pretty much whatever he liked, due to his fast metabolism and hefty training regime, yet they both enjoyed pasta and they vowed that once everything was settled, they would go out and eat Italian food together. Sam had just suggested that maybe she had not yet met the right guy, but somehow, she was starting to believe that perhaps she had.

'Oh, you might be wrong about that, Sam,' Erica said as she held out her hand to help the young man up off the floor, 'I may have met someone just last week.'

Last week? I was in a coma last week, Sam thought, his

disappointment sudden as he realised that she was not talking about him.

'Lucky guy,' Sam said as he took Erica's outstretched hand and she helped him to his feet.

Erica shot Sam a sly smile before she winked at him, 'Yes, and I may be a lucky gal.'

Suddenly Sam shuddered with pain and his body began to stretch again as Anubis brought his form into service, ripping the t-shirt that the young man was wearing and filling the baggy track pants that Sam had taken to wearing.

'Geez, Anubis!' Sam complained as he spoke through the canid mouth. 'You could have given me some warning to take my shirt off!'

Anubis snorted loudly, 'My apologies, Samuel, but there is no time for this.' His long, erect ears swivelled atop his head, like a radar dish may do, and his nose twitched as he snorted savagely at a scent upon the air, which was undetectable by the mortal nose.

Sam's eyes reappeared on the beast, 'What the heck is that stench?'

'It is the scent of impending death, murder to be precise. The thief is upon his next victim. We have not a moment to lose!' the god growled as he took control of his body and sped out of the theatre, heading toward the source of the smell.

Sam glimpsed Erica's concerned expression before Anubis took off. 'Be safe you two!' she shouted after them, but by the time her words pierced the air, both man and beast were gone.

The thief had silently found his way into his victim's apartment, despite the hulking size of his demon-form. He found he was unable to use Kurt's body for anything other than lifting small random items, and his mental influence over his host was not yet strong enough to guide Kurt into the building. Yet there he was, spying on the pregnant woman as she stepped naked from the shower. Jalel decided not to strike her inside the bathroom, *too cramped, too small.*

He waited until the woman had entered her bedroom before making his move, his footfalls softened by the carpeted floors. But his stench could not be masked and consequently, the woman spun around startled. She screamed, her eyes wide with fear as the monster swiped for her head, which she barely managed to evade as she moved back. The momentum of the demon's swing sent him crashing onto the bed and the terrified woman quickly moved past him, holding her swollen belly as she waddled out of the room.

The panicked mother-to-be ran down the hall and into the living room – straight into the arms of Sam.

'Whoa, are you okay? I saw someone come into your house and I heard your screams,' Sam asked, his eyes darting about the place looking for Jalel.

'Please help me!' the hysterical woman pleaded to Sam, not caring that he was another stranger in her house, at least he was human.

He shushed her and spoke softly, 'You have to get out of here, quickly!'

'There's a monster in the bedroom!' she whimpered. She turned to nod toward the direction of the assailant down the hall as the demon came lumbering into view. She released another blood-curdling scream as she saw the abomination stride towards them. Sam positioned the woman against the wall behind him – fear had rooted her to the spot. Sam considered attempting to take the woman into his arms and flee, but he knew that his god-speed would be dangerous for her unborn child, so he decided to stand his ground.

Jalel scoffed at the framer, 'Ha, is the dog now sending a pathetic boy to do his dirty work?'

'Actually, I was just in the neighbourhood and saw your light on,' Sam chirped with a mock seductive tone. The joke was clearly lost on the thief, who was quick to retort. 'Well, it matters not! Ha, fool to come here, boy! You will die!'

'Today? I don't think so, thief!' Sam said, smiling.

The demon's smug expression turned to shock as he saw that Sam's eyes now started to glow bright red. 'Dog? What manner of trick is this?'

'You will not take this woman's child, nor her life this night,' Anubis snorted as the transformation into his form took place.

The frightened woman, who was cowering in the corner of the room, let out a gasp of shock at the sight of Anubis, who maintained his defensive stance before her, an indication that he was there to help and would not harm her.

The thief came at Anubis with claws swinging and Sam moved the god's body, easily blocking the successive blows as the demon continued to strike out. Sam moved to counterstrike the thief with great speed and power, landing several bruising blows upon the demonic body and finishing with a reverse side kick, which sent the thief flying backward, smashing him into the drywall and leaving a large indentation there. Frustrated, Jalel let out a scream of anger. 'Enough of this!' he howled, his words spewing forth copious amounts of foul saliva from his misshapen mouth. His right hand travelled around behind him, to his back, and he produced a sheathed blade from under the folds of mottled flesh.

'Osir!' Anubis gasped in shock at seeing his old friend. Taking control of his body, the god retreated several steps away from the weapon.

Is that Osir? Sam asked the god telepathically.

'It is indeed – we must be extremely cautious, Samuel. One cut of the steel upon our flesh and I will perish,' Anubis replied shakily.

Sam attempted to bring his consciousness forward, to take control, 'Anubis, I can disarm the thief.'

'No, Samuel! It is too dangerous. We must take the woman and flee. We have insufficient practice working together to be effective against such a weapon.' Anubis turned to collect the huddled woman and escape, but Sam pushed on with his mind, determined to act as Jalel swung the now naked blade at the retreating god.

Sam spun back around toward the thief, raising his right leg as he did so, and extended his foot at the optimum moment, striking the blade free from the thief's hand. Sam raised the god's left leg into a powerful front-heel kick, directed at Jalel's right thigh, before finishing the assault with a perfectly timed right-leg side kick to his throat, sending him crashing through the living-room window. Anubis moved quickly to recover Osir and then ran over to the broken window, but the thief was gone.

'That could have gone horribly wrong!' the god scolded Sam as he turned from the window.

'But it didn't go wrong. Anubis, you must trust me and have a little faith that I can help you,' Sam responded calmly, returning to his own form as he walked over to the frightened woman, so as not to scare her any further.

'That was him wasn't it, the prenatal killer?' she whimpered.

'I'm afraid so, but you don't have to be scared now, he is gone,' Sam said as he covered her nakedness with a nearby throw rug.

The relieved woman hugged her rescuer tightly and Sam picked her up into his arms, with a little extra strength provided by Anubis, and carried her into her bedroom.

Sam gently lay the woman down upon her bed and sat down next to her. 'It's okay, rest now.'

'Thank you … Oh, I don't know your name.'

Sam felt Anubis nudge him in his mind, '*She cannot give your name to the police, Samuel. We need to operate in secrecy if we are to stop the thief.*'

'My name is – Brandon,' Sam replied, providing the name of one of his Kung Fu heroes.

'Thank you, Brandon. I had better call the police.'

'Sure … but I guess that you'll have a difficult time trying to explain what happened.'

'What did happen? What was that thing and … sorry, but what are you? Some type of werewolf?'

The suggestion brought a hearty laugh to Sam. He had not considered that he may very well be such a creature. 'Um, not quite, no – not a werewolf. Just think of me as an angel, sent to save you from that demon.'

'So, an angel named Brandon? That thing was a demon? He was going to kill me, wasn't he?'

'Yes, he was here for you and your unborn child, but don't worry – you're safe now. What is your name?' Sam asked the still trembling woman.

'Amy.'

'Well, Amy, here's the problem we have: you see, you won't be able to tell anyone what really happened here tonight.'

A look of confusion appeared upon Amy's face, 'Why not?'

'For starters, people simply will not believe you, they will think you mad. Secondly, you have a baby on the way and you need to be thinking of your family. If you tell the truth, you will have the news people hounding you – not to mention every other kook knocking on your door.'

'Okay, I understand, but what am I to say?'

'It was a robbery. Someone entered your home while you were in the shower and you disturbed the thief when you came into the living room. Then a passer-by heard you scream and came to help. There was a scuffle and the thief was pushed into the wall, before he escaped by jumping through the window. The passer-by ran after him and you did not see either of them again.'

Amy seemed comfortable regarding the cover story. 'You're right, Brandon, that does seem like a much saner explanation.'

'Good, then it is settled. Now you should call the police and your husband. I will wait across the street until one of them arrive to help you. I'm sorry, Amy, but I cannot be seen here. I must leave now.'

'Wait, before you go, please come a little closer.'

Sam moved closer to Amy and she reached up her hands to bring his head down to her and she kissed him softly on the forehead. 'Thank you, Brandon, for saving our lives.'

'Oh, it was nothing, besides, I really was just in the neighbourhood and saw your light on,' Sam replied with a wink. With that, the framer got to his feet.

'Okay, now remember,' he said as he walked away, 'I'll be watching from across the street. Good luck with everything, Amy, and take good care of that baby.'

'I will. Thank you again, angel Brandon.'

CHAPTER THIRTEEN

Desperate Measures

JALEL HAD BEEN SOUNDLY beaten by Anubis and his human host. After the fight, the thief retreated to Kurt's apartment with several injuries, mostly cuts and bruises, but most especially a severely bruised ego. Up until tonight, he felt superior to the dog, believing that he had the upper hand and that he was more powerful than Anubis. However, something had changed, some type of alliance between the god and the human had been forged, facilitating greater strength and ability. And what of the foreign fighting style which was so aptly applied to the demon's sorry frame? Jalel felt that he was facing an otherworldly opponent, and for the next few hours, he felt deeply concerned, somehow vulnerable at the concept of losing his wicked gambit. He had worked so hard to get to where he was and the taking of innocent lives had provided him with great sport up until now. Jalel felt his energy begin to fall away as he slipped into a deep depression and with little resistance, he let himself recede into the dark depths of unconsciousness.

It was a different atmosphere at the hotel Rosales, where Anubis and his comrades were staying. Sam was met at the room door by an anxious Erica, who after a quick check that he was as fine as he seemed at first glance, hugged Sam tightly before ushering him into the room.

Donovan was also present, his eyes equally appraising in checking for any damage to Sam. Following was a jumbled and fevered barrage of questions from both Erica and Donovan, and it was Anubis, speaking through Sam, who moved to reassure them, 'Friends, please be calmed – all is well. Both Sam and I are uninjured.'

'What happened? Did you stop the thief?' Erica inquired, wide-eyed.

'He was soundly defeated, thanks mostly to Samuel's fighting skills. He was exceptional,' the god replied proudly.

Sam did not respond to such praise, rather, he let the god continue to answer questions on his behalf.

'What of Kurt? Is he okay?' Donovan asked, clearly concerned about the welfare of his son.

'He is, Donovan, and unfortunately so is the thief. We defeated him, but he managed to escape. Yet, there is some good news.' Anubis produced his sacred blade and held it out for all to see.

Donovan beamed as he lay eyes upon the knife, 'Osir, you found it!'

'Indeed, we did. It was in the possession of the thief as we suspected,' Anubis replied.

'Wow, it's beautiful,' Erica commented, admiring the weapon. 'So, this is what has caused so much trouble for you?'

'Yes, Erica, it is of course not the fault of Osir – it simply does what it was created to do. In the wrong hands this weapon can wreak terrible havoc.'

'What of the demon's victim, did she survive?' Donovan asked, his demeanour now much more relaxed.

'She did – not even a scratch was inflicted upon her. We left her safe and very grateful for us having saved her soul and that of her unborn. So thankful in fact that she kissed us as a reward.'

Erica raised an eyebrow at hearing this and her jaw dropped, her smile turning into stunned silence as her eyes searched Sam's face. Seeing her reaction brought Sam rapidly into the conversation.

'Um, it was not a reward and it was barely a kiss – she was just grateful that she was alive,' Sam sputtered nervously, then facing Erica, he continued his defence, 'Really, it was nothing, just a light kiss on my forehead.'

Erica, frowned and made a disbelieving smile, 'Why are you telling me? What do I care if you want to go around kissing pregnant women that you have never met before?' She crossed her arms, incredulous, and Sam was caught off guard by her dramatic reaction.

'No, I don't, I mean I wouldn't ... She was married,' Sam realised what he had just said a moment too late, *What a ridiculous thing to say, she was married!*

'Oh, she was married, oh, that's okay then I guess. Nothing wrong with kissing married women then is there?' Erica laughed as she spoke, relishing that she had Sam on a string and enjoying his awkwardness. She could imagine the woman's thankfulness manifesting in a small kiss of gratitude, but her banter was covering a hint of jealousy that she did not wish to admit. Whilst Sam and Anubis were away, she found herself daydreaming about the framer. From the moment she first met him, laying helpless in the hospital, she had a soft spot for him. Then when she had interviewed him, learning about the fire, the loss of his job and his recent memory, made her feel for the young man, she could sense his despair. Furthermore, over the past several days of being by his side, she had grown quite attached to Sam, and his sense of humour and strength of character had begun to warm her heart. He was also attractive, she thought, but the thing that she admired the most, was that he did not appear to be aware of how attractive he was. 'Sam,' Erica continued to chuckle, 'I am just playing with you.'

'Oh, great, anyway it wasn't me she was kissing – it was Anubis, and he's a god, irresistible to mortal women,' Sam quipped spryly.

The comment brought raucous laughter from all except Anubis, who came forward as quickly as Sam had, to defend himself, 'Me? Oh, no she did not kiss me. You are mistaken, Samuel. I am a god – I do not seek to become intimate with mortals!' The seriousness of the god's tone produced a further round of laughter.

The group continued to discuss the events of the previous couple of days, and finally Donovan insisted that they all retire for the evening, before taking his leave.

Erica faced Sam and smiled warmly. 'I'm so relieved that the two of you are okay,' she said as she placed a hand on his forearm. 'Um, Anubis, do you think it would be possible for you to rest now too? I would very much like to talk a while with Sam.'

'But of course, it has been a big evening for us. Goodnight, Erica Murphy, may the gods lay their blessing upon you as you slumber.' The red glow of the god's eyes vanished as Sam's gaze returned, his face now also appeared weary.

Erica smiled, and she led Sam by the hand over to the bed. She could feel his hand tighten slightly around hers. 'Relax, Sam,' she said, sensing his nerves were aflutter, 'I just want to lay next to you. I feel safer when I am by your side.'

'Oh, sure, I'd like that,' Sam replied as he lay down upon the bed and Erica joined him by his side. Sam lifted his right arm, inviting Erica to rest her head on his chest. She nestled into him.

'Are you scared, Sam?' Erica asked softly.

'Scared? Scared of what?'

'All of this craziness.'

'Craziness? Hmm, you may need to be a little more specific, Erica.'

'Aren't you scared that you might die?'

Sam was quiet for a few moments before he answered, 'Not really, I mean we all have to get off this rock somehow, right?'

'Oh, you know what I mean,' Erica smiled, her tone serious as she adjusted her shoulders to lay closer to him.

'Well, the truth is that I've never really thought too much about dying. I believe that there is a new life after this one and I guess that Anubis kind of proves that. I am afraid to leave certain things and particular people behind, but death itself does not frighten me.'

Erica turned her face upward to look into Sam's eyes, allowing her concern to show. 'Well, I would care if you die, Sam. Damn, I wish I had your strength and courage. I am petrified of death, not so much death itself, but the process, you know, how it happens – the pain.'

Sam smiled, 'Don't worry, if I pass before you, I will keep an eye out for you in the afterlife.'

Sam's words melted away the last vestige of hesitation in Erica's heart. Perhaps he was the man that she had been waiting for, the one that she could love for eternity, if she could. She had never believed in soulmates, but at that moment it appeared that Sam was the perfect other part of her. She raised her hand up to the side of Sam's face and she guided his lips to meet hers. The kiss was so tender that she felt as if she were melting into him.

Sam responded with equal affection, his lips gently brushing hers before he opened himself fully. He was suddenly lost, the world blurred away as he kissed Erica, with her soft lips and gentle yet persistent tongue eagerly feeling its way around the inside of his mouth. It was Sam that eventually broke the kiss, as he slowly pulled away from her, 'Wow,' he exclaimed softly. 'What does this mean?'

'I think that I am falling for you, Samuel Baker. The framer closed his eyes as he savoured the moment. He had wanted this woman from the moment they had met, during the last several days and through the insanity of the events that had transpired. And now, here she was in his arms. It was almost too much to believe, but precious moments such as these were rare, especially given the circumstance that now governed their lives. 'Erica, I don't know what to say.'

'Shhhh,' she replied, placing her lips lightly against his.

'This is my gift to you. So, being a gift, it's yours to receive. There doesn't have to be any more words,' Erica said softly as she snuggled back down onto Sam's chest.

Sam felt his heart pulsing rhythmically against the weight

of Erica's cheek as he closed his eyes and holding her in his arms, he steadied his breathing. His chest rose and fell, and he sensed that Erica had been rocked to sleep. The framer soon followed, as he sank down into the sweet depths of the sea of unconsciousness, with his darling Erica floating like a boat upon the gentle waves above.

Kurt woke the next morning to the sound of his mobile phone ringing – it was his boss. Kurt answered the call, 'Hey, Tom, what's happening?'

His boss's tone was one of great excitement and urgency, 'There was an attempted murder last night, but the victim survived unharmed. It looks like the prenatal killer was interrupted and frightened off by a passer-by.'

'Okay, text me the address and I'll get right over there.'

'Already sent it to you. This is a huge story, Kurt, apparently the killer left fingerprints and DNA evidence at the scene. The police are awaiting the results.'

Jalel was furious at the use of the words 'frightened off' as Tom had stated. The thief was not frightened by the dog – he was overpowered, and he needed to make a tactical retreat. His rage grew to bursting and as a result, he took control of Kurt's body and threw the phone across the room. It smashed against the wall, promptly breaking into many small parts.

A new concern quickly quelled the thief's rage. Tom said that the killer had left behind evidence at the scene. He could not take the chance that he had inadvertently left some trace of Kurt's identity behind, so he decided to leave the apartment and go into hiding. He was now well and truly past the point of no return regarding his dark mission, and he would not allow an end to come so soon, without realising his plans into fruition.

What now? Jalel wondered, his desperation providing just

enough energy to steer his host's body down the street and into the nearby subway station. Once there, the thief scurried along the side wall until he located an access door into the subway tunnel and he ventured into the darkness. After several hundred meters Jalel came to an old service room, and he forced the door open by repeatedly throwing his heavy frame against it, then he slipped inside. The room was dark and dank, the air thick with the smell of mould and diesel. He fumbled along the wall of the darkened room, where he found a switch. A dim, solitary lightbulb flickered into life as Jalel turned on the switch, providing just enough light to see the extent of his new lodgings. There were various old pieces of paper and rags littering the floor, and here and there were old tools, abandoned, as they were no longer serviceable. Jalel closed the door behind him and sat down with his back against the adjacent wall. After some minutes of deep thought, the cunning thief had come up with a new plan of action. He desperately needed two things right now, more energy and more power, and there was a way to get both.

Taking on the guise of a god was not an easy task, especially when the god being imitated was as recognisable as Anubis. That was the very task that Apep had been busying himself with for the past several thousand years. After the entrapment of Anubis, Apep quickly realised that the great god of death's absence would be noticed by Horus and the other gods of the underworld. If his plan to lay siege to the afterlife and its lord Osiris was to succeed, he needed to hold secret his devious deceit from his brother and sister gods, at least until he had received the knowledge of Anubis by devouring his essence. Yet, there he was once again helping a recently deceased man navigate through the vast and frightening dimension of the underworld.

Being the serpent god of chaos, Apep had the ability to change his appearance at will, and even become invisible if the need arose. His disguise as Anubis was far from perfect, but at a quick glance or from a distance he could fool anybody. It was for that very reason that he did not approach too closely toward Horus as he led the human soul toward the scales of judgement. The silver lining for Apep, as he continued the ongoing masquerade, was the moment when the human heart was judged, and this particular mortal did not possess a book of the dead. The reptile considered the fact that this soul had successfully passed the four previous trials as nothing short of a miracle and yet, his judgement was an almost foregone conclusion. The heart scarab was the spiritual representation of the human heart and it was this very creature that was placed upon the scale. The feather of truth was then placed upon the scale by Thoth, the ibis-headed god of wisdom, and the scale lock released.

The human soul watched nervously as the scale began to dip under the weight of the scarab, raising the feather high. His judgement was complete: he was not worthy to progress through the final gate, into the afterlife. The mortal man fell to his knees and began pleading to the gods for salvation, but Horus simply shook his head, showing not one ounce of pity. The god of the air raised his staff high and brought it down firmly onto the stone floor, producing an ear-piercing sound.

From out of the darkness sprung the terrifying god Ammit, the devourer of souls, called forth by the tone of the staff. The condemned man screamed with sheer terror, his eyes frozen wide with dread. The crocodile jaws of the god opened wide and closed rapidly about the torso of the unworthy soul, cleaving the essence in two. The creature then went about ravenously consuming the remains of the soul, which were left lying about the floor of the chamber.

Apep liked the god Ammit, and one could say that they were almost kindred spirits, both part reptilian and both had the ability to devour souls. It was always a thrill to see his brother god eat the essence of mortal man with such fervour, and at length, a smile spread across the disguised god Apep's lips.

The smile was not lost upon Horus, his hawk head cocking violently to one side as he looked at the fake Anubis, 'Does something amuse you, brother Anubis?'

The smile quickly faded from Apep, and he dared not speak as he could not emulate the voice of Anubis. Instead he grunted, shaking his head and bowing low, before turning and leaving the chamber with haste.

Upon exiting the veneer of the dimensional gate of the underworld and returning to earth, Apep shed his disguise. Shifting to his own form, he hastened to moisten his eyes. His tongue worked furiously to slather saliva over his beady, exposed eyes and once his dryness had been slaked, he set about stilling his body to focus on the vibrations that ran invisibly through the air. These vibrations brought the god his extra-sensory information. He could hear conversations from anywhere in the world, and know how fresh the information was depending on how long the soundwaves took to reach his senses.

Apep was a simple creature at heart. He was created and designed for one very important purpose: the testing of human spirit. He was not evil, nor was he good; he was designed to be a truly neutral entity. Although he was responsible for many great evildoings, he was never the one to commit the actual deed himself. Apep had a purpose – a very important purpose – as did all the gods. The reptile was humanity's moral evaluator. He would help the soul be stained with ill deeds, or enlightened with good works, both crucial cargo for the human spirit when the soul was weighed at the hall of judgement. The choice of doing right or wrong a matter of human free will.

Perhaps it was the worst of humanity that had begun to imprint upon the lizard's patience and sense of his own standing among the hierarchy of the gods. He had witnessed many low and dastardly deeds, many more than good or righteous ones, such was the nature of humanity to fail, for the ego of mankind would often seek to pacify its insatiable hunger. He started to take pity on those who had damned their souls to an afterlife of endless pain and torture. Yes, the thousands of years spent playing the great tempter were beginning to wear at the impartiality of the god, and so Apep began to seek out the disembodied spirits of evil men and women – his disenchanted, or demons as the humans call them. These demons, such as the thief, had been sent about with various tasks, taking some of Apep's hefty workload and pushing their ill will among living humanity. As such, the world now heavily gravitated toward darkness, rather than the light, with so-called 'possessions', the result of madness brought about by dark whispers in the ear of man.

It was hardly fair, Apep reckoned, that Osiris hid himself along with his purist soul children behind the veil of creation, in an eternal paradise, where any whim may be serviced. Nor was it fair for the disenchanted to be so brutally punished for a few moments of poor judgement and human weakness. Being the moral gauge that he was, Apep could see that the scales of judgement were indeed prejudiced toward the darkness and that counterbalance would have to be corrected by him. The consequence of Apep's rebellious plans would of course bring forth the wrath of Horus and his golden army of eagle-men, or even the great Osiris himself. However, great rewards do not come without great risk and if Apep was the one to take that risk, then so be it. Perhaps there was even a chance that he could reconcile his actions with the father god, that he could give the great creator a chance at showing true benevolence. Apep had to try – he desperately sought the opportunity to retire from his long life of servitude and bask in the glory of the afterlife.

Meanwhile, he would bide his time and play the game. He would be the one who would be responsible for creating situations that would sample the best and worst of humanity. The serpent could arrange for two people to meet, via what humanity may consider to be a chance occurrence. Several weeks ago, he arranged for a young woman to have a flat tyre on her car and he watched on as a very handsome, yet very married, man stopped to render assistance.

The sound vibrations tickled his senses, and he could hear that same married man in New York talking dirty to his new mistress and lover, the same damsel in distress with the flat tyre, as the cheaters made passionate love to each other. He could also hear the man's unsuspecting wife complaining to her friend about how distant her husband had become of late.

He could hear the screams of a shop assistant in France, who was being robbed, held at knifepoint as the thieves busied themselves with their looting. He could hear the lies of the politicians, the unrelenting gospel-bashing of the preachers and the ever-constant deceit of the very young and the very old: everything will be okay, little Jennifer, no matter what, you deserve to be treated like a princess and one day you will find the perfect prince; don't worry, John, your suffering with arthritis will soon be over and you will go to heaven, where you shall regain your youth and you will never be in pain or want for anything ever again.

Lies, lies and more lies, Apep mused. The truth was that

humans were dragged kicking and screaming into this world at birth, they lived their lives kicking and screaming and they died the same, their souls dragged out of their bodies, kicking and screaming. Oh, how the serpent was pleased to not have such fears, for his life was an eternal one … well almost.

'Apep!'

The serpent heard his name being called and he recognised the voice instantly – it was his spy, the thief Jalel. *Ah, surely my minion has word of the fate of Anubis! At last!* Apep became quite excited at the thought of devouring the essence of his brother god. *Soon, the underworld and the afterlife will bow at my feet!*

The thief had prepared his trap with great foresight and extreme caution as he could ill afford to provide Apep any opportunity to fight back. Jalel had broken into an animal shelter after the sun had gone down, a few hours after closing time, his demon-form causing great alarm among the animals temporarily residing in the cages at the back of the property. He took his time perusing the selection of dogs available and at length, his eyes fell upon a suitable source of bait for his trap. A large black Rottweiler barked and snapped ferociously at the demon as he stared at the animal from the safety of the opposite side of the cage. *Perfect,* the thief smiled, *yes, this will do nicely.*

Jalel decided not to kill the dog, he would merely knock the beast unconscious. The frightened animal put up quite a struggle, savagely biting the demon's arm, the wound drawing blood and pus-like fluid. Once the canine was down and out, the thief dragged the dog over into a dark corner of the courtyard, and after taking several paces back away from the animal, he concluded that the positioning of the dog was perfect for his plan.

A mewing litter of kittens drew the attention of the thief and he moved over to the cage where the soft cries were coming from. He had many cats as a child, indeed almost all of Egypt was fascinated by the mystical creatures. There was even a goddess named after the cat, Bastet, the fierce lioness warrior of Osiris. The creatures made Jalel nervous as a child, for he believed that felines could see into his soul and that did not sit well with him as a youngster. The demon, still reminiscing, opened the cage and drew out a small, fragile ginger ball of a kitten and held it snuggly in one arm. He looked down blankly at the baby cat as he remembered how he remedied such childhood fears – surely the creature could not see into his soul without sight? His demon claws travelled across the kitten's face and, finding the eyes, he effortlessly slid his sharp nails into the sockets. A terrible scream came bellowing out of the feline, its tiny claws wildly scratching at the air, before finding purchase on the demon's flesh of the forearm. The frightened, agonized kitten clambered up his arm and dug its needle-like claws into the folds of skin at Jalel's neck. Jalel calmly lifted his hand to the nape of the kitten and brought it back down into his arm, where he held it tightly – too tightly – squeezing the air from its chest.

Still looking into his memories, he grasped the top of the feline's head and began to twist it clockwise. There was a very brief moment of resistance before a small crack was heard. Jalel continued twisting the dead kitten's head clockwise, around and around, the tiny little bones grinding and cracking together, like a pepper mill. The thief emulated the actions of his youth past, until his memory began to fade. The thief looked down coldly at the sight of the little head flopping around, attached by only skin and veins, which were now stretched and ruptured.

Ah, memories, he thought, *oh well, waste not, want not.*

The thief opened his mouth and chewed down upon the deceased kitten's skull and he could taste the small offering of essence that slid down his gullet. The flavour was predictably unpleasant, but it was still sustenance. He remembered back to the many times when he had to forage to find any meagre scraps of food to stay alive, and so the kitten's death had not been in vain as far as he was concerned.

Apep appeared abruptly, emerging from a dull blue cloud of mist. The serpent's beady eyes darted about as he searched for his minion, 'Thief? You summoned me forth, show yourself.' The reptile continued to glance about the scene with great caution. After a moment, Apep's eyes fell upon a dark, hulking mass lying on the ground, barely noticeable against the shadows of the courtyard. Cautiously, the serpent crept toward the body, until he was merely a few feet away. It was then that he recognised the form as a large black dog.

'Brother Anubis? Is that you? Are you wounded?' the serpent enquired with mock concern. The dog let out a soft groan at the sound of Apep's voice, bringing a smile to the reptile as he crept closer to the beast. 'Fear not, brother. I shall help you. Your long-standing sufferance will soon be at an end.'

Apep licked his eyes as he closed the final few steps to the beast, which lay helplessly upon the ground in front of him. 'Augupte,' the serpent spoke the sacred words of soul harvest, summoning the canid spirit from the flesh and the black beast gave one final breath as its life was rendered void.

The reptile stood upright, his eyes pointed skyward as he let the essence become absorbed into his being. However, something was not right – he could taste no divinity in the spirit and the only sensation that came to him was for want of freedom, to run carefree through the streets. The very next sensation that came to the serpent was a sudden impact to the back of his skull, which duly rendered him unconscious. Just before his senses left him, his hearing lit upon the sound of rambunctious laughter, then his very last ever thought, *well played, thief!*

Jalel was well pleased with himself as he penetrated the top of his former master's spine, his claws once again proving to be an invaluable tool. Jalel continued to chuckle softly at the brilliance of his deception. He pulled out Apep's spinal column and peered into the wound, looking for the faint blue glow of his soul, only to discover that it was not blue, rather it was a bright green colour which shone brilliantly, illuminating the bloody tunnel of flesh which led to its origin. The thief placed his demonic mouth over the wound and sucked at the fluids which had pooled at the spot, and as before, the essence of the soul was extracted. Such sweet nectar it was. The flavour was not like the warm, roasted lamb taste of the human soul. The flavour of the serpent god's soul reminded him of the finest sweet tobacco that Jalel used to smoke when he was back in Egypt. It was moist and richly fragranced, spiced with exotic ingredients of deepest Africa, earthy, yet clean. The thief drew the serpent essence deep into his lungs, as he did when he used to smoke, and he held it there, allowing the god to be fully absorbed into his cells.

Jalel was ill-prepared for what came after the inhalation – pain, unbearable and agonising pain. So intense was his suffering that the demon dropped to his knees, then contorting into a fetal position, he laid on his side, curling into a ball. The thief's heart pounded inside his chest, the vibrations travelling up into his brain and into the pineal gland. The sensation was blindingly painful. A severe stabbing pain shot through the demon body, and just as Jalel was considering that he had made a terrible mistake, the pain abruptly ceased.

The soul of a god was not naturally compatible with that of a mortal human and as such, the combination of the serpent god and the already demonic-form of the Jalel-Kurt union resulted in an even more nightmarish abomination. The demon had now developed an elongated maw, filled with razor-sharp teeth, but as before, the teeth were all severely twisted and crooked, fractures threating to render such a potentially damaging weapon into a comically fragile embarrassment.

The skin of the demon had also changed, with various patches of scales breaking through its raw and fluid oozing flesh, and here and there thick, black hairs sprouted forth.

At his groin, the penis had been malformed and now resembled a reptilian tail, albeit only about seven centimetres in length. *No cock?* the thief questioned. *Well, how am I to piss?* The answer came sooner than he expected. He concentrated on urinating so that he may discover from where the flow would come. For a few moments, there was nothing, then he felt a familiar sensation welling up above his groin. He felt a strong pulsing at the top and back of his tongue. A hard, fleshy lump appeared and opened like an eye of a penis, spraying urine out of the demon's mouth like a jet of water, several feet in front of him.

'Ugh! Foul piss!' Jalel sputtered as his mouth and nostrils were filled with the strong taste and smell of urine. *Gods have cursed me. Is this your attempt at revenge, lizard? Making me piss from my mouth?* A thought sent a shudder through the demon, *if that is from where I must piss, then I do not wish to discover from where my shit will come!* The thief shot his hand down to his anus, only to discover that there was no such orifice to be found there. *Great! Something to look forward to!*

A whole new world of sensations violently assaulted the thief, his skin alive with microscopic tremors, rippling through his being, travelling through his nervous system and into his brain, where they were transitioned into sound.

His head spun wildly as he attempted to focus on the jumbled mess of noise. He could hear an ungodly cacophony of voices, mashed with sounds of the city: babies crying, dogs barking, car horns honking and the odd guffaw of laughter. Just as Jalel believed that things could not get any worse, more sounds came to him. All the languages of the world now began to infiltrate the Australian English language bouncing around his brain, pulsing in and out of hearing, like a radio searching through channels for stable signal.

The thief became enraged at his inability to focus his senses and his anger surged forward, but the rage only intensified the jumble of sounds. *This is useless, I have made a grave error in consuming the serpent,* he conceded, his failure bringing a deep depression upon the thief like a dark blanket being drawn down over his whole body and as it fell, his rage slipped away. As his anger left him, the noises began to quieten. Then he heard several words string together and soon, he could hear whole sentences. *So, calmness brings control, control brings clarity?*

Jalel was enjoying the sense of feeling empowered and over the next half hour or so, he had the basics of extrasensory hearing under control. Although he could not turn the noise off, he could turn the volume down by slowing his breathing and trying to still his body.

Aside from his new extra-sensitive hearing, the thief found that all his senses had received a hefty upgrade, propelling him into the position of demi-god. He could smell all the scents of the animal shelter, the fur, hair, shit, blood and piss. The scents were so strong that the thief almost gagged, his stomach churning as it threatened to flip.

Jalel decided to leave, but before he did so, he used his demonic strength to rip apart the corpse of Apep, tearing lumps of flesh and bone apart with ease. He then threw the remains to the dogs, who eagerly devoured the morsels.

The demon took one last look over the scene of his triumph and, without thinking, his newly lengthened tongue slathered out of his foul mouth and flicked upward, over his dry eyes, covering them with thick, sulphur-scented mucus – the nervous remnant of his former master Apep providing yet another unwelcome gift. Stench aside, the thief felt great relief at having wet eyeballs and with a jagged, toothy smile, he made his way toward his new home in the subway.

CHAPTER FOURTEEN

Man Down

OLD MAN DONOVAN DID not pass the night well. He was thrilled with Anubis and Sam's success in defeating Jalel the previous evening, but he was also deeply concerned for the welfare of his son, Kurt. Due to his worry, the restless night seemed to have no end and so he had been awake for several hours. His watch showed that it was now shortly after six in the morning. *The others will be awake soon, Better go freshen up.*

Standing in front of the mirror, the old man stared at his frail form. He was saddened to be growing old. Perhaps if he had the strength and vigour of his son, he could have been more of a direct assistance in the ongoing battle with the thief. *Ah, the thief, aptly named*, Donovan conceded, for Jalel had indeed stolen from both him and his son. He had stolen Kurt's life, his soul, and who knows when will come the point of no return for him. The thought saddened the old man to tears, his grief leaving a deep bruise on his soul. 'Oh, Kurt, where are you, son?'

Erica woke before Sam and she felt well-rested having spent the night by his side. She felt safe whenever she was near him. The reporter had always been independent, making her own way and never seeking the protection of any man. Sam was different, it appeared that he had no hidden agenda, nor did he display any false pretenses toward her. She could just lay in his arms, without the expectation of giving more of herself, this made its impact on her heart. He held her and comforted her ever-racing mind, so Erica was rather content to allow herself to be a little vulnerable toward him.

Now she lay silently next to Sam and she took the time to look over him as he slept, taking note of every fine detail of his appearance. She counted every breath that he took, watching as his chest rose and fell, the amulet of Osiris still securely fastened around his neck, and she couldn't help but wonder what it felt like to wear such an ancient and powerful piece of jewellery. Sam had fallen asleep fully clothed, except for his shoes which he had managed to discard to the floor sometime during the night. She slowly ran her eyes over Sam's body and Erica soon found herself wondering, for the first time, how he would look naked. When they had first met, she knew that there was something unique about Sam. Now she loved the idea of spending all her free time with Sam, and the thought of becoming intimate with him sent a little tremor of pleasure through her body, tingling from deep within.

Ah, come on Erica, times and places, times and places. Bigger things happening now. Dangerous things happening now and more danger to come ... And then what? The question brought an abrupt end to her swelling arousal, but quickened her heart. The thought of losing Sam, when she had only just realised her feelings for him, was too much to bear. Life had suddenly become chaotic, and she felt slightly unhinged, out of place and out of time. She did not want to waste any opportunity to show him how much he meant to her and so she leaned over him and she kissed him softly, delicately. She then felt her kiss returned by Sam, who put his arms around her and pulled her down onto him, before rolling the two of them over so that he was atop her.

When he first felt Erica's warm lips against his, Sam thought that he was still dreaming, until the memory of her sweet words and loving kisses the night before perforated the veil of sleep. She was real and his affection for her would be denied no longer. 'Good morning, beautiful,' Sam said as he looked down upon Erica's pretty, lightly freckled face, her porcelain skin glowing softly in the early morning light. Sam moved to kiss Erica again, but stopped millimetres from her lips as he sighed heavily. 'Good morning, Anubis,' Sam croaked, his voice shaking of the lethargy of sleep.

'Oh, good morning, Samuel. I trust that you slept well?' the god replied with a playful tone. Anubis was well aware of what had transpired in his absence – and the fact that Sam was hovering over Erica who was displaying a full blush to her cheeks like a mischievous child that had been caught out, added to the evidence that they had been up to no good. *'I am pleased that the two of you are able to find some happiness in*

all this chaos. However, you must forgive my lack of comprehension of your primitive emotions – they seem unnecessarily complicated.'

Sam moved himself to sit on the edge of the bed, the young man barely containing his excitement as he spoke telepathically with Anubis, *'I can't ask for your understanding, I can only ask for your patience. I will try to be discrete; I don't want you to feel uncomfortable around us. I guess that we'll just have to hold off our physical affections until you are resting. No doubt it is very weird for Erica too, she has to share me with you. It must be like dating two people at the same time, or perhaps dealing with a boyfriend that has a split personality or something. She's just so perfect and I can hardly believe that she is interested in the likes of me.'*

Erica cleared her throat, 'Are you two having a lovely conversation?' she quipped sarcastically as she playfully flopped her arms over Sam's shoulders. 'Not talking about me I hope?' she whispered into Sam's ear.

At this point Anubis came forward as his eyes glowed red. 'Hello, Erica. Firstly, please accept my congratulations upon your and Sam's budding relationship.'

A broad smile came to Erica's lips and she placed her hand over her heart, displaying a gesture of sincere gratitude. 'Aw, thank you, Anubis, that's very kind of you. Well, now that you know about us, please take good care of my Sam,' she said with a wink.

The god moved to respond but was halted abruptly by a call for help from the room next door. It was Donovan.

Sam's eyes appeared briefly to Erica, 'Stay here and lock the door behind us!'

Anubis took control and the beast-form was again brought into service. Using god-speed, the duo was inside the doorway of Donovan's room within heartbeats.

At first Anubis could not see anything out of the ordinary, until his eyes fell upon Donovan lying face down on the floor at the foot of the bed. The old man was still alive; Anubis stood watching Donovan's back as it expanded and contracted with breath. Yet the god refrained from moving beyond the doorway, his senses urging his immobility.

'Maybe he had a bad dream and fell from the bed?' Sam offered.

'Perhaps. Samuel, all does not appear well. I can sense that something is wrong,' Anubis responded with great concern.

The god sniffed at the air until a faint, yet familiar smell came to him, the smell of the serpent. 'Brother? Have you finally come for me?' Anubis prompted. There was no response from the otherwise quiet room. 'Apep? I am addressing you – come forth and show yourself. I am ready to face you, brother!' the beast shouted, but still there was no movement.

'This does not bode well, Samuel. I can smell my brother Apep,' the concerned god confided to his host.

'But, Anubis, you called his name. Is he not supposed to appear when his name is called out?'

'Yes, indeed he should. That is why I am concerned. My brother can change appearance – perhaps he has taken on the guise of Donovan, as means to lay a wicked trap for us.'

'Okay, then we need to do something. We can't stand in this doorway all day.'

'Hmm.'

'Come on, Anubis, we need to act. We'll just be extra vigilant … Wait, perhaps we should have brought Osir with us, just in case.'

'Argh!' the god growled mentally to Sam. *'We were lured here too easily, Samuel, that cannot happen again.'*

Anubis took several cautious steps toward Donovan as Sam mentally ran through his defensive options, imagining what types of blocks and counter-strikes may be needed.

'Donovan, can you hear me?' the beast growled. The old man did not respond.

'Anubis, wait!' Sam shouted. *'That smell – sulphur and rotted meat – familiar isn't it?'*

Again, the god sniffed at the air, this time more deeply, resulting in a loud snorting from his nose as he did so. *'Yes, it must be the thief, but what of Apep? I can smell him too.'*

Sam had grown weary of playing the waiting game. 'Thief! Your plan to catch us unaware will not work. Now, show yourself!' he said aloud, taking temporary control of the god-body.

At first there was no response, not from the unconscious body of Donovan, nor from anywhere else in the room. Then a wet, squelching sound came from the far side of the bed and a demonic hand appeared, slowly rising above the edge of the bed and resting on top of the mattress. A mangled mound of flesh heaved itself up from where it was hiding behind the bed, revealing a repulsive, twisted form.

Relishing his new horrific appearance, the demon took its time to fully upright its body. Anubis and Sam could now see the horrifying source of the stench, which held both scents of the thief and the serpent. Traits of Apep's reptilian appearance had melded into the festering body of the demon-thief, and as if to extinguish any lingering doubt about the matter, a long, pustule-riddled tongue slathered upward over the black beady eyes of the monster.

'What manner of madness is this?' Anubis spluttered. 'You have devoured my brother?'

The thief did not respond to the god's bewildered, somewhat rhetorical question, his cold, dark stare piercing the pungent, stench-infused air of the room.

'Why is he just standing there?' Sam thought to Anubis. *'Why does he not attack?'* The god did not answer Sam, his stoic focus aimed at the thief.

For what seemed like an age, the standoff continued until finally the demon spoke, 'Well, this situation comes as much of a surprise to me as it does to you. You see, I was soundly sleeping back at my new home, resting after my new … acquisition,' the demon smiled as he opened his arms to show off his twisted new form. 'I was indeed deep in slumber, imagining the glorious carnage that I will very shortly unleash upon this world. Suddenly I heard a name being called in the darkness and the voice which spoke that single word was carried upon the sound of such immense sadness.'

The thief stopped his speech at this point, his face pointed slightly upward and forward as a school teacher may do as if awaiting a response from a slow-witted student. 'Well? Can you guess the name that was spoken, dog?'

Anubis did not indulge the thief's mocking and after a few seconds, the demon provided the answer with an exaggerated sigh of disappointment, 'Kurt! It was Kurt Banks. You see, that old fool summoned me!' The demon released a bout of raucous laughter as he pointed his clawed hand at Donovan. 'I guess that there must be some weak presence of the son still residing in me. That will not be the case for much longer,' he purred.

'Summoned? How did that happen? Magic?' Sam queried Anubis.

'*Yes, of sorts,*' the god replied. '*It was one of Apep's abilities. He could travel to any location almost instantly, provided he could hear a voice or sound that belonged to that destination.*'

'*So, Donovan must have called out to Kurt somehow. Anubis, we should attack the thief now – let me take control,*' Sam said eagerly, his energy frantic and ready to pounce.

The god was about to argue the decision with his co-host, when the demon surged around the side of the bed and gathered up the unconscious body of Donovan, holding him up off the ground by the back of the neck.

Sam took control of the god-body and moved to rush forward when the thief shouted, 'Do not come any closer, fool, or I will kill him!'

Sam immediately stopped his attack and put his hands out to show that he had no weapon, 'Okay, okay. Look, I am unarmed. Please, just don't do anything stu–'

Sam stopped abruptly as the demon opened his maw wide, large enough to encompass the top of Donovan's head and, with a sickening crunch, the monster bit into the old man's skull. Bright red fluid oozed from the cracked, busted teeth and gums of the demon, which mixed with the dark red blood pulsing from Donovan's head. Then a loud crack could be heard as the demon bit through and removed the top, front section of Donovan's head. The old man's eyes sprung forward from the bloodied sockets and swung wildly by the optical nerves.

Sam lurched at the demon, now chewing ferociously, and struck him strongly with a front-heel kick to the stomach, forcing the air rapidly out of the monster. This caused the demon to spit the remains of the head out, spreading skull, blood, brain and foul mucus across the bed. Sam followed up with a series of rapid blows about the face and torso of the demon. However, the strikes did little damage to the thief, resulting in guffaws of manic laughter from him, which only further enraged Sam, who struck out with increased ferocity. The crazed laughter of the demon was halted as Sam landed a powerful uppercut underneath his chin. His tongue was caught between his ragged teeth as they smashed together from the savage punch, severing the grotesque organ from his mouth.

Jalel howled and spat profuse amounts of blood, broken teeth and saliva about the place as he flailed about. The thief rushed viciously at Sam, who promptly flipped himself sideways through the air, landing close to the wall of the room. Sam rose quickly, ready to defend himself, but the demon continued his momentum out the door and hurled himself down the hall.

Anubis took control and ran after the abomination and, just as he was about to close the gap between them, the thief vanished with a wavy mirage-like effect, as one may see hovering just above a hot desert road.

Anubis turned about and rushed back into Donovan's room, dropping to the floor beside the old man's body. The god feverishly searched the remains for any sign of Donovan's soul, but none was to be found there, nor anywhere nearby. The repulsive demon thief had devoured the old man's soul.

Anubis howled with frightening ferocity, his rage filling every part of him. His closest and oldest human friend had perished at the hands of the demented thief and there was nothing that Sam, nor himself, could have done to prevent the murder of the old man.

Sam was equally upset at the devastating turn of events. However, he had the presence of mind to know that the commotion and Anubis's howl of anguish would surely have caught the attention of the surrounding guests, and no sooner had the thought appeared, than the sounds of doors opening out in the hall could be heard.

'Help! Somebody call the police!' Sam yelled with all his might.

'Sam! What are you doing?' Anubis growled angrily. *'We need to take care of Donovan!'*

'Anubis, Donovan is dead, and his soul is not trapped inside his body. There is nothing to be done for him now. We must be smart about this and remove ourselves from the suspicion of the police. We must act as if we have just discovered Donovan's body. You know that it will be impossible to catch the thief if we are behind bars.'

Anubis knew that what Sam was saying made complete, logical sense and as such, he decided to allow Sam to take control of the oncoming situation. *'Yes, you are right, Sam. Please forgive my abrupt nature. I need to retreat into your consciousness for now. I am currently too incensed to think clearly.'*

The framer did his utmost to reassure the god. In truth, Sam needed a rest himself, respite from having to share his mind and body with the god of death. *'I understand, Anubis. Please take the time that you need to grieve and regain your strength and composure. I'll handle this situation and I'll be waiting for you when you are ready.'*

Grieve? The god had never had to grieve before, not for anyone. Grief was indeed what he felt, at least that was the label that Anubis had decided to place upon the feelings that had welled up inside of his soul. Feelings? A god should have no feelings, yet they were indeed present within him. Perhaps he had spent far too much time in the presence of mortals, that their primitive, mostly irrational emotions had somehow leeched into his being. Maybe spending too much time co-inhabiting the body and consciousness of Samuel had made the god weak to the ways of human sentiment. The framer's blossoming love for Erica had awoken such primitive feelings of affection, fear and anger, perhaps even jealousy? For these reasons, Anubis decided to withdraw from Samuel for a while, to be freed from the concoction of emotions that he had to bear witness to.

'Sam?' Erica whispered as she crept cautiously into the room.

'Erica, don't come in here!' Sam urged. It was too late as the reporter's eyes fell upon the bloody carnage that had unfolded in the room.

'Oh my god! Oh my god!' Erica squealed with horror, a strained panic arising in her throat, 'Is that Donovan?'

'Erica, please don't look,' Sam rose to his feet and attempted to turn her from the blood and gore, but she would not be removed from the scene and consequently, she came closer to inspect the body of the old man, her trembling hand hovering just above his destroyed face. 'Sam, what happened in here?'

'It was the thief. He was too fast, too powerful. He has absorbed the soul of Anubis's brother god. He is … a monster.'

Sam gently urged Erica to her feet and she, in turn, fell into his arms, sobbing with ragged breaths. He led her out into the hallway and there the two stayed, until hotel management arrived, soon followed by the police. In one terrible moment, four had become three and with Anubis retreating, there were now just two.

.

CHAPTER FIFTEEN

The Age of Jalel

THE POLICE HAD CONDUCTED a rushed investigation into the murder of Donovan Banks over the next couple days and, although Sam was initially considered a suspect, no trace evidence of Sam was found on the victim, nor directly at the spot of the killing. The only evidence that they did find was some partial bloody fingerprints and some bodily fluids, both of which were soon proven to be a match to the victim's missing son, Kurt Banks. They also found some dog hair, which had also been found at the scenes of the prenatal killings. The police already had DNA evidence linking Kurt to the residence of the only surviving victim: Amy, the trace evidence from the Hotel Rosales instantly finding a match in the police database. The police department had concluded that the spate of gruesome murders had been carried out by Kurt Banks, possibly in the company of a large black dog. It seemed that Kurt's motive behind the killings were to advance his career, and that somehow Donovan Banks had learned of his son's murderous activities. The motive was a tenuous conclusion, a desperate effort to force the pieces of information into a package that may pacify the ever-growing panic spreading throughout the populace.

Sam and Erica needed to recover emotionally from the gruesome murder of their new-found friend and ally, so they decided to leave the Hotel Rosales and lay low at Sam's place following the murder of Donovan. The choice seemed easy, especially since the police had warned Sam not to leave town.

Sam was unaware of how long Anubis would be absent from his waking mind, but he was comforted by the fact that he could call for the god when they had word or sight of Jalel. The thief had been badly wounded and wasted no time in fleeing from Donovan's hotel room and the way the demon simply vanished left Sam feeling extremely uneasy, so he and Erica decided to refrain from saying the names of Jalel, Kurt or Donovan out aloud. They were not ready to face the thief just yet. They needed to formulate a plan if they were to finally overpower Jalel, whose strength and abilities had been boosted significantly.

Training proved to be rather therapeutic for Sam, and he spent almost all his waking hours honing his martial arts skills as sharply as he could manage. Outrage at the murder of Donovan burned deep inside of Sam and that burn provided ample inspiration to push his body to the limits. Osir proved to be a valuable training partner for Sam as he toiled with the weapon, man and blade eventually functioning as one entity, the steel becoming a lethal extension of Sam's arm.

Late one afternoon, a storm came rolling over the suburb in which Sam's apartment was situated. Erica sat on the top stair of his back patio, her mind numb to all around her as she watched the lightning sprawl across the dark grey sky, followed shortly after by the rumble of thunder. It was early winter and the cool air caressed her face as she sat – her pale blue jeans and a dark green knitted jumper providing ample comfort as she watched the stormy sky brew. A sentimental ballad from the eighties played softly in the background, the music drowned out on occasion by the random roll of thunder.

'It's kind of beautiful, don't you think? The storm?' Sam asked as he sat next to Erica, offering her a cup of strong tea.

"It is,' Erica replied with a smile as she took the cup from Sam. She sniffed deeply at the scent rising from the brew, 'Irish Breakfast?'

'Uh-huh, yes.' Sam paused a second and smiled as he continued, 'Don't you think it's kind of funny that I seem to be attracted to Irish things?'

Erica laughed, 'Oh, yes, well let's see if you say that after you try your first pint of Irish ale.'

'Just so happens that I like black beer too,' Sam replied.

'Good! Then after this is all over, we will go out to an Irish pub,' Erica said as she turned her gaze back to the incoming storm.

When this is all over? The question hung about the air, as if a spirit of foreboding had been summoned into existence. It was a question that had plagued Erica over the past several days. The future was only full of danger and uncertainty for the couple. Who knew what was coming at them, victory or defeat, and defeat was just a kinder word for death. Erica was extremely concerned that she would lose her new love to the demon-thief. She found herself becoming more and more smitten with Sam, and her desire for emotional and physical connection with him grew steadily to the point of yearning. She wished she could do more to help Sam in the battle that lay ahead; she wanted to be more to him, wanted more of him. Erica sipped at her tea. Sam was sweet, and he had made the drink with love, as if a part of himself was present in the brew. By drinking it, Erica felt that she could take Sam into her, that he could warm and comfort her inside. She took a long drink of the love-laced tea before placing the cup down beside her. Erica let out a soft sigh as her thoughts continued to swell and she rested her hand on Sam's inner thigh, her fingers caressing his jeans rhythmically as she observed the skyline.

Sam, seemingly sensing her want, turned to look at Erica. Her face was taught with purpose, her eyes eager as she returned his gaze. He leaned in and kissed her with tender affection, a breathy groan of desire escaping his mouth as their lips parted briefly. Erica lifted herself onto his lap, facing him with her legs wrapped around his waist, and kissed Sam with all her desire, pouring her heart and soul into him. 'I love you, Samuel,' she said between kisses. There was slight pain in her words as she spoke her precious confession, 'And I don't want to lose you.'

'I'm not going to leave you. I am a part of you now. I love you,' Sam said with certainty in his voice.

Sam stood up with Erica still tightly clamped about his waist and he carried her into the bedroom. He lay her down upon the bed and kissed her more passionately this time. He felt Erica explode with desire as she grabbed the back of his head and kissed him, her mouth locked around his, her soft tongue stroking his rhythmically. Sam removed Erica's jumper, followed by her white singlet and jeans, his hands moving lovingly over her body as he did so. Her skin was as Sam had imagined, pale and soft, like a porcelain doll – broken only by her black underwear.

Sam removed his sweater and t-shirt. Erica's eyes danced over his body as he undressed, her smile an unspoken compliment. A flash of lightning burst through the sliver between the curtains as Erica leaned up to kiss Sam's chest and rigid abdomen. Then, arching her back against the bed, she bit at her bottom lip while working to take off her bra.

Sam was captivated as his eyes scanned Erica's shapely figure. She was beautiful, and her breasts were soft, flushed with desire – her passion for him clear to see. Yet he hesitated before going any further, as if seeking final permission to proceed, looking at Erica's pretty face, her dark hair splayed across the mattress behind her head. In response, Erica sat up and reached out, grabbing Sam's belt, her nimble fingers fumbling briefly at the buckle before unzipping his jeans. Her soft kisses worked across his stomach, sending a tremor through Sam's body. She raised her hands, reaching for Sam to come to her, then smiling – he did just that.

Anubis finally returned to Sam three days after he had taken his leave of absence, following Donovan's murder. 'Greetings, Samuel and Erica,' the god said as Sam's eyes glowed red. 'I apologise for being away for so long. It was necessary for me to gather my thoughts and use my solitude to formulate a plan.'

Erica was seated on Sam's sofa, working on some notes for her article. She rose to her feet and came over to where Sam was standing and looked sincerely into the glowing eyes, 'It's good to see you again, Anubis. Sam and I missed you.'

'Welcome back, my friend,' Sam said with a tone of relief. 'You said that you were trying to come up with a plan, so do you have any ideas?'

Anubis forced Sam's mouth into a smile, 'Yes, Samuel, I believe that I might have found a way that we may succeed.'

The thief awoke abruptly from his slumber. Severe pain filled his mouth and his severed tongue throbbed persistently, sending wave after wave of searing shocks up into his brain. His mouth was dry and caked with blood and it was only with much difficulty that the thief could swallow. He groaned and sobbed uncontrollably as he rocked back and forth on the ground.

He would have stayed to finish the dog after killing Donovan Banks. The benefit of hindsight had Jalel fully aware that all he needed to do was utter one word, a word learned from the memories of Apep – 'Augupte'. If he had spoken it, he could have easily devoured the soul of Anubis and his human host, but the young man had taken the thief's words and Jalel could not tolerate the blinding pain of losing his tongue. The severed and exposed nerves threatened to render Jalel unconscious with agony and as such, he refused be disappointed with himself for fleeing from the fight.

The thief had lost count of the days since his injury, such was his sufferance that he drifted in and out of consciousness. He had only found one means of alleviating the pain, albeit temporarily, and now it was clear that he needed some more pain relief. He concentrated hard and after several seconds he felt the sweet release of his bladder, followed by the opening of his oral penis eye and his mouth filled with urine. At first it stung and burned his wound making the thief bash his hand against the floor repeatedly, but soon the pain was replaced with relief as he allowed the stump of the severed tongue to float about his full mouth. After a few minutes, his cheeks became numb and weary and he could hold the piss no longer, so he ejected it from his mouth, staining the floor with dark orange fluid.

It was at this time that the thief took stock of his life and the most recent events leading up to his current situation. *So, you have done well, Jalel. You are a shining example of what it means to be successful, and your mother would be proud,* the thief thought sarcastically. In actuality, the thief could only think now, as he had lost the privilege of speech, due to his severed tongue.

He hated the god of the dead for countless centuries, but now he found a new level of hatred for not only the dog, but also his human host – the framer. For it was the human who had taken his tongue, taken his speech, and for that he would make the mortal suffer greatly.

Over the next few days, the thief's pain began to subside. It seemed that the urine baths had an antiseptic effect upon his wound, assisting the end to clot and form a seal.

As the afternoon approached, a deep hunger gnawed at the thief's gut as he had not eaten for days, and so he could stand the stomach-ache no longer. Tonight, he would sneak out and find some food and after that he would find a soul or two for dessert. The only small comfort that Jalel found in his current condition was that he was finally rid of Kurt's essence. How poetic it was that Donovan's soul was the one to bring about the demise of his son. Once Jalel had feasted on the old man, he had sufficient energy to devour Kurt's soul once and for all – the essence being absorbed fully by the thief. Now he was the proud owner of the twisted mass of flesh that was his body.

The hours passed slowly in his pathetic lodgings, but eventually he could feel the heat escape from the concrete wall at his back, signalling that the heat of the day had eased, and night was imminent. The moon had begun its silent vigil over the city as the thief made his way down the main thoroughfare of the city centre.

He had managed to change his appearance to something that more or less resembled a man. The thief felt great discomfort in this, for his flesh was still a twisted mess, giving the appearance of a severely disfigured person. His face was the only part of his form that even remotely looked like Kurt and he did the best he could to fit the tissues together, but he struggled to hold the form and each step that he took was agony.

To avoid unwanted attention, Jalel had covered his pathetic body with an old blanket he had found near the subway and moved as quickly as he could, trying his best to stick to the shadows as he made his way along. He looked enviously upon the various cafes and eateries that peppered the bustling avenue. The smell of food and coffee forced his stomach into violent spasms and he felt his form shift slightly before he managed to recompose himself.

Soon he noticed some alfresco tables at the front of a bistro with uneaten food on their plates. The thief quickly sat at a table and started shovelling the leftover food into his mouth, his ravenous hunger would be denied no longer. His wounded tongue spasmed wildly as the thief chewed and he could taste blood as he swallowed the morsels, his stump rupturing with the friction of food against it. The thief cared not, such was his hunger that the pain in his gut was stronger than that in his mouth.

'What are you doing? Get out of here!' snarled a waitress who had rushed out of the bistro to shoo the dirty vagrant away from the eatery.

Jalel attempted to respond to the waitress, but as he opened his mouth, chewed food and blood fell out onto the plate in front of him. Suddenly he was reminded that he was unable to speak. This enraged the thief and he screamed at the shocked woman, spraying blood and spittle across her face and shirt.

The waitress screamed, her voice shrill with fear and disgust. The thief stood up abruptly, flipping the table over as he did so. Again, the woman screamed and ran back inside the bistro, locking the door behind her. 'Somebody call the police! I think that is the man they are looking for!'

Police? Looking for me? Must go, must get out of here! The thief took several steps before he stopped, looking at all the people on the street that were standing there watching him. A few of the onlookers held their phones out, filming the unfolding drama. Why was he the one who should run? Why should he have to hide? Was he not stronger than all of them? Was he not a god now? He had hidden from the world for far too long. Now was the time that he should reveal his beautiful horror to the world. Now was the time to take the world by the throat and bring it crashing to its knees. Now was the time for blood and havoc, a time for death and despair, for he was the true god of death, the ender of life and swallower of souls. Yes, they would all fill his gut and he would shit them all out, empty and void of substance. Now was the age of the thief. Now was the age of Jalel.

Sirens filled the cold night air as the respective emergency service vehicles made their way toward the city centre. Standing in the middle of the street was a creature of indescribable terror, indescribable because nobody could agree on just what the thing was. Was it some sort of sick joke, a publicity stunt – full of visual-effects wizardry? Was it some type of alien – an extra-terrestrial from another planet?

The thief, not caring to hide his appearance any longer, had reverted to the comfort of his twisted, demonic-form – the pus-riddled, sulphur-stinking contorted mass of broken flesh and bone that he had somehow grown to love. The monster was in no hurry to move from his spot amidst several vehicles that had been left abandoned by their frightened drivers as they happened upon the area, the headlights bathing Jalel in harsh illumination. *Let them see, let them lay their eyes upon their new master, let the meat know who shall be devouring them.*

The sound of the sirens reached their crescendo as they screamed into the street, tires screeched angrily as they were brought to a stop. Dozens of police exited their vehicles and sheltered behind them, guns drawn and trained steadfast on the monster before them.

'You there! Don't move! Place your hands high above your head and get down on your knees!' came the directives from the police sergeant.

The demon did not respond. He stayed still, smiling at the officers, his broken, bloody maw a sign of true maniacal menace.

'Identify yourself!' came another demand from the sergeant, and no sooner had the words left his lips than the creature began to shimmer, like a heat mirage, waving rapidly, translucently from side to side and then the monster vanished.

After a few moments, a bewildered police officer cautiously crept forward to where the creature was standing, and upon close inspection found nothing. 'It's gone, sir!' the officer called out as he turned to face his sergeant.

Suddenly the creature reappeared behind the officer and smashed its clawed fist through the man's chest, punching his heart clean out of his body. The organ bounced several times before coming to rest meters away, the heart beating for a few seconds longer before ceasing. The demon opened its vulgar mouth and chomped down upon the officer's neck, ripping his throat out sideways and forcing the head to flop over to one side. The body fell to the ground and the monster fell upon it, sinking sharp, busted teeth into the dead man's brain, absorbing his life essence as he did so.

The police opened fire, but the creature moved rapidly, avoiding the flying projectiles with not one bullet finding its target. Ricochets flew about the place and, fearing that innocent bystanders may be injured or killed, the sergeant called out, 'Hold your fire! Hold fire!'

Again, the demon stood still, blood dripping from its maw, the dead mutilated body of the police officer at its feet. The thief realised that he did not need his tongue, words were not necessary, his deeds would speak his intent. The abomination snorted before exhaling forcibly out of its open mouth, the foul stench of decay and murder lacing the stilled air as if the night itself was petrified of the monster which was present among its substance.

The monster took several slow and deliberate steps toward the horrified police officers, who remained sheltering behind their vehicles. Seeming nervous and unsure of the reality before him, the police sergeant refrained from giving the open-fire order.

'Enough, thief!' a deep, grizzled voice rang out, piercing through the silence, echoing off the street and along the glazed shopfronts along the avenue.

The frightened onlookers turned their attention down the street, from where the voice had billowed. There, moving steadfastly toward the scene, was another monster. Echoes of the word 'werewolf' were heard among the whispers of the onlookers.

Anubis strode with pointed determination as he reached out a pointed finger toward the demon, 'You will pay for your crimes against humanity! I will render you to oblivion. This ends tonight.'

The thief was shocked to see the beast approach with such bravado, with such confidence and, for the briefest of moments, he felt admiration for Anubis. But his focus quickly returned, and the monster turned to face the dog. The thief spread his arms out wide, as if to say 'come get me'.

'No words, thief? No grand speeches about how you will be the end of me?' Anubis snarled. 'Oh, that's right, you have no tongue. It must pain you greatly that a mere mortal could take away such a precious belonging of yours,' the god continued, chiding Jalel as he approached ever closer. 'So, the thief has turned victim? How does it feel, Jalel? How does it feel to have something stolen from you?'

The monster raged at the insulting taunts from the god as he sprayed mucus from his mouth and nose. Jalel was stronger than Anubis and he would have great pleasure in taking the dog's life and eating his soul.

Anubis rushed at the thief with his god speed, striking him hard across the head, sending the twisted body crashing to the bitumen. At the sight of this, the crowd erupted with raucous cheer as it appeared that the people now had a champion.

Anubis quickly glanced over his shoulder, there was Erica, skulking about twenty meters behind him, in a semi-crouched walk. Anubis discretely motioned to her with a stop gesture and returned his attention toward the thief.

'*Now, Samuel!*' Anubis shouted mentally to his host, and as soon as the instruction was given, Sam took control of the god-body.

Jalel had clumsily found his feet and rushed forward, his claws swinging wildly at Sam, who in turn blocked the savage blows, but rage had infused the demon with great strength and its aggression weakened Sam's forearms as they became bruised and fatigued. Sliding out of the blocks, Sam moved to counterstrike the monster repeatedly about the torso and the face before pushing the demon backward and connecting with a front heel kick, switching rapidly into a side kick. The thief was again sent thundering onto the road with a satisfying slap. At this, the onlookers, including the police, cheered loudly for their potential saviour.

The demon raged again, its howl vibrating in the chests of the closest spectators, who in return took several steps backward. The abomination writhed as it rose once again to its haunches.

'*Okay, it's now or never,*' Sam said to Anubis as he readied his next attack.

'*Good luck, my friend!*' Anubis replied with concern.

Sam ran at the demon who responded by lunging forward, swiping his claws savagely at the framer's face. Sam was too fast for him and, using his momentum, he dropped down onto his thigh and kicked up at the thief, striking his lower leg, sending the demon down onto one knee. Sam rose and brought his knee up to Jalel's face, his nose busting on impact. The thief was stunned as Sam moved quickly to position himself behind Jalel and place his arms up from under its foul arms, securing him in a strong headlock with Sam's hands at the back of the thief's nape. '*Okay! I'm ready, Anubis. I don't know how long I can hold him in my form!*' Sam shouted to the god.

Without further hesitation, Anubis withdrew his consciousness and Samuel regained his human-form, which drew a gasp of shock from the crowd that had grown to fill the now packed sidewalk. Sam had managed to talk Anubis into allowing him to wear a black singlet and baggy track pants so that he did not feel so exposed when in his own form, the garments were rather stretchy and they could facilitate the larger Anubis-body. Though the god still struggled with the constricting nature of clothing, he was happy to compromise for Sam's comfort.

The thief struggled and squirmed to be free, but Sam's headlock held firm. Sam felt the thief's form buzz and parts of his outline went translucent momentarily, but the lack of movement prevented his phase shift. Sam puffed out a hot breath of relief. The thief continued squirming in his arms until he craned his neck, looking at Erica. Sam turned him away roughly.

Sam raised his face to look skyward, the almost full moon seemed to be gazing lovingly into his eyes. Such beauty has the moon, would this be the last time that he would gaze upon it? There was no time to consider its magnificence and thus, Sam opened wide his mouth.

Anubis had gathered all his essence, as a vacating squatter may do when packing all his belongings into a suitcase. The god forced himself out from Sam's lungs and climbed steadily up the oesophagus, up the throat, and with a last concerted push, the god sprung free from his human host.

It felt bizarre to be once again without form, but it would only be a brief feeling of disembodiment for the god as he focused his energy toward Erica, who upon seeing Sam cough savagely, opened her own mouth wide.

Anubis glided into Erica's lungs with relative ease before settling himself into her cells and opening communication with her, *'Erica Murphy, are you okay!?*

The god's words thundered inside Erica's mind, more like thunder than language. The pain forced the reporter to her knees, and she felt as if her head would surely split open. She screamed out loud, her torment forcing the sound from her.

'Erica! The collar – put it around your neck!' Sam shouted as he swung his legs around Jalel's waist to better secure the thief. Sam had removed the collar and given it to Erica prior to their arrival at the scene. Because Anubis had inhabited Sam's body for so long, the human had built up some immunity to the side effects of telepathic communication and as such he was able to manage the pain without the amulet.

Erica brought her left hand from around her back and, trembling, she slid the half crescent collar around her neck, securing it in place. To her relief, the pain echoed away, until she could finally hear her own mind again, and she took several deep breaths before standing up.

The thief was totally befuddled as to Erica's strange behaviour and he once again attempted to struggle free from Sam's hold. The human had positioned himself perfectly against the demon's form and as such, the technique had stripped the thief of his mobility. *Must be sure to devour his soul last,* thought the thief. *I must have the combat knowledge that he possesses, then I will be unstoppable.* Momentarily giving up struggling, Jalel looked back at Erica who was standing bolt upright, her pretty face looking blankly at the thief, red and blue flashing lights of the emergency vehicles licking her face rhythmically.

'Erica Murphy, are you okay now? Can you hear me?' Anubis softly inquired, his voice now pulsing gently through the young woman's mind.

'Yes, I am okay. I forgot to put the collar on in all the excitement. It all just happened so fast!'

'All is well, Erica, but we have no further time to lose – we must get to work.'

'Yes, okay, I'm ready. Let's finish this! Oh, one more thing – will it hurt a lot?'

'I'm sorry, but yes it will hurt very much for several seconds.'

'Okay, Anubis. Let's dance, big guy.'

The pain was as terrible as the god had promised, Erica felt her entire body struck with fire as her muscles and tendons tore and stretched. She felt her bones grind as they grew and lengthened. Her teeth and jaw cracked and popped as it was reshaped into canine-form. Throughout the transformation all she could think was *how could Sam endure this?* She drew strength from her own womanhood, from the collective maternal power of bringing forth life through pain – and knowing it was a hope she held for her future. Erica had learned from Sam's experiences and, as such, she had made the wise decision to wear a baggy sweatshirt that was three sizes too large for her, along with matching pants that were fastened with safety pins, which sprung open as her form grew – and what a beautifully monstrous form it was. Erica's body had taken on the appearance of Anubis, but with definitively feminine features. There were curves and mounds that the god was not used to having and the canine hair at the back of the head and neck was long, silken and still kissed with the black and blue sheen of his coat.

As the transformation completed, Erica heard a gasp ripple through the gathering crowd. She saw hope etched on the faces of the people gathered there. Her own adrenaline surging, she felt her arm reach up and back over her shoulder to reach the secret weapon stowed away there. It was Osir.

CHAPTER SIXTEEN

Spirited Exodus

ANUBIS'S PLAN WAS A good one and everything was going well – with Jalel still secure in Sam's hold.

In a moment tethered with eternal consequences, Anubis, in the god-form of Erica's body, would use Osir to stab the thief repeatedly, releasing the devoured souls one at a time, starting with the most recent victim and working backward to the point where Jalel had entered Kurt's body.

It was to that end that Anubis came at the thief, Osir humming happily in its master's hand. Jalel thrashed about as the god approached, with fear etched on his face as his wide eyes followed every move of Osir. Yet Jalel's struggle was futile as Sam bore down on the thief's nape, reducing his movements to desperate thrusts.

Osir sung as it was thrust forward into the thief's abdomen, gliding with ease into the twisted stomach of the fiend. Anubis took a second to inspect the vile substance that oozed from the wound and to his delight, he could see the pale blue glow of a soul as it seeped its way to freedom. Within a few moments the essence of the slain police officer moved to stand a few feet away, staring incredulously at the scene before him.

Wasting no further time, Anubis deliberately placed the blade of Osir into the areas of the demon-form that would be less likely to inflict a lethal wound to Kurt's body. The thief howled, gasping as the blade slid against his thigh bone, cutting into the marrow.

Having shared Anubis's senses and vision, Sam was surprised to discover that he could also see the disembodied spirits, bringing a smile to the framer's lips. The plan was working. He watched as the next batch of blue, glowing mist stirred and took on a familiar form. It was Donovan Banks. Sam watched as the soul of the old man glided over to place his face mere centimetres away from Jalel's face. *'You vile creature! You will burn in Durat and I will be glad to bear witness to your destruction!'* the old man hissed at the thief, before turning his attention to Anubis, *'Clever, my lord! Very clever, I knew that you would find a way to defeat the thief.'*

Next out into the world was Apep, who chose not to acknowledge Anubis, nor Sam. Instead, he lingered well behind the action, glaring intently at Jalel as he paced back and forth, and even though there was no necessity to do so, the reptile continued to send its ethereal tongue sliding up over its beady eyes.

Osir then found its way into the demon's upper chest, finding little resistance from the rib cage, the wound giving birth to the little ghost kitten, which quickly scurried along the sidewalk, passing effortlessly through the legs of the crowd.

Sam was growing weary from his struggle with the demon, yet he was pleasantly surprised that he was able to restrain the monstrosity, who continued attempting to squirm free, Jalel's rigid body leaning forward as he savagely grunted, his twisted gut rumbling ferociously. Sam's thoughts of pride were quickly dashed as he felt a warm, thick, sticky mass of fluid expel from the armpits of the demon. The sensation was quickly followed by the foulest odour that he had ever smelled, as the stench of sickness, rotted meat and sulphur accosted his senses. The demon had shat itself from under its arms, and the viscous substance was running down Sam's forearms, making his skin sting and his arms slippery.

'Anubis! Hurry, I can't hold on much longer!' Sam screamed as he adjusted his grip.

Anubis looked up to see Sam struggling with the thief, his arms slipping as the demon thrashed about. The god struck out with Osir again, plunging the blade into the thief's side, and the spirit of Jennifer's murdered baby emerged. The infant gave out a cry, taking the first breath that it was denied in life and no sooner had the cry sounded than the spirit of the child's mother, Jennifer, emerged. She bent down and gathered her baby into her arms, smiling down at the child that she never had the chance to meet in the physical world. Jennifer then took notice of the struggle that was occurring on the street behind her and, with babe in arms, she floated over to stand with the other onlookers.

Jalel heaved with an almighty thrash and Sam's arms finally gave way. The thief shimmered as he phase-shifted out of view. Anubis was striking out with Osir as the thief vanished and the blade found purchase in another body. Osir had struck Sam in the upper abdomen, the blade entering to the hilt.

'Noooooo, no, no, no, no!' Erica screamed as Anubis relinquished control of her body and she reverted to her own form, quickly removing the blade. Sam fell onto his back, blood rapidly spreading from the wound. She placed her hands over the wound, desperately attempting to stem the flow of blood, but the damage was done.

'No, Sam! No! Not now! Not here! I've only just found you. I can't lose you now!' Erica gasped, her eyes filling with tears.

'I love you, Erica. I'm so sorry,' Sam grunted, wheezing heavily.

'I love you, Sam. Please don't leave me!' she pleaded, her voice breaking into a deep sob.

Anubis spoke to Erica, his voice somewhat urgent, '*Erica, I can re-enter Sam's body. I can save him. Lean into him, get close to his mouth.*'

Erica needed no further prompting, 'Sam, Anubis says he can save you. He will have to join with you again,' she said with a glimmer of hope in her voice and a small smile on her lips.

Sam looked up into Erica's beautiful face, admiring the love of his life that he had ironically found at the end of his life. Erica gently leaned in to kiss him and allow Anubis to pass into Sam. But Sam withdrew and urgently moved passed her face to look behind her. With as much strength as he could muster, he called out, 'Anubis, behind you!'

The god was quickly stirred back into action, taking control of Erica's body. He rose and turned just in time to see Jalel phase into view. The demon lashed out at Erica and ripped the amulet from her body, clawing her chest as he did so. The blinding pain of having a god inside her mind again accosted Erica, her head pounding violently, forcing her to the ground, but her thoughts managed to turn to her dying Sam. Shakily, she got to her feet only to come face-to-face with the thief, who was wearing the most evil smile that the monstrous face could muster.

Jalel struck out violently, his goliath left hand smashing into the side of Erica's head, sending her sprawling across the road. Anubis had managed to bring his consciousness forward just before the thief struck and, as such, he took the full brunt of the blow rendering him unconscious, as too his host, Erica.

Sam watched on helplessly as Erica's body lay motionless on the bitumen. With desperation, he turned onto his stomach and crawled toward Osir, which was only a few metres away. After much effort, he reached the still glowing blade and felt its warmth in his hand. Sam had little strength left and realised that he was powerless to do anything. He looked up to see Jalel walking toward Erica, 'Jalel! Please ... Don't do it ... Don't hurt her!'

The thief smiled as he heard the plea from over his shoulder. Then he turned and started toward Sam. The framer had most of his essence in the spirit world now and he could hear Jalel telepathically, '*Oh, Samuel, is it? That is what they call you? You must not take this all too personally. After all, I am simply doing what I do best: I am stealing – I am taking it all. Besides, you stole from me. You took my tongue, so it is only fair that I take the life of those that you love the most. Do not be*

*sad, Samuel, for soon your loved ones will live on forever ...
inside my gut!'*

Samuel heard a familiar voice beside him, *'Samuel, my
boy,'* it was Donovan, *'Samuel, you must let go. You have to
die – it is of the utmost importance.'*

'Die? I'm already doing that, seems like I have no choice,'
Sam replied weakly.

*'Yes, yes, you do have a choice – you need to die quicker, you
need to come with me.'*

'What? Why?'

*'Always with the questions! Come boy, hurry up and die.
Anubis wasn't the only one with a plan,'* the old man's words
had such urgency to them and Sam knew that Donovan
could be trusted.

Sam struggled to roll onto his back and after doing so he
raised Osir with both hands as high as he could manage.
With all his remaining strength, he thrust Osir down into his
heart, his hands falling to his side and his eyes, looking up at
the moon, lost their light, lost their life.

The thief stopped dead in his tracks rather impressed with the
courage of the framer for taking his own life. Jalel was also
bitterly disappointed, *Clever lad,* he thought, for now he
could not devour Sam's soul, as the framer had successfully
released his soul from the flesh. The thief watched on as the
young man and the old man hurried away from the scene.

*Hmpf, cowards! Not even staying to watch their loved ones
being devoured,* thought Jalel and with no one and nothing
left to stop him, the demon turned his attention to the
unconscious Erica and Anubis. The bleeding of souls left the
demon feeling weak, especially after losing Apep, but soon he
would have another god soul inside of him. *Hmm, tonight I
think that there is dog on the menu.*

After spending the last few weeks sharing his body with the god of the dead, Sam adjusted quickly to his ethereal existence, as his form felt light and clean and he was aware of all around him. Furthermore, the sliding back and forth in consciousness with Anubis was more than adequate training for the spirit world. All the framer had to do was will his movement with his mind and his soul would move accordingly.

Once Sam was freed from his fleshy shell, he followed as Donovan ushered the young man out of the mind field of Jalel, so that their plan would not be heard by the thief. Once the old man was certain that there was sufficient distance between themselves and the thief, he turned to face Sam, *'Samuel, thank you for trusting me. We must move quickly if we are to save Erica and Anubis.'*

'Okay, well, what's your plan?' Sam inquired eagerly, his eyes searching Donovan's for answers.

'We must travel to the underworld to seek an audience with Osiris himself. Only he can help us now.'

'Wait, Osiris? Okay ... but how? Surely if you knew how to get in touch with him, we could have done that a long time ago?' Sam responded sharply.

'Samuel, I could not have done this before – I had not the waking knowledge, nor the skills to be able to open a doorway into the underworld,' Donovan replied sheepishly.

'But you do have that knowledge now, right?'

The question made Donovan squirm as he adjusted his ghostly collar, a nervous remnant from his living years. *'Well, not quite, no. You see, we shall require some assistance from someone who knows how to access the underworld,'* Donovan replied with a reluctant nod over Sam's shoulder, indicating that their source of assistance was standing behind the young man.

Sam didn't need to turn around to know whom Donovan was referring to, '*Apep, I presume?*'

'*Yes, it is I, Apep, son of Osiris and brother to Anubis,*' the serpent answered as he slid around to face the two men, his head bowed in a gesture of humility.

'*You son of a bitch!*' Sam hissed, his voice on the brink of breaking with rage. '*You did this – this is all your fault! You claim family ties with the divine and we are supposed to trust you!?*'

'*Please, Samuel, I do know the error of my deeds and although I could stand here to argue what I had caused, or what the thief had taken upon himself to do – we simply have not the time,*' Apep pleaded.

'*Samuel, Apep has offered to open the passage to the underworld and guide us through the five trials of the soul. He is our only chance of saving Erica's life!*' Donovan said in a tone designed to snap Sam out of his rage.

Sam relaxed his stance and his demeanour slightly at realising that Donovan was right. '*Okay, lord Apep,*' Sam said with mock sincerity, '*sorry for my ignorance, but won't such a journey take a long time? Time that we do not have?*'

'*It is true, it will take some time yes, but fear not, for time moves very slowly when we are in spirit and once in the underworld it will cease to exist – there is no concept of time on the other side. So, once we have crossed into the underworld it will be as if this world is frozen in time. Samuel, if we hurry, we may be able to return in time to save your love,*' Apep stated confidently.

Sam nodded his acceptance. '*Then let's get our asses to the underworld. Oh, and one more thing, will everyone stop calling me Samuel! It's Sam – just Sam.*'

With no further words exchanged, Apep spoke the sacred prayer into the cool night air. A loud crack ripped through the fabric of reality that is called earth. Bright red lightning and fine tendrils of fluorescent green spread through the air like pulsing veins, which began to swell and contort until they formed a small stone archway. The air became devoid of life, devoid of oxygen, but it bothered the three spirits not, for they did not need to breathe. Through the doorway, a disturbing foreign land could be vaguely discerned. The realm of the dead was waiting, and it was Sam who moved first, the young man gliding toward the arch. He stopped momentarily to inspect the stonework, only to discover it was not stone he was looking at – the bricks were made up of millions of maggots, all tightly packed, squirming about, fighting to burrow underneath each other to avoid the fresh air of the earth realm. Sam then turned his focus forward and glided into the underworld, with Donovan and Apep following behind.

CHAPTER SEVENTEEN

Trials and Tribulations

NO SOONER HAD THEY entered the underworld than the maggot doorway closed behind them. A foul stench confronted the senses of the trio, and it was only then that Sam and Donovan realised that they had regained their physical forms once more.

'Are we back in our bodies?' Sam asked, as he patted his hands over his body to check if it was solid.

'No, not your actual body, that is in fact dead – in the earth realm. This is your afterlife body, the form that you will carry forward for the rest of your time here. It is as real as your earth body, so please be aware that you can die here, the same as in your home world. If you die here, you will cease to exist,' Apep replied with a matter-of-fact tone.

Sam took a step forward and felt that his footfall had landed in a soft, squelchy substance. He was shocked to see that the doorway was merely the beginning of the nightmarish landscape before them, for underfoot were countless more maggots, the unsightly floor a writhing mass crawling about in putrescent, congealed blood and here and there were large bones laying half buried in the maggot floor. Sam soon discovered that these bones were so large that they looked like femur bones from giants, which formed the outline of a pathway. The entirety of this world was oddly lit with deep, unsettling red and green tones, with the occasional splash of a dirty blue hue. The foul smell of maggots and rot gave the underworld such a dreadful feeling of hopelessness and, sensing the discomfort of the mortals, Apep slid to the front to take the lead. 'Come, we must move forward,' he said as he moved down the grotesque path.

After what seemed like several hours, two large doors appeared in the distance. The doors were very tall, about ten times taller than Sam and he stood at over six feet. Framed on either side of the doors were two tall spinal columns made of bone that reached slightly higher. The doors themselves were made of massive, smooth heavy stones of varying size and irregular shapes, all placed neatly together, like an ancient oversized jigsaw puzzle. The doors seemed to be free-standing, attached to nothing, like a replica of a door and not actually real, with no visible lock, hinges or handles.

Apep motioned to the gate ahead, 'This is the first trial of the soul – it is the Gate of Greeting. The gatekeeper will know if a person has lived an honest life. He will ask you one question for which he already knows the answer, and if you lie you will be destroyed immediately.

'Donovan Banks, perhaps you should wait here, just to be sure. I will guide Sam through the rest of the way,' Apep said.

The old man began to protest, but was interrupted by Sam, 'He's right, Donovan. We can't risk losing your soul. Please wait for us here and if, for some reason we don't return, you can try your luck at getting through?'

Donovan nodded his agreement. 'Well okay, Sam, but please take care,' he turned to the serpent, 'and, Apep, you must do the honourable thing and make good on your promise to help us.'

'Actually,' Sam said to Apep, 'Donovan has a good point. Are you sure that you will pass the lie detector test? Excuse me, but you seem like one who may be prone to fibbing.'

'I have and will mislead, but I have never lied,' the serpent replied confidently.

'Okay then, well let's move on,' Sam said gesturing toward the doors.

As Apep and Sam approached the gate, an entity materialised out of nowhere. This creature was not dissimilar in appearance to Apep, except that it was three times as large and was shaped more like an actual snake. The creature presented itself into a tight coil, seemingly ready to strike out and end them at any moment. Its large beady eyes stared fiercely at the framer, as if it was scanning his mind. After a few seconds the creature spoke, 'You are known as Samuel Baker, this is known to be true. Samuel Baker, I have but one question for you. If you answer it true, entry through the gate will be granted. If it is untrue, you will be destroyed.'

Sam straightened his posture to display an air of confidence toward the serpent, 'And I will answer your question, my lord.'

'Have you come here to take your place in heaven, or have you come here to confess your sins and be unmade in the depths of hell?'

Apep shot a nervous look at Sam. *What kind of question is that? It is impossible for Sam to answer, because he is here for neither of those reasons,* the reptile thought.

Sam continued to look directly into the serpent's eyes for a few moments before answering.

'I am not here for either of those reasons. I have come here to save my love.'

Clever boy! thought Apep. *He has answered honestly without giving away too much.* It was true that each gate guardian was responsible for protecting Osiris and the father god was never to be seen by mortal souls, for Osiris was a being of perfection, and the human soul is faulty, impure – a stain – and perfection must not be stained.

The serpent entity considered Sam's response for a moment, before nodding, a sign that Sam had passed. Next, the guard turned his attention toward Apep.

'Brother Apep, you have been rendered spirit. No doubt you long to return to our father, but as you are in spirit, you are not exempt from the trials.'

Apep raised his head proudly, 'I accept your trial, brother, and I too shall answer your question.'

'So be it,' the guardian responded.

'You are guiding this human through the trials. Do you intend to betray him?'

Apep did not pause for a moment of hesitation as he answered, 'No, brother, I do not intend to betray him.'

Again, the serpent nodded and turned toward the gate. The gatekeeper climbed up to the middle of the door, forming the infinity symbol – that of the number eight upon its side. The large gates rumbled like thunder and the door opened several metres to allow Sam and Apep to pass through.

The landscape of the underworld was uniformly sparse and disappointing in appearance everywhere, it seemed to Sam. Apart from the writhing maggot-covered ground, and the occasional giant bone scattered about, there was very little to hold one's interest. There were no buildings or roads, no people or animals roaming about, no birds to take wing overhead. There weren't any mountains, nor rivers – just those damn maggots and their offensive odour. As he walked, Sam wondered from where the land of the dead was lit, as there was no sun or moon in the sky, but the entire land was constantly bathed in that deep, unsettling glow – like some kind of ghastly night-light.

The second gate was not as far as the first one had been and appeared to be constructed differently to the first. There were no doors visible on this gate, merely a massive piece of rock, which appeared to vanish high into the dirty blue sky above. Upon the gargantuan rock slab there were several impossibly tall ladders bolted parallel to the door, leading all the way up, beyond the limits of eyesight. As the two approached, Sam looked about nervously for the guardian, 'Where is the doorkeeper?'

'This is the gate of justice and the gate *is* the doorkeeper. It is a living entity,' the reptile replied. 'Those ladders are our trial, and we must climb them.'

'That will be easy,' Sam said confidently.

'Perhaps, we shall see. Each rung of the ladder represents one year of your life. You must climb every year until the year of your death. Here is the catch, for every crime that you have committed against another, and has not been answered to in life, the ladder will slide down by one length of your

body and if you touch the ground before you reach the year
of your death, you shall not pass any further.' Apep smiled as
he headed over to his ladder and climbed with such speed and
agility that he ascended several hundred feet in the matter of
moments.

Sam moved to his ladder and began the ascent. The
rungs were larger than he expected, and it felt as if he were a
small child, the space between each rung was about half the
height of his body and it took some effort to clamber up to
the next one.

At the age of seven, Sam's ladder slipped down and the
memory of his first crime came into his mind: he had stolen a
toy from his cousin, an action figure of his favourite
superhero. He could remember that he had soon lost interest
in the toy and sold it to a neighbourhood kid for fifty cents.
A moment of panic struck Sam – he had forgotten all about
the petty theft. How many more crimes had he committed
and forgotten about?

At the thirteenth rung, the ladder dropped again: he had
taken a drink from the refrigerator of his local corner store
without paying for it. He could remember how good it tasted
as he tilted his face to the sun to drink the last of the sweet
brown soda. The sweet victory of that day was now just a
sour memory. Before Sam could climb another year, the
ladder fell again. Still at thirteen, he had vandalised the side
of the same corner store with graffiti. It was a difficult year
for Sam, he had become associated with a group of rowdy
teenagers and they had little compunction about stealing and
causing general mayhem.

Sam looked down to the maggot-infested floor, he was
now only three or four metres away. He then turned his gaze
upward, Apep was so far up that he could not be seen, as the
reptile had lived for thousands of years. Shakily, Sam climbed

to fourteen, then fifteen, sixteen, seventeen, eighteen – again, the ladder slipped down. The memory of a fight entered his mind: he had become infatuated with a young woman that he had met at a local bar. He had spent most of the night attempting to gain her affection, only to have another man swoop in and catch her eye. It was the first time that Sam had combined alcohol and jealousy and the cocktail did not taste good. He promptly strode over and broke the man's jaw with a rage-fuelled right hook. It took several people to drag Sam off his target and he was ejected from the establishment.

'Damn it!' Sam cursed to himself. He tried to be a good man, with the emphasis on the word 'man', but he was a foolish teenager and he had made many mistakes. He had learned his lessons and made a conscious effort to do the right thing.

Nineteen, twenty, twenty-one, twenty-two, twenty-three, twenty-four. No sooner had Sam climbed onto the twenty-fourth rung than the ladder shuddered violently and slid back away from the rock wall, before turning sideways with Sam on top. The ladder slid forward, on a collision course with the rock surface of the wall and Sam closed his eyes as he braced for the violent impact. No such collision occurred as the ladder passed through the stone, which seemed as if it now had no substance. It felt as if he was passing through a thick, cold, grey fog and, once all the way through, the ladder flipped and returned to its upright position on the other side of the stone wall, which then solidified once more. The framer wasted no time in descending to the maggot floor.

Sam made it through the gate. He passed the trial, but Apep was nowhere to be seen. The framer took a few deep breaths and pondered if the reptile had failed his trial. What was Apep's motivation anyway? Why had he suddenly decided to play nice with others? Sam suspected that revenge was the goal for the serpent god. He had been killed by Jalel, so no doubt Apep was out for blood.

What felt like an hour had passed before Sam heard a very faint grinding sound from high above and he looked up to see a ladder sliding down the face of the wall, but still no sign of Apep. After a while or so, a tiny grey dot of reptile flesh appeared way up the ladder and the dot slowly became larger as Apep slid rapidly down, his tough, leather-like claws providing ample resistance to the friction of letting the sides of the ladder slip through.

'Sam, you made it!' Apep grinned as he reached the ground.

'You could have let me go first,' Sam responded with a tone of distrust.

'I could have, but I had much further to travel than you and I have already kept you waiting long enough. Let us move on,' Apep said over his shoulder as he walked away from Sam.

Eventually, the two travellers came to the third gate, and to Sam's surprise, it was a large yet human-sized door, made of thick, heavy timber beams. Even more shocking was that the door was already opened. Sensing Sam's relief, Apep cautioned the framer, 'Do not be overly complacent, Sam, for the next trial awaits us just beyond those gates,' and surely enough, as they passed the large gateway, an incredible scene greeted them.

Laying ahead of the duo was a mighty lake, still and stagnant, dark green in colour. The gag-worthy smell of the lake struck Sam heavily as soon as he entered through the gate. It was a sickly concoction of mould, moss, rotting vegetation and decaying flesh. The air carried about it an unsettling presence, as if it were void of any substance, and a dreadful, deathly and unearthly silence shrouded the entire expanse of the area.

At the water's edge were five very old, long canoe-shaped boats, although Sam very much doubted that the ancient, half-rotted crafts would provide adequate transport for each of them. Sam scanned the area for any signs of a bridge, or some other more reliable means of crossing the foul lake, but to his disappointment he found none.

On the far side of the gruesome expanse of water, a few hundred metres away, was another gate, also open, with what appeared to be the orange glow of sunlight shining through, illuminating the ground in front of the exit as an usher might do, indicating the way out of a theatre.

'This is the trial of levity,' said Apep. 'We must each choose a boat in which to ride and make our way across the lake to the other side.'

'Sounds simple enough,' Sam quipped.

'Don't be foolish, boy. That's what you said about the ladders!' the reptile spoke with a stern voice. 'The weight of all of the bad deeds that you have done throughout your life is also carried with you on this boat. If the weight is too great, you shall sink into the depths before you reach the other side.

'Oh ... well, yes, I can see how that may be a challenge then,' Sam replied with a flash of dismay upon his face.

'Indeed, and if you sink, you will find yourself being dragged down into the bottomless abyss where you will continue to fall until rot renders your corpse into pieces. Those parts of you will float to the surface, but your soul will stay in the waters forever, always sinking, forever drowning,' Apep replied, his dark beady eyes appearing even more menacing than usual as he stared intently at Sam.

The young man was too scared to respond, instead, he walked over to the nearest boat. Climbing inside, he took a seat on the floor, which was growing a decent patch of bright green moss, and it gave off a strong scent when disturbed. The boat itself was not very wide and was only designed for a single passenger. The sides of the boat came to the height of Sam's armpits, which suited the young man well, for he did not care to inspect the contents of the stale water too long for fear that he may soon be taking a swim. Without warning, the boat lurched free from the bank and slowly drifted toward the opposite shore.

No sooner had the boat begun its journey than Sam felt the boat dip ever so slightly down into the water, and for a moment it rose briefly before falling at a very slow but steady rate, as if the boat was being pulled into the foul, fettered water.

'It's the weight of your bad deeds dragging you down!' shouted Apep from his boat, which was still riding high.

Sam investigated the thick, sickly dark green water and as he looked, a human head floated up and broke the surface beside him. Half of the flesh had completely rotted away and the rancid, water-logged meat that remained was tenuously attached to the bone, pale blue and bloated, with broken skin lesions at several spots. There were no eyeballs present, and long optic nerves protruded from the sockets, floating about like thin lengths of spaghetti in a pot of cold water. As Sam looked more carefully about the area, he noticed that here and there were different body parts at the surface in varying stages of rot. The sight made Sam look away in disgust. Was he to end up like these unfortunate souls?

'Do not feel too much pity for them, Sam. There are always consequences for our bad deeds, and we truly do reap what we sow. No one is immune, not even me,' Apep called out to Sam, who looked over to see the reptile's boat begin to sink. It was almost completely under water, and Apep still had about fifteen metres left to travel.

'Apep! You're almost sunk!' Sam yelled.

'So I am, but then again, I never needed the boat,' the god replied, with nonchalance. Abruptly, the reptile stood up and dove into the water, only to resurface a metre out from the boat. Then, with speed and agility, Apep snaked his way effortlessly through the water toward the opposite shore.

Asshole! Sam thought, but he had more urgent issues at hand. His boat was now getting very low in the water and, like Apep, he still had fifty odd metres of the lake left to traverse.

In an act of desperation, Sam decided to use his hands as a makeshift paddle and, reluctantly, he slid his left hand into the foul, viscous dark water. Searing pain burned his hand as it entered the water – it felt as if the lake was on fire, although there were no flames present. The young man quickly pulled his hand back into the boat and noticed that blisters had started to appear. The intense pain caused his hand to throb strongly, his skin turning bright pink, as if it had been immersed in boiling water.

Sam desperately looked toward the shore and the open gate waiting there. The welcoming, warm orange glow appeared as a beacon of hope shining upon the lake of hopelessness. Sam noticed that his boat was no longer sinking, and it was now ambling along steadily. It appeared that the weight of his bad deeds was insufficient to send him to the burning depths of the abyss below, and soon enough the boat came to a grinding halt up upon the safety of the bank.

Sam angrily held his wounded hand up to show Apep as he hurried up the embankment, 'You could've mentioned the burning lake!'

'Oh, I did forget to mention that, didn't I?' the serpent replied with a shrug.

'Hey, wait a minute! You dove into that lake and you swam in the water – how did you not get burned?' Sam asked, pointing his finger at the reptile.

'I may be dead, but I am still a reptilian god, meaning that I still possess the same abilities here in the underworld that I had in life. I have thick, leather-like skin, made of small scales and these scales provide excellent heat insulation for my cold-blooded physiology. If that lake were freezing cold, then I would have certainly perished.'

Apep looked down at Sam's wounded hand, 'The pain is very real here, isn't it? This place, the underworld, is designed to put the soul through the ultimate test and I'm afraid that pain is also one of those trials. Perhaps we should take some time to rest?'

Sam huffed as he reached the gate, 'Yeah sure, but let's be on the other side of this door first!' He scowled as he glared back at the lake.

Disappointments seemed to be ample in the land of the underworld – the majestic, welcoming orange glow that Sam had witnessed shining through the open third gate was not sunlight, it was instead the immense glow of distant fires.

Noticing the look of dismay upon the framer's face, Apep followed Sam's gaze, 'They are the mighty fires of final judgement. They burn just beyond the fourth gate. We must still pass that gate before we can enter the hall of judgement, and on to the final trial.'

'Great, so literally out of the pot and into the fire, huh?' Sam grumbled sarcastically, before realising that the reptile was unfamiliar with the saying. 'Because, you know, the lake is like a pot of boiling water?'

'And what of the fire?' Apep enquired. 'What was in the pot?'

Sam shrugged with impatience, he did not want to waste his energy on attempting to explain the idiom, 'You know what? Forget about it. It's just a silly saying that we have on earth.'

The serpent came closer to the framer and looked deeply into his eyes, 'You are weary Sam. We should rest a while here. You will need all your strength for the last two gates.'

Reluctantly, Sam agreed that they should take a break, but where to rest his aching frame? He sure as hell was not about to sit down upon a floor of stinking maggots.

'Maybe we should have rested on the bank of the lake after all,' Sam conceded. 'At least the foul stench of the water would be better than a wet, maggot-filled ass.'

'No need, we can rest over there,' Apep pointed as he spoke. A large, long bone lay about twenty metres from where they stood, and it was there that the duo sat.

An uncomfortable silence arose between the two as they rested. Apep took to closing his beady black eyes – to avoid eye contact with him, Sam guessed. Likewise the framer sat quietly and stared at his scalded hand, which had begun to throb intensely, his skin tight and broken in places was raw to the touch and a deep headache had settled in. After some time, Sam broke the long silence, 'Why did you do it, Apep? Why did you want to kill Anubis?'

The reptile took a deep breath before exhaling and when his eyes finally flickered open, he said, 'I did not kill my brother, that was an act of self-defence upon the thief's part, that night in the temple. Anubis had already been wounded by the time I happened upon him. I simply watched as the consequential events unfolded. After I learned of the papyrus, I picked up the thief's trail and recruited his assistance.'

'You recruited Jalel to destroy Anubis? To take the lives of innocent souls?' Sam asked with remarkable calmness.

'No, I recruited the thief to stand witness over the papyrus, awaiting the day that Anubis's soul would be freed.'

'And? What were you going to do then? Eat him?' Sam questioned with a pang of disgust, his temper growing quickly.

'Yes, I desired his knowledge. I wanted to guide my disenchanted through the fifth gate and into paradise. Only a worthy human soul, Anubis or Osiris himself, can do that. I could only gain such knowledge by devouring my brother god's essence.'

'Wait! Is that why you are helping us now? So that you can pass through the final gate on my back?' Sam's anger boiled over as he stood up and pushed the reptile over backward, onto the writhing maggot floor.

Apep stood to his feet, casually brushing of hundreds of pulsating larvae, the stench of the creatures pervading the stale air, 'Sam, I will not betray you; remember at the first gate? The question that was asked of me?'

Sam did remember, but his anger still flushed his cheeks.

Apep gently continued to speak to reassure Sam, 'The first gatekeeper asked me if I would betray you and I answered no, and that was the truth, for I would not have been able to continue any further if I had lied. Even if I had intentions of betrayal, I could not follow you past the scales of judgement, you see, I cannot pass into paradise – I am forbidden entry.' Apep licked his eyes as he continued, his tone sincere, 'I promised Donovan Banks that I would guide you through the five trials and onward to beseech the help of Osiris. Besides, once my deeds have been uncovered, I will be destroyed,' the reptile responded matter-of-factly.

'But, why? Why help us now?' Sam asked, his emotions somewhat calmer now.

'At first, after I was freed from the thief's flesh, I had my fixation upon exacting revenge against Jalel for ending my life. Then I witnessed Ms Murphy, so devastated by your impending death. It was truly a powerful display of love and devotion, the pain in her heart was palpable to say the least. Revenge is a sweet type of chaos. But the unhinged, almost chaotic love – the seemingly boundless bond that I witnessed between two humans today – is quite rare. You see, I am the instigator of chaos, the creator of opportunities for the human condition to thrive, or succumb. I have seen many great lovers over the eons, but I have very rarely witnessed such power as the love that the two of you share,' Apep nodded his head as if he was admitting simple truths to himself. Then he continued to explain, 'You know, a god should not feel human emotions, but my countless years upon the earth has taught me to develop such feelings as jealousy for my father Osiris's favouritism over Anubis, hatred for the thief for his betrayal and, most recently, compassion for lovers, who fight for the right to love and be loved in return.'

Sam felt humbled and a little embarrassed for lashing out at the reptile. He had judged the god too harshly it seemed. Perhaps there was some good in even the most spiteful of hearts. 'I apologise, Apep. I am very grateful for your assistance,' the framer said, extending his uninjured right hand toward the reptile, who smiled and took it in a firm shake.

'Perhaps we should just move forward then?' Apep asked.

'Lead on, lord Apep,' the framer replied.

CHAPTER EIGHTEEN

Heartfelt

THE FOURTH GATE WAS a wall, a very long wall, straight and high, stretching far both left and right beyond the scope of sight. It was made entirely of old white marble, massive blocks stacked steadfastly upon one another, all interlocking and covered with cracks and mould.

As the duo approached, the ancient blocks reminded Sam of the derelict tombstones at the old town cemetery. It appeared that this gate was actually a cemetery, for along the wall, every four metres or so, an arch shape was carved into the marble, tall and deep enough for a man to stand in. Several metres directly in front of each arch was a marble casket, standing upon two thick marble columns around one metre high. These arches and caskets spanned the entire wall.

'Wow, are these all the dead, from all over the world?' Sam enquired with a look of awe upon his now very weary face.

'Not quite, Sam. These are all of the dead mummies from ancient Egypt. Trust me there must be millions of them here. This is the Gate of the Starving Dead,' Apep said grimly.

'The gate of the what and what now? Why does that sound so unpleasant?' Sam inquired shakily, not sure if he really wanted to know the answer.

'Oh, you will not enjoy what is to come, I'm afraid,' Apep smiled nervously as he spoke. 'You must choose one of these mummies. You must wake it and you must feed it.'

'Um, okay … Probably a stupid question, but I don't see any burger joints around here – what exactly are we meant to feed the mummy?' Sam asked, his nervous eyes darting about the grim scene.

'Yourself, you must feed it a part of yourself,' Apep replied, his tongue now working overtime on his eyes.

'What? Oh, this place is so horrible, a nightmare! Why would anyone want to go through all of this?' Sam asked with exasperation, his hands resting on his upper thighs as he doubled over, feeling like he was about to vomit.

'The promise of heaven, Sam, only the best souls get to go to the kingdom of Osiris. That is why the tests are so extremely brutal. The prize is beyond bliss, I am told. Besides, what is worse: an eternity of roaming as a spirit, unable to interact with the world and the ones you love, or a chance at spending the rest of time in paradise, where you shall want for nothing? I wish that a lowly creature such as myself could have an opportunity to experience such a prize,' Apep replied calmly.

In truth, the reptile could use his magic to pass himself through this trial, as he had done many times when he guided deceased souls through the underworld while disguised as Anubis. He had decided that he would undergo each trial as Sam had to do, to somehow test his own worth.

'All I want is to save Erica and Anubis. That is the only reason why I am doing this,' Sam said as he straightened himself, then taking a deep breath, he continued, 'Okay, let's get this over with.'

Apep guided Sam over to inspect the open tombs in which the mummies rested. 'You must choose one, any one you wish.'

Sam looked at several corpses before he came across the mummy of a small child. Sam guessed that the child was around the age of six years old, the gender indiscernible, as the body was still mostly wrapped with brittle linen fabric, except for the hands and the right forearm, along with the legs and both feet. 'This one. I choose this child, in honour of the innocent children taken by the thief.'

'Very good,' Apep said with a smile. 'Now you must say the following words whilst touching the body: *Akpet kahmun pashir.*'

Sam braced himself and took a deep breath, then placing his hand upon the small body, he spoke the ancient words of resurrection, '*Akpet kahmun pashir.*' For a few moments, nothing happened, 'Did I say that correctly? Should I try ag–' A shudder erupted from the child-mummy, stopping Sam's enquiry in its tracks. The child raised its withered hands up to its head bindings, savagely scratching at the fabric trying to remove them. *My god, it can't breathe!* Sam thought, and he rushed to help the child, rapidly unwinding the linen wraps.

For some reason, Sam was expecting to discover a rabid, zombie-like monster, desperately clawing for his brains. Instead, the child was a young boy, disturbingly difficult to look at with his dry, leather-like retracted face showing teeth and jaw bone through large decay holes, his empty eyes sockets frozen wide, yet the boy showed no sign of menace. The little corpse moved rigidly, like an animated toy or doll, his deteriorated face looking up at Sam as he clambered out of his marble cot, and made his way toward him.

'Now what?' Sam called out to Apep, who had selected his own mummy and was just about to resurrect it.

'You must offer a part of yourself to the child, a sacrifice if you will.'

'My blood?'

'No, your flesh. You will find a dagger inside of the casket. Just cut something off.'

'Just cut something off?' Sam mumbled under his breath as he looked inside the casket and found the dagger, just as the reptile had promised.

The dagger looked far from sanitary, but it mattered not to Sam. He had already been through so much. He had taken the ultimate lie detector test, braved the heights of the ladders, almost sunk into the abyss of the lake, and cooked his left hand. The injury had seized the young man's joints, his fingers swollen with fluid, his hand felt useless and strange, as if it no longer belonged to him. The extreme pain had worked upon his mind, intensifying to the point that Sam wished the appendage gone. *That's it! My hand. Let the child have my hand.*

Without thinking further on the task, Sam removed one of his shoelaces, and with the aid of his teeth, he tied a crude tourniquet above his left elbow. The young man began to cut above his wounded hand, at the wrist joint. He reckoned that it would be far easier to cut through skin and sinew than skin and bone. The skin was tough, and the blade was dull, and as they say – the first cut truly is the deepest, the cold sting of the blade making Sam cringe with pain.

Sam yelled in agony as he ran the blade back and forth only to discover that he was not getting very far through with that technique, so he desperately began to stab at his wrist with the old dagger, occasionally misjudging his strikes and hitting bone.

'God damn it!' he huffed as he continued to plunge the blade into his mangled wound. Despite his tourniquet, a large amount of blood began to spray from his veins and arteries as he toiled away. Intense pain struck Sam as he sliced into a nerve, his brain peppered with sharp shocks, his vision leaving him blinded in a haze of white, yet he fought to bring his sight back to continue his gruesome labour. When he felt like he had weakened the joint sufficiently, he pulled upon his busted hand.

Sam groaned, saliva and spittle sprayed forth as he forced air from between gritted teeth, he briefly considered taking a quick break, but the agony of his throbbing wound urged him to complete the amputation. Desperation seized Sam and he began twisting his hand, the bones cracked and popped as they finally gave away at the joint. Veins and nerves stretched as he pulled the hand from his body, and Sam realised that he still had to cut through the bloody cables to be finally free of the hand.

He ambled over to the casket with the hungry corpse watching on intently as Sam placed the hanging hand on one side of the marble coffin and his forearm stump on the other. Using the marble as a cutting board, he sliced at the nerves and again the tremors of pain shot up his arm, accosting his brain and hazing his vision. He felt his face flush with alternating hot and cold waves as he struggled to hold his consciousness in place. His martial arts training had taught him to manage pain, but the agony that he felt was on another level. He remembered his teachings. He focused on steadying his breathing and slowing his heart. The pain abated slightly and his sight cleared as the nerves were cut one by one, the bloody ropes recoiling up into Sam's forearm, like snapped rubber bands. Next were the veins, but they were extremely rubbery and the blade was not cutting through. Sam was so close to being rid of the hand – he felt a rush of adrenalin and the framer felt almost manic as waves of warmth pulsed through him, so he took to the vessels with his teeth and after a few mighty chews of his incisors, his hand was at last loose.

Once the limb was severed, Sam fell to his knees, his head light from loss of blood and his stomach abruptly turned, evacuating it's contents as he vomited against the white marble casket. Sam held up his arm and noticed his spirit-hand was still attached, shining brightly, but there was no sensation in the ghostly digits, just the near-blinding pain of the bloody, fresh mutilation of his forearm stump. Sam struggled to remove his singlet and he wrapped it as tightly as he could manage around his mangled wrist.

Sam turned to see the hungry boy-corpse standing with his hands outstretched like a beggar. The framer was now feeling weak and disorientated, yet he shakily reached out and gave his severed hand to the child, who in turn devoured the flesh from the bone with great fervour. Blood and morsels of flesh dribbled from the mouth of the long-deceased child as he ate, his eyes fixed upon Sam as he chewed heartily upon his meal.

Abruptly, the mummy ceased its chewing and dropped the mangled remnants of the hand to the floor. Great convulsions seized the child, as if he were choking on his food, followed by violent gagging, before he bent over and vomited. The resulting fluid was the foulest brew that Sam had ever seen, an unholy rainbow of gruesomeness, strands of viscous blood streaking the dark brown, green and black fluid, with the occasional fleck of bright yellow. Furthermore, the stench of the puke made the river of souls smell like a fresh summer breeze. The mummy spewed the rancid fluid into its cupped hands, until there was no further content left to be ejected.

The child once again stood deathly still, like a doll, albeit a nightmarish one, his face as expressionless as it had been throughout the entire ordeal. The mummy's hands were still cupped, with almost all the thick vomit strained through his thin bony fingers. Sam noticed something moving in the remains of the spew – it was a beetle – and the framer instantly recognised it as a scarab beetle. The insect seemed to be looking directly at Sam, perhaps as if it were pleading to be rescued from its vile surrounds and, taking pity on the small creature, the young man picked the scarab up by the top of its shell.

No sooner had Sam removed the beetle than the boy-mummy began to shake violently, almost vibrating. An unsettling gasp, like the death rattle of a dying man echoed up from the throat of the nightmarish doll before the child simply crumbled away, rapidly turning to coarse dust and peppering the maggots that writhed upon the floor.

Sam stood up in shock at the spectacle of the mummy's disintegration before his eyes when he felt the scarab break free of his grasp. The beetle quickly scurried up Sam's right arm, but he could not grab the insect with his stump, which reflexively flailed about. He could not reach it with his good hand as it moved around the back of his arm and up over his left shoulder. The scarab was too fast as it moved quickly down onto Sam's chest, over his heart, and began to chew into his skin. Sam desperately took hold of the scarab, but his slippery, bloodied fingers failed him. He was unable to find purchase on the beetle or pull it free from his chest.

'Try not to panic, Sam!' Apep called to the young man, the reptile busy cutting through a segment of his tail to feed to his mummy. 'This is all a part of the process. Lay yourself inside the casket and try to relax!'

Relax? Easier said than done when there is an insect eating its way into your chest! Sam thought. Nonetheless, the framer did as the reptile had instructed and bundled his sorry frame into the casket, positioning himself onto his back.

Deep, sharp pain surged through his chest as the scarab burrowed, its pincers slicing effortlessly through the soft tissues and weaving between the rib cage with great ease.

Sam howled with pain as the scarab reached the outer lining of his heart and chewed at the cardiac tissue, sending strong, unbearable cramps throbbing throughout his upper torso. Intense pulses of electricity struck his brain like lightning and he felt his heart twitch violently under the assault. One last severe cramp seized Sam's heart and this time it stayed still, frozen as the muscle ceased to function.

In the very next instant, Sam felt his soul become violently expelled from his body and the pain was abruptly gone. *Thank god for that!* Sam thought, with great relief that his sufferance was finally at an end.

Sam looked over to where Apep had been tending to his mummy. He saw that the reptile had already fed the corpse and was in the throes of dying as he watched on, Apep's hands thrashing above the walls of his casket.

A few moments passed before Sam watched Apep approach. 'Feeling better?' Apep asked as he joined Sam's side, the reptile also now in spirit.

'Yes, thanks. You know you really need to start providing more detailed instructions on these trials – might have saved me some grief,' Sam replied dryly.

'What, and deprive you of the thrill of surprise?'

'I think I've had quite enough surprises over the last month, thank you. That was truly a nightmare. What was the purpose of all that?'

'This was all very necessary, Sam. Remember when we first arrived here in the underworld and we regained our bodies, our afterlife bodies?'

'Yes, you said that we would have those bodies for the rest of our time here … Kind of not applicable now is it? We are spirits again,' Sam spread out his arms to illustrate his point as he spoke.

'The afterlife bodies are needed so that one may suffer the trials of the soul. Without the body, there is no pain and without pain there can be no trials, for only when a man suffers does he learn the true value of his spirit.'

'Okay, I get it, but why are we spirit again now? Why did we have to die again?' Sam asked, his face knotted with confusion.

'We had to be freed from the flesh so that we may pass through the fourth gate. Tell me, do you see any door, any way through, around or over this wall?'

Sam didn't have to look too hard to know the answer to the question. 'No, I don't see any way through.'

'Precisely. We could never have passed this gate in our physical form. However, our spirits can easily move through the wall.'

'Oh, I see. Well what about the mummy and the scarab? Surely we could have simply taken our own lives?'

'No, Sam, everything in nature is a cycle. The mummies that you see here are the previous successful participants. It

was not them that you woke; it was not them that you fed
your flesh. It was the scarab that lay dormant in the stomach
of the corpse, moving the dead flesh like a puppet. The scarab
had to taste your flesh so that it could discover if your body
was pure, free of toxic impurities. What they say is true: pure
of body, pure of soul.'

'Hmm, lucky I was in training for the national fight. I
usually like a beer or two, and I used to smoke the occasional
joint back in the day,' Sam said with a tone of relief.

Apep looked slightly puzzled, he did not partake in such
indulgences and as such, he didn't know much about beer
and he certainly had no idea what type of joint could be
smoked, perhaps lamb or chicken? Regardless, he continued,
'Once the scarab judged you as worthy, it set about eating
your heart. This is necessary for the next part of the trial, the
Hall of Judgement, where your heart will be weighed.' Apep
pointed to Sam's body as he continued, 'The scarab has
devoured your heart so that it may carry the weight of your
heart's essence, for you could not physically take the essence
through the wall. When we are ready to pass through this
gate, we will command the beetle to follow us. It will climb
the wall and join us on the other side. Once we reach the
Scales of the True Heart, the scarab will be weighed, and
regardless of the outcome, it will be cleansed by Horus and
sent back here. Your body will join the rest of the dead here,
with the scarab lying dormant becoming a new mummy,
waiting for a future participant, as was the body of the child
before you. This is the cycle of which I speak.'

Sam filled his ghostly cheeks with air, before expelling it
forcefully from his lips, making the sound of a horse braying,
'Okay, right then. Let's move on, shall we?'

Apep nodded in agreement before calling to his beetle, 'Brother Khepri, follow behind thee!' At the command the reptile's scarab scampered out of the casket and across the maggots toward him.

Sam peered at the hole in the chest of his now still body. He could see the scarab sitting in a pool of thick blood – it was as lifeless-looking as his corpse.

'Khepri, come!' Sam barked the order and just as obediently, the scarab scuttled out of the wound, out of the casket and stopped below Sam's floating body. Then, looking down at the beetle, he said, 'Come on, boy. Let's go walkies!"

CHAPTER NINETEEN

Moment of Truth

PASSING THROUGH THE WALL was as effortless as Apep had suggested, and there was no resistance as the spirits entered the thick marble. Sam experienced a brief moment of panic as they traversed through the wall, his vision filling with only the white of the stone. The framer feared that he may become disorientated as the marble was everywhere, and the thickness of the wall was so deep that he lost his sense of space. He could see Apep moving steadily in one direction and so he followed close behind the reptile.

The duo soon passed clear of the marble wall, and the sight that greeted them was truly awesome. Ahead was a very large, wide and long hall, the entirety of which was constructed with a shiny, black onyx type of material, with large veins of richly coloured gold running throughout. Along the left-hand side of the entire length of the hall, every five or six metres, were large rectangular openings, like unglazed windows, and shining through each window was the intense, orange glow that Sam had previously mistaken for sunlight.

Sam floated over to the first window and peered out. He saw a hellish landscape of raging fires burning ferociously above an endless ocean of lava. As he watched, he fancied that he could make out the shadows of human-like forms thrashing about the sea of molten fluid.

'That is Durat, well the upper surface of it at least,' Apep spoke with a slight hint of fear to his tone. 'That is the place you may know as hell.'

'I can see people there, breaking the surface briefly,' Sam replied grimly.

'Think of the lava as the seas of your earth, it lies above the surface of Durat. The lava is thin at ground level, almost like a burning hot mist, but it becomes thicker as it goes higher. The souls that you see are trying to escape – they attempt to float out of the lava, but it is futile. They will only be burned by the fires and the ocean will drag them back down to the depths. Nobody has ever escaped Durat.'

Sam nodded his understanding, 'And what is on the bottom?'

'I do not know to be sure, some of my brother and sister gods have heard rumours. They say that it is a place where you are pulled apart, unmade very, very slowly and painfully, and when you think that your punishment is over, you are made whole again only to be destroyed over and over for all of time.'

'Well, that sounds rather unpleasant. Let's try not to end up there, huh?' Sam said dryly.

'Oh, I'm sure that you will be fine. Love has given you strength and has brought you this far. We will see if you have enough left for the final trial. As for me? I will soon discover the intimate terrors of Durat, I think,' Apep said with great dread.

Sam turned to look at the god, there was much fear in the reptile's eyes. The framer felt a sudden pang of sorrow for Apep and he instinctively placed his ghost hand upon the god's shoulder, only for it to pass through with a buzzing electrical sound.

Apep smiled, 'I truly appreciate the gesture, Sam, but it is okay. Truth is, that is why I wanted so desperately to have the knowledge of Anubis, to be able to pass into the kingdom of my father and avoid the hell that was waiting for me and my disenchanted. But you and Erica have shown me that there is hope for humanity, that there are very good people in the world and that even though you have flaws, those defects can be made void, thanks to the love for another. I was foolish, so please do not feel sympathy for me. I will get what is coming to me at the end of this hall.'

'The disenchanted? You love them … in your own way. That is why you started down the wrong path, Apep. You too are here because of love,' Sam nodded as he spoke, finally understanding that the serpent had developed his own rudimentary form of affection. Humanity had worn him down, and mortal emotions had stained the god, scarring him with vulnerability. Sam watched as Apep huffed his chest, his throat full of hard gulps and his ghostly eyes appeared moist, as if the reptile was holding back tears.

The moment was interrupted by a scuttling sound and Sam turned to see the scarab beetles scurrying across the onyx stone floor toward them. It was only then that Sam noticed that the floor was clean. 'Hey, there is not one single maggot here.'

'Remember, nothing physical can pass through the wall, only spirit – and the wall is too high for us to climb. The scarab makes good use of the joins between the blocks, but it takes them some time to climb the wall.' Apep smiled at his scarab as he spoke, 'They will follow us. We should move on.'

The light from the raging fires outside cast thick beams of orange across the floor as the pair glided down the hall. The rich gold veins of the black stone gleamed proudly at the touch of the hell-glow, a constant reminder of the possible fate that may await them. The design of the dreaded effect was no accident, Sam guessed, as the entire underworld was one big, elaborate torture test. Every small detail of the place was created to instil ultimate fear and despair for the soul that was attempting to gain access to heaven.

Sam was stirred from his grim pondering, courtesy of an image coming into his mind, the image of Erica. She was still in danger and it felt as if he had spent a small eternity battling through this nightmare of a place. He felt a surge of energy flow through him. He would succeed – he must, if not for Erica, then for Anubis, as he had promised the god that he would do all in his power to help defeat the thief. With renewed purpose, Sam increased his speed of movement, determined to put an end to the trials, one way or another. As Sam sailed down the passage, he could make out a golden glow at the end of the hall.

'Ahead is the end of our journey, Sam. The Scales of the True Heart awaits us,' Apep called out as he too increased his speed to match the young man's.

The pair slowed down as they approached the final room, and it was immense. Inside the Hall of Final Judgement, the walls were lined entirely with brilliant gold, and covered with perfectly carved hieroglyphs, as if they had been engraved with a laser. Tall black-and-gold onyx columns held up a ceiling that appeared to be made of a dark, metallic liquid-like substance, the surface of which acted as a perfect mirror. As Sam looked up into the liquid mirror, he felt as if he would fall upward into it. He suddenly felt nauseous and disorientated.

'Focus ahead of you, Sam. Do not look into the ceiling – it is merely another test of fortitude,' Apep hissed softly.

Sam did as he was instructed and, as his focus returned, he could make out several tall figures who had appeared ahead. The most notable of the characters was the god Horus, a majestic, imposing figure to be sure, standing at twice the height of Sam. The hawk-headed god was strong and muscular, with pure white feathers layered over his golden skin. Large folded wings sat proudly at the back of his shoulders, looking like some type of spring-loaded weapon, capable of removing a man's head in the blink of an eye. He would have no need for such a weapon, because, in his left hand, the hawk held a long spear, the head of which looked as if it was made of a large sharpened ruby that was about the length of Sam's forearm. The god's head twitched sharply from side to side at odd angles as he inspected the approaching duo.

At his right-hand side was Thoth the scribe, the ibis-headed god of written language and record keeper of the underworld. He stood erect and was also studying Sam and Apep as they slowly approached. His physique was much slenderer than Horus, and a little shorter in stature. His avian head was layered with fine, delicate feathers which were the colour of teal, these feathers became smaller and thinner as they progressed down his long neck to his feather-free chest.

To the right of Thoth was a large, elaborate scale made of solid gold. The dishes of the scale were deathly still, completely absent of any form of practicality, as if the entire weigh station was one solid piece, like a statue.

Sam heard Apep whisper as he glided slightly behind the framer, 'Sam, beware of Ammit, the soul-devourer. He lurks in the shadows, beyond brother Horus.'

Sam would have been completely unaware of Ammit, if Apep had not given fair warning. Sam could barely make out the shape of the monstrosity that was brooding in the shadows. 'Let's hope that we will not have to deal with him!' Sam hissed quietly.

'Halt!' the booming command pierced the air, reverberating off the gilded walls of the immense room. It was Horus who spoke, and with such authority that Sam ceased his movement immediately.

'You, human, be still and silent for now,' the hawk god demanded. 'Brother Apep, what has become of you? You are in spirit, why?'

'I was killed, brother. It is a very long tale, one of which I shall be more than happy to regale unto you in time,' Apep responded respectfully, as he bowed his head.

Horus snorted, 'Even so, you need not have tested the trials of the soul. You could have traversed the underworld in your afterlife body. You know the spells of safe passage.'

Apep continued to hold his head low as he responded, 'No, brother, I had to take the trials. I had to prove that I was worthy of standing rightfully before you. Furthermore, I had to prove to my human companion that I was true to my word.'

Sam looked over at Apep, the reptile looking more like a scolded child than a god. The framer nodded that his trust had indeed been earned.

The hawk looked confused as his head twitched, his small, steely eyes searching the reptile for some glimpse of trickery, 'What word did you give to the mortal, brother?'

'That, my brother, is between Sam and myself. It is of no importance to you,' Apep replied firmly, his tongue flicking across his eyes as he now raised his head to meet the gaze of Horus.

Ammit stirred deep in the shadows, perhaps sensing a growing tension between the brothers, yet for now, the monster remained shrouded in darkness.

Horus turned his attention toward the framer, 'You, mortal, what is your name?'

'Samuel Baker, my lord,' Sam replied, bowing his head as a sign of respect.

'Welcome here, Samuel Baker. You have completed the trials of the underworld, and you have been judged as worthy to face the last and final trial. We will weigh the essence of your heart against the Feather of Truth. If your heart is light with good deeds, the feather shall be lowered. If your heart has known many bad works, it will be heavier than the feather and you will fail. The reward for success is passage into the Kingdom of Osiris. The punishment for failure is to be devoured by Ammit and carried in his belly to spend an eternity in Durat. Do you accept these terms?'

Sam did not need time to mull over his options. For the sake of his love and his friend, the choice was easy. 'I accept, my lord.'

Horus nodded his head, his right hand gesturing toward the large gold scales next to Thoth, 'Approach with your scarab, Samuel Baker, and be judged.'

Thoth was busy writing down Sam's name and taking base measurements from the scale onto a scroll of papyrus as the young man approached with his scarab.

'Born year?' the ibis enquired as Sam drew near.

'1995.'

'Death year?'

'2019.'

'Occupation?'

'Picture framer.'

Thoth looked befuddled at Sam's answer, 'I am unfamiliar with that vocation.'

The framer thought quickly, *Which job in ancient Egypt would best correspond to what I do now?*

Politician? Philosopher? Builder? Slave? Soldier? I can fight, that will have to do. 'Um, okay, I was a fighter?' Sam's answer came in the form of a question. He was unsure what to say to the god. Apart from being a framer, Sam was proficient with only his martial arts.

'He is a warrior, brother Thoth. Inscribe him as a warrior,' Apep suggested confidently.

'Warrior? So be it!' Thoth huffed as he wrote down the answer. 'Wife?'

The question stung Sam in his soul as he thought of his sweet Erica. Marriage? It felt like Erica had provided Sam more love and affection in a few days than what he had experienced in his whole life. Her love for him was pure and intense and the thought of what may have been settled heavily on the framer's mind. Will he ever have the chance to hold her again? 'No wife,' he replied solemnly.

'Children?'

'None.'

The ibis god must have been content with the information, as no further questions followed. Thoth leaned down and collected Sam's scarab from the onyx floor and placed it onto the right scale dish. The god then moved to the other side of the scale and produced a large golden-coloured feather that was secreted away behind the shaft of the device. He carefully balanced the feather onto the left dish and Sam was amazed to see that the feather remained bolt upright, standing on its point in the centre of the scale. Thoth then moved to the centre of the weigh station and removed the locking pin that held the arm of the scale still. The boom began to move and if Sam still had breath to breathe, he would have held it.

To Sam's delight, his scarab rose triumphantly as the feather sank. The young man smiled as he looked over at Apep. The reptile did not return his smile, rather, there was a look of sadness upon the god's face. Sam looked back just in time to see that the scale's decision had reversed itself, the feather was now riding high. Sam stared hard at the scale, willing the feather to drop, and after a moment, it did just that. The feather lowered slowly, as his scarab was raised, and after what felt to be another lifetime, the scale had made its decision and stopped still.

'The scales are even. The result is equilibrium,' Thoth announced as he inscribed the result on the papyrus.

'Wha– what does that mean?' Sam asked tentatively, his voice awash with desperation.

Horus raised his spear high into the air, before bringing it down heavily onto the stone floor. 'Judgement has been made! Samuel Baker, you have achieved equilibrium with the Feather of Truth. You have been judged as neither pious, nor malicious of heart.'

Sam bowed his head low in front of Horus, 'Forgive my ignorance, my lord, but I do not understand the judgement. Did I pass? Did I f–'

Horus cut off Sam's query abruptly, 'You have reached synchronicity with truth. You have not done excessive good deeds, nor have you wronged too much. Equilibrium is a very rare result. In the eyes of us gods, your nature is as close to ours as a mortal human's can be. You have passed the trial of the true heart, Samuel Baker. You may pass through the final gate.'

Sam turned to Apep, who was now smiling broadly as he spoke, 'Well done, Sam. I never doubted you ... well maybe for a moment or two.'

'Apep, is there no possibility that you can come with me? Surely there is a way?'

'No, Sam. I am forbidden to enter the high realm of my father. My words were true – I did not deceive you. You must go on, and I must stay here and face my judgement.'

'I will tell Osiris what you have done here today. Surely he will understand?'

Apep smiled repentantly, 'You did not understand me at first, my motivations. He will not understand either, besides I have wronged my brother and consequently I was responsible for ending the lives of many innocents. Now, I must face the Scales of the True Heart.'

'Is there some problem?' Horus demanded, impatient with the prolonged goodbye between his brother god and the human. 'Most folk do not stay in this realm any longer than is necessary. Please move on, Samuel Baker.'

The framer nodded, 'Goodbye, lord Apep. I will always be grateful to you for helping me,' Sam whispered to the reptile.

Apep took several steps away from Sam as a cue for the young man to leave, 'Goodbye, Sam, now go and save your woman and rescue my brother. Oh, and Sam ... tell him that I regret what I have done.'

Sam smiled and nodded as he floated toward Horus. 'I'm sorry to keep you waiting, lord Horus. I am ready to go now.'

CHAPTER TWENTY

Slice of Heaven

AFTER THEY LEFT THE great Hall of Judgement, Horus led Sam down a narrow hallway, some hundred metres long. The god walked at a steady pace and Sam, still in his spirit-form, glided along next to him. As the two travelled, Sam noticed that the dark onyx and gold walls started to lose their opacity and in place of the stone the structure took a more crystal-like appearance, black at first, then changing to a smoky quartz colour, through to pink, into yellow, before finally becoming completely clear. It eventually appeared that there were no walls at all, just nothing, only complete darkness. Eventually the floor too had disappeared, and

Horus stopped on the last of the remaining translucent floor tiles. Sam did not notice that the god had stopped walking as he glided onward into the darkness, and he soon found himself gently floating about in empty space.

'Where are we? What is this place?' Sam asked as he turned around to face Horus.

'We are here, Samuel Baker. Welcome to the Kingdom of Osiris, or as you mortal humans call it, heaven,' Horus announced, his voice echoing ferociously throughout the void.

Sam was beyond confused. Of all the things that he had witnessed over the past month, this was the most unsettling by far. 'What? This is heaven? But there is nothing here … just nothing! Where is everyone? Where is Osiris?'

'Everyone is here, Samuel. They are all in their own heaven. Father Osiris is where he belongs, in his temple, far away from his creations.'

'Creations? You mean humans?'

'Not only humans, but life from all over the many worlds and realms of his domain.'

'So, if everyone is here … in their own heaven, why can I not see them?'

'You cannot see them because you have not opened the door.'

'The door … I don't see any door,' Sam replied, investigating the empty blackness around him.

Horus huffed loudly. It was clear that his patience was wearing thin. 'Did you not receive the teachings of the afterlife? Surely Apep tutored you?'

'You would think so, but I'm afraid he did not tell me anything about what happens here.'

The hawk groaned with displeasure. 'Human, you must create the door, the door to your heaven.' Horus abruptly turned and began to move away from Sam, 'Good luck in the afterlife, Samuel Baker, somehow I believe that you will need it.'

Sam was about to protest against Horus abandoning him in the void, but decided to try to focus on what the god had told him. Okay, create a door, open the door. How hard can that be? It was obvious that he had to create a door with the power of his mind, for that was all that was left of him now. The density of the darkness was so intense, Sam could not even see his own spirit-body anymore. He had no legs, feet, arms or hands. He could hold no tools or implements, even if there were any available. *My mind? Wait, where is my mind?* Sam questioned, his panic now rising. He had no brain – so, no mind? Then where were his thoughts coming from? The framer turned around, desperately trying to find the beginning of the pathway back to Horus, but it was all for naught, as he was indeed completely enveloped in nothing.

Just when it seemed that he was about to go insane with fear, the memory of Anubis's teachings came to him. He and the god had switched control of Sam's body by shifting their consciousness forward and back, like changing drivers in a car. There didn't need to be a body, and there didn't need to be a brain or a mind for that matter. He was and always had been consciousness, spirit, merely wearing the meat of humanity. The body was just the means by which the soul experienced life.

Right! You want a door? I'll give you a bloody door! Sam's thoughts echoed about the void. *A doorway is just a frame, right? Well I'm a framer, so let's choose a nice timber moulding.*

Sam pictured some lengths of wide, beautifully carved timber, the grain and swirls of the wood running like veins across the planks. He pictured the wood as red cedar, with white marbling throughout, and he imagined how smooth it was, with a gorgeous satin varnish. Next, he imagined cutting the timber at forty-five-degree angles and joined them with adhesive and nails, then finally, he willed the frame upright. Next, he imagined placing vertical timber planks of the same grain and colour as the outer frame to create a door and, finally, he conjured a beautifully carved handle.

The framer moved a few metres away from his creation to inspect his handiwork. *Not too shabby. Now, show me a door.* Just as Sam thought the words, the structure steadily appeared as more solid and, at length, there was a beautiful door standing before him. With great excitement, Sam reached for the handle, only to discover that he could find no purchase upon it. *Oh, right, no body!* he mused. It was clear that this new form of existence would take some getting used to. Again, he focused, then imagined pulling the door toward him, it immediately glided open and Sam stepped through the open door.

The other side of the door was as equally perplexing as Sam stepped from a place of intense darkness into the polar opposite of that. There was nothing but pure white light as far as he could see.

'Oh, really? What the ...? A little help would be nice!' Sam shouted out, feeling weary of the afterlife already. No sooner had the words been said than the shadow of a figure appeared a little way off in the distance, slowly gliding toward him. Sam felt a sense of panic as the figure approached.

'Hello gorgeous!' the figure shouted joyfully. It was Erica.

Sam felt his energy collapse and he fell to his knees. In that same moment he realised that he had his body back once again, even his severed hand was back in its place, firmly attached to his arm and as good as new. He looked up desperately at his love, 'Erica! What are you doing here?'

Erica smiled as she knelt to him and kissed him tenderly. He could taste her lips, feel her softness, her warmth, and he could smell her perfume. This was no trick. She was here with him – of that he was certain.

Erica gazed lovingly into Sam's eyes and she spoke to reassure him, 'Sam, it's okay. I'm here now, and I've been waiting for you.'

'Waiting for me?'

'Yes, I didn't make it, Sam. The thief killed me shortly after you died,' Erica replied, narrowing her eyes as she spoke. Sam had grown to know that look – grown to love that look. It meant that she was deadly serious on the matter. She had used that same look the first time she told Sam that she loved him.

'No, no! I was trying to save you. I came here to get help.' Sam started shaking as he spoke, 'How … How did you get here before me? I didn't see you throughout any of the trials.'

'Anubis – he brought me directly here after we died.'

'We died?' Sam looked around, eagerly searching for the god. 'Anubis is dead too?'

'He is not here, Sam. He has gone to be with his father. It's just you and me now, but Sam it's all going to be okay. We can be together forever now. You and I will live here in … paradise.'

Sam was anxious as he looked about the bright void, 'Paradise? Do you see any paradise here?'

Erica looked into Sam's eyes and smiled warmly, 'Yes … Yes, I do. I see you.' Again, she kissed him, the scent of her shampoo now met Sam's nose.

'Oh, Erica, I'm sorry I couldn't save you.'

'Enough of that talk now, Samuel!' Erica spoke with mock admonishment. 'There is no judgement here in heaven, only unconditional love. You did your best. I watched your trials. I saw your pain and your bravery, and I'm so very proud of you.'

Sam stood to his feet, urging Erica to stand with him, and he took her delicate hand in his. 'Okay, so now what? Where is this paradise that you speak of?'

'We will create it, Sam, together. Come walk with me.'

Erica led Sam by the hand and as they walked an old, narrow, cobbled road appeared underfoot. Thick, green grass kissed the edges of the path and rapidly grew outward, creating a lush meadow with rolling hills at the horizon. To the right, the sounds of a babbling creek laced the air as a little brook materialised, winding lazily beside the road. The air became crisp and very cool and smelled sweet of moss and greenery.

The path ahead began to undulate away from the couple as they strolled along. Furthermore, at the very base of one of the closest hills, a little cottage appeared, with walls of white rock and a thatched roof, upon which perched a smoking chimney. The surrounds of the cottage were sprinkled with various fruit trees and vegetables growing nearby.

As they approached, toward the house, the smell of Irish stew permeated the air, sending Sam's stomach into ravenous convulsions. 'Erica, are you doing all of this?'

Erica smiled happily, 'Do you like it? This is what my childhood home was like, back in Ireland. This is my idea of paradise.'

Sam ceased in his tracks, causing Erica to come to a jarring stop. 'Wait, what did you just say?' he asked.

'I said that this is my idea of paradise. Why?'

Sam pulled Erica close to him and looked into her eyes. They were beautiful – perfect. He looked at her face, at her hair – flawless. He took his hands to her blouse and quickly worked to unfasten the buttons.

'Oh, Sam, you could've waited till we were inside the cottage!' Erica gasped with pleasure as she playfully slapped his hands away, before she continued to undress herself.

Erica slipped off her shirt and unhooked her bra strap, exposing her perfectly sized breasts, the cold air bringing her rosy nipples to attention. She needed no further encouragement from Sam as she lowered her jeans. Her panties quickly followed them to the ground. Erica stepped toward Sam, biting her bottom lip as she did so. 'Come here, my love. We will make Osiris blush in his own kingdom.'

Sam's forehead creased with confusion and he took a step back away from Erica, while holding his palm up to stop her. 'No, wait. I just want to look at you.'

Erica stood still as she was directed, her perfect body fully exposed to the idyllic countryside of her own creation. Sam loved her more than he had ever loved anyone or anything before. She was his ideal woman.

'Sam, is something wrong?' Erica asked, shivering slightly as the crisp Irish air licked at her skin, peppering it with goosebumps.

'Yes, yes there is. You are perfect. You have no flaws, not a single scar, mark or wrinkle. You have no unpleasant odour, no bad breath. You are squeaky clean, and the whites of your eyes are ... well, white. Your body is too perfect, your breasts, your thighs, everything. You are not really Erica. Are you?'

Erica flashed a pained expression at the suggestion, 'Samuel! How could you say such things? I am here with you. I am your Erica!'

'Yes, you are Erica, but you are not real. You did not die. You are a projection of perfection and that is not my Erica. My Erica has flaws – she is not perfect. She is human and that is why I love her. I think that you are a creation of my mind, born of my desperation to see you again. I bet that this is not what your childhood home was like. No, this is all my projection of what I think you would want, because all that I truly want is for you to be happy.'

Erica shook her head softly, tears rolling down her flawless cheeks, 'Oh, Sam, are you sure that this is what you want? You want me to be gone?'

'No, Erica, I want to save you and I cannot do that if I am here playing make-believe with a copy of the real you.'

'Well then, I guess that I should probably let you get back to saving the real me then. Good luck, my love. One way or another, I'll see you soon.' With no more to say, Erica gathered up her clothing and headed up the hill toward her little cottage. Then turning back to Sam, she said, 'Oh and Sam, if things don't work out, you know where to find me.' Then she winked and continued on her way.

Sam now realised that heaven was truly an amazing place, full of unlimited possibilities. There was no physical pain here, no bills to pay or people to argue with. One could eat, drink, smoke and do pretty much anything that one desires, without any negative consequences. Heaven could be whatever one wanted it to be. But, right now Sam needed heaven to be the home of Osiris, and he needed to find the father god, but how?

Think, Sam, think! the framer urged himself to concentrate. Horus said that Osiris was far away from his creations. Then he is unlikely to be residing in someone else's heaven. His kingdom must be apart from all of this. Sam soon realised that he was looking in the wrong place. He had to go back through his door, back into the void.

Turning on the spot, Sam saw his door in the distance and he ran along the cobblestones toward the exit. Upon reaching the door, the young man took a deep breath. He was happy to have his body back, and he realised that in a few moments he would once again be spirit, so he enjoyed a few last breaths, before he swung the door wide and stepped into the abyss.

Once again Sam was floating about in pure blackness. He was relieved to see that his door was still there. At least he would have somewhere to go if he could not locate Osiris.

Sam moved his vision about the blackness, but he could see nothing besides his door. *Why can't I see anything but blackness? Why can't I see anyone else's door? Maybe one can only see their own door to their own heaven. Maybe only a god can see through the darkness. A god?*

Sam had shared consciousness with Anubis and as such, he had seen with the eyes of a god. He remembered how Anubis could speed up his vision, causing reality to move in slow motion. With a shudder of realisation, Sam tried to remember how it felt to see with the eyes of Anubis. He forced his consciousness to condense, like a spring being compressed to the point of maximum tension, and then he looked forward, holding his mind-spring in place. Slowly he started to see bright flashes all about the void and gradually, the flashes lingered longer, until at length, they stayed on.

Sam had retained the god-vision he gained as host to Anubis and he could now perceive that which mortal souls could not. Each of those countless numbers of bright white lights were actually other doorways, other people's heavens, all of them closed but radiant, as if they had all left a porch-light on, and it reminded Sam of the stars in the night sky, in the milky way galaxy that he had seen many times, on many nights. Was heaven there in the sky all along? Could mortal man catch a glimpse of the afterlife from earth – only visible at night, that magical time when one could see with the eyes of a god? Was the universe actually the afterlife? Had the astronauts of earth reached out, rising from the planet to touch the face of the divine? Sam guessed that the answer to all those questions was 'maybe' and they would have to be left to be pondered upon some other time.

Looking about, Sam could see a golden light way off in the distance. The light was perfect, pure and magnificent, almost as if the light itself was made of gold crystal. *That must be it, the Kingdom of Osiris,* he thought, and with no further hesitation, the framer glided toward the divine light.

CHAPTER TWENTY·ONE

Weapon of Choice

THE ENTRANCE TO THE Kingdom of Osiris was as grand as one might expect, with large double doors forming an arch – exceedingly tall, perhaps some twenty metres high, and made of rich, solid gold. Around the entire perimeter of the door were stones, each about the size of a large apple. They were no ordinary stones, being of all types and colours, one stone of every gem, rock and mineral known to man, alongside other strange looking stones from elsewhere in Osiris's dominion.

There were no visible handles or knobs with which to open the doors, so Sam figured that once again the power of the mind would do the trick. As he concentrated, the gargantuan doors slowly swung open and as soon as there was sufficient space, Sam glided through into the kingdom of the father god.

Sam was unprepared for the sight that met him once inside the doors. He had expected to see a glorious world, made entirely of gold, with bright and vivid blue skies above and lusciously perfumed flowers everywhere. Instead, the land of Osiris was exceedingly simple, made entirely of dense, translucent crystal which gave a metallic rainbow sheen, as petroleum does upon water. The ground itself was merely large slabs of the same crystal, from which the constructions of the kingdom emerged. Numerous large buildings and palaces were scattered about the land, above which a violet sky, so dark that it was almost black, loomed as far as Sam's sight could discern. The air was not perfumed with flowers, rather, it smelled of burnt toast, sweet and pungent. Soft, delicate sounds of vibrating crystal, like the ringing sound made when one's finger runs along the rim of a wine glass, also pervaded the clean air.

Curious, Sam thought. *Where to now?*

After a moment of hesitation, the framer decided to head directly forward, along the smooth, humming avenue that lay before him. A realisation came upon the young man as he walked along – he was in fact walking. Yes, he once again had a physical body and he was happy to have it back. He enjoyed the feeling of walking on solid ground once more, having the sensation of smell, and looking through his physical eyes. As Sam travelled, he took the time to stop by a large window in the side of one of the buildings.

There was no glass in the window and through the opening Sam could see no furnishings or decorations inside, nor any occupants, only the soft glow of a couple of lights.

The lights appeared to be floating, as if they were being carried about by some gentle breeze, although no such breeze was present. The lights were rather small, about the size of a tennis ball, and quite delicate in luminosity, changing colours rhythmically, in tune with the crystalline ringing that filled the air above.

Sam then turned his attention to the wondrous city all around him, only to discover that it too was empty, not a single person, animal, angel, god or demon to be seen, merely the occasional appearance of those bizarre glowing lights.

Osiris must really value his privacy, Sam thought, concluding that being the father god of all creation is perhaps a task worthy of such solitary focus and devotion.

The framer continued to walk along when, finally, the vacant landscape and continuous ringing of the toast-scented air began to work upon Sam's nerves. His mind was becoming more erratic, his thoughts undulating between past, present and possible future events. The ability to focus his attention was slipping and a strong headache began throbbing through his skull. No longer was he walking along steadily, he was jarring forward – violently at times – as a learner driver who has not yet mastered the smooth operation of the clutch and gas pedal might do. Sam wobbled from side to side and at one point he collided hard against the side of a building. The impact was real and hurt somewhat, leaving no doubt that the Kingdom of Osiris was actually a physical location, perhaps somewhere in another dimension.

Just when his composure was reaching its breaking point, a great building appeared off to Sam's right, bringing the young man to a stop. *A pyramid? Of course it would be a pyramid!* And what a pyramid it was, covered with seamless, glass-like gold, cutting sharply up into the dark violet sky.

With a renewed feeling of exuberance, Sam focused and ran toward the great building. As he approached, he spotted a large doorway at the base of the pyramid, and within moments, he was inside.

'Are you just going to stand there and gander at me, child?' Osiris was facing the one entrance of the room as Sam entered, as if the god was expecting him. He was standing in the middle of a cavernous place, which must have been the very apex of the pyramid. The top third of the sloped walls were window-like and outside of these windows was the black void of the afterlife, with countless stars of varying size, brightness and colour. There were no decorations, furniture or embellishments about the room, as were all the other buildings in this simple, clean world. Everything was pure.

'Well, child? Have you no words for me?' Osiris asked nonchalantly, his lingering intimidation shrouded just below the surface of his expression. At first Sam had no words as shock seized him, rendering the young man both motionless and speechless. Certainly, the framer had searched – striving long and hard to find the father god, yet, he was ill-prepared for the greatness of Osiris's presence. The almighty lord did not resemble a man, nor any god that Sam had thus far encountered. One could not even go so far as to call the being alien, for Sam could not conjure an impression of any extraterrestrial, of screen or word, that could compare to the extraordinary appearance of Osiris.

Sam had seen ancient Egyptian images of the father god and, just as such illustrations indicated, his skin had a matte-toned, turquoise-green pallor to it. The god had an elongated cranium and his neck was a mass of meat and sinew, necessarily providing strength to hold the large skull aloft. The elongated, hairless head resembled the bodice of a squid, with thousands of tiny black thread-like veins criss-crossing underneath the skin.

The god's face resembled that of the sphinx, minus the headpiece, and long earlobes dangled below cat-like pointy apexes of his ears. The lord had a broad chest and shoulders, which angled sharply down toward an incredibly narrow waist, before rounding out into a bulbous pelvis, from which four long, yet muscular, insectoid legs protruded. Osiris had two human-shaped arms, rather slender and lacking any noticeable muscle tone, and at the end of his arms two, large oversized hands hung heavily.

Despite his disturbing appearance, Osiris had a gentle, kind energy about him and as such, Sam was not afraid for his life. So, after a few moments he answered the god, 'My lord Osiris, please forgive my rudeness. I, I, I ...'

'You, you, you?' the god interrupted, playfully mocking the mortal before him.

Sam let loose a laugh. He was well pleased that the father had a sense of humour. 'Ha, yes, I am unsure of how to talk to you, my lord. I have been searching for you, to beseech your help.'

'My help? Hmm, I have a few questions for you first, my child. Firstly' – the father god erupted with violent malice in his words – 'how did you get into my kingdom!?' his face twisting as he spat the question at Sam. The god's entire appearance was changing, his mass shifting rapidly into a new form.

Sam took several steps backward, only to find that there was no longer an entrance behind him. He was trapped. As Sam turned his attention back to Osiris, he was shocked to see that the god had now taken on the appearance that was instantly familiar from the ancient depiction that Sam had seen on the Anubis scroll. He was now human in body shape, standing at least three times the height of Sam. The god had retained his elongated head and green skin, albeit his face was strikingly beautiful, neither masculine, nor feminine, but decidedly human looking.

Osiris's handsome face bore an expression of great anger, and still the questions spewed forth, 'Now you see my true form, boy! Answer my questions or else I will destroy you! Who are you? Why have you invaded my privacy?'

The changing of body was clearly a display of power, designed to show that Osiris could look however he pleased, a ridiculous conglomeration of forms – human, animal and the otherworldly, perhaps to frighten away unwanted visitors, but Sam had come too far to be scared off, or to be shouted down, regardless of who it was that berated him so savagely. 'My Lord!' Sam shouted back to the god, marching forward abruptly, not caring if he was to be rendered into oblivion, 'Please hear me!'

Osiris was a little shocked that the human had dared to show such courage toward him and consequently, he relaxed his aggression. 'Very well. Speak – but mind your tongue!' The god watched as Sam gulped hard before speaking, his mouth seemingly finding it difficult to articulate his thoughts. 'My lord Osiris, I bring word of your son Anubis. He is in great peril.'

Osiris twitched his head violently at the name of his son, his expression changing from anger to cautious curiosity. 'And? What of him? What of my son?'

'He has been trapped on earth for thousands of years, my lord. He–'

'Enough talk, boy!' Osiris shot his hand up before beckoning for Sam, 'Come to me, boy. I will not harm you.'

Sam was past caring for his own welfare, but he knew that he must obey the god's instructions without question if he was to help Anubis and Erica, so he walked over to Osiris. As he drew near, Sam could smell the scent of the divine and it reminded him of Turkish delight – of roses and chocolate, the fragrance somehow pacifying him.

The god placed his huge hands upon Sam's head and closed his eyes. Sam felt his mind slip out of him, like running and falling upon wet, slippery ice. The feeling of racing adrenalin stung in his nose and for a few moments he had no thoughts, no presence and absolutely no consciousness. He was nobody and nothing. Had the father god destroyed him, rendered him void? No, soon enough Sam had his awareness back in place and all was as it were.

'I have borrowed your mind, child. I have seen everything that has transpired,' Osiris said with an expression of deep concern. 'I have been careless not to have noticed the absence of my son, to have neglected the earth for such a vast amount of time. Unfortunately, earth is just one of my many worlds and my attention has been scanning across the furthest reaches of matter, where my other realms exist,' Osiris waved his hands toward the star-filled windows overhead as he spoke. 'I am the creator, you see. It is what I do. To create a world takes much time, and time is different here, to me it is literally nothing. That is why I created so many gods – they are the sentinels of your little planet, and if Anubis's absence was not noticed by Horus or Toth, then I can only surmise that the presence of Anubis was not missed. Perhaps Apep may have had something to do with that,' Osiris smirked as he attempted to justify his lack of attention regarding Earth.

Sam nodded his understanding of the situation and offered Osiris a respectful bow before cautiously addressing the great god, 'Lord Osiris, is there anything that you may be able to do to help us?'

Osiris shot Sam a measured look, before nodding slowly. 'There are a great many things that I can do to remedy the situation. I cannot go to earth myself, for I must not leave my children, nor my great work.'

'Your children, lord?'

'Yes, the children who live here in my kingdom. Surely you saw them on your way here?'

A look of confusion crossed Sam's face, 'Sorry, my lord, but I saw no children. I saw nobody at all, only those lights … Oh … they were your children?'

'Ha!' a loud guffaw erupted from Osiris, his delight with Sam's sudden comprehension clearly evident. 'Yes, they are my children. They are what you may call souls – pure souls. You see I create each soul in existence, every one of them is my child and they must go forth and do what children must do. They must live, play and they must learn, they must grow, they must mature, and they must die. Then they go back and do it all again, over and over, until they have lived every life, played every game, learned every lesson, felt every pain, every joy and every death. They must do it all until they are pure souls, perfect souls and then they can come home – forever.'

Sam became even more confused, 'What? So, I have lived before?'

'Yes, child, you have, many times. Without death, there is no fear and it is the fear of death that compels one to live. You do not fear death, Samuel Baker, as most men do. Perhaps you have not learned to live?'

'I do want to live. I have found love, my lord. I want to live for her and I want to live for me.'

'Ah, love – one of my creations, you know. I must confess, it actually began as a little joke or an experiment, if you will. You see, it goes like this: the young man wants her body, the middle-aged man wants her heart and the old man wants her mind. What do you want from this ... Erica, Mr Baker?'

Sam considered the question for a moment before he replied, 'Well ... I want all of her, but I will only take what she is willing to give.'

'Hmm, you are perhaps an older soul than I had guessed, Samuel. Some men take the young woman's body and leave her when her fruits have bruised. Middle-aged men settle for a happy wife until their hearts find another and the old man just wants to be remembered by the woman by his side, until ...'

'He dies. What about heaven? Hell?'

'In the beginning there was nothing in existence, except me and I ... Well I was nothing more than a little light, a star if you will. I sat still in the darkness for many millennia and I began to think. I began to create consciousness. As I sat and pondered, I grew restless, so I decided to grow. I grew and grew until I was so big and powerful that I became the first entity – the true father of all creation, an entity known as Atum-Ra, or as humanity came to call me – the Sun. Then I began creating planets and life, of which I looked upon with a fiery gaze. As I watched my creations spin around me, I desired to be among them, so eventually I withdrew my consciousness from the sun, created a physical body and became the first pharaoh of Egypt – Osiris. Sometime later, I had my fill of humanity, so I created the gods to watch over the Earth and I made myself my own kingdom, a place from which I could continue my great work, and a home for the purified souls of my children to live in. What you call heaven, where you imagined an idyllic life with your Erica, that is a place of rest, a place to recover from your previous life before you move on to the next. Hell is real, but it too is temporary. It is a place to pay for wicked deeds done, and it is truly a place of pain and unimaginable horror. Out of such terrors, great lessons can be learned and once they are, the damned are reborn into life yet again.'

'And what of the trials of the underworld?'

'Simple, it is the way to reward or ruin, for great rewards await great souls and the trial of the soul is the only way for good souls to become great. I can see that you are a good soul, Samuel. Obviously you would not be standing before me if you were not an exceptional being, but you are far from perfect. You even managed to curb the wicked nature of my serpent child. Apep was created to be chaotic. He was designed to be impartial, yet his years of dealing with the worst facets of humanity made him … weak. Do you know why he helped you? Why his nature was so abruptly pacified?'

'He told me that he wanted to see if love could endure, to see if humanity could once again find hope. I think that perhaps in helping me, he could find some hope for his own soul.'

'Apep helped because he was killed and as such, he could no longer influence the world. He could no longer interact with the living, nor could he create events or situations to test the human spirit. Apep was no longer chaos, he was merely a ghost. He had no choice but to either roam the earth-realm or the underworld, and he would not be able to pass into the afterlife. Only Durat would have him, and gladly so. Apep helped you because he had little else to do. He was curious about your spirit and perhaps along the way he developed compassion for you. Maybe he started to see you as his champion, but the one thing he did not expect was to be loved – to have your appreciation and affection. You destroyed him as a god when you took his hand in friendship. I no longer have a god of chaos.'

Osiris looked coldly at the framer for a moment before continuing, 'My child, I am faced with an unusual dilemma. What am I to do with you now? You have bonded minds with a god, my son Anubis, and in doing so you have absorbed a trace of his being. In essence, you have become more than human.'

'More than human?' Sam queried.

'Yes, you are ... what would you call it? A hybrid? You are part god now, your soul eternally stained, and as such you can no longer travel the path of a human soul.'

Sam felt a sense of panic at hearing the revelation, *No longer human?* He feared that Osiris would simply destroy him, as he was no longer capable of being a perfect soul. Osiris seemed to read the look of dread upon the framer's face and moved to reassure him, 'Do not worry, child. Although it is true that you should not exist, I will not harm you. Now, I could dispatch Horus to deal with the thief and that whole mess. No, I have a better proposal: if I am to help you with saving Anubis and Erica Murphy, you must obey my will and pledge servitude to me from this moment forward, as my other gods do, such as Anubis and Horus and all the others spread throughout my creation.'

Sam was unsure of the father god's intentions, and he was a little worried by the term 'servitude'. He knew that Osiris was the great creator, and that he sent his children, his perfect souls, out into the world, out into the universe. It appeared that he had nothing but the most noble and loving of intentions for them, to grow and eventually return to live in his glorious kingdom. If Sam was to save Anubis and Erica, of course there was no question that he would do whatever

Osiris demanded. 'I will do as you ask of me, lord Osiris. Now please tell me what must be done.'

Osiris smiled broadly as he approached Sam, 'Excellent. Firstly, I shall require the assistance of an old friend.'

The father god held out his right hand from his side, as if he was waiting for something to come to him, and after a few seconds a green glow appeared at the god's palm, the glow rapidly becoming an object – a familiar object, an object that had recently been used by Sam. It was the blade Osir.

Sam was about to comment on seeing Osir, when Osiris abruptly struck out at the framer, driving the blade deep into his chest. The familiar blinding pain of Osir once again accosted Sam and he gasped, his flesh burning savagely, his heart cramping around the point of the blade. Flabbergasted, he looked down at his chest and grasped at the blade, holding it still as he pulled himself away from Osiris.

'My son, forgive me, but you must die. You simply cannot exist,' Osiris said, his face displaying sincere sympathy for the young man's plight.

Sam stumbled backward a few feet before his legs could hold him no longer and the framer fell hard to the cold, gilded floor, 'You said that you would not harm me!'

'A father must sometimes lie if he is to bend a child to his will. Besides, I have not destroyed you, not really. You see, before you can live anew, you must die, only then can you be born again as the god that you must become. Anubis has been a good and loyal servant, but his time has passed. His legend has been lost to the sands of time and the world has moved on without him. He will need to be replaced by a new god.'

'Wha ... but Anubis ... he is my friend. I will not let him die!' Sam hissed as his body started shaking, desperately attempting to hold death at bay.

'Die? Why should he die? No, he shall come home to me, his duty to his master fully realised. You will do my will upon the earth. You will fight against the evil of the world. The earth needs a new god of the dead, protector of souls and you, my son, you will die and you will become my Anubis reborn.'

A savage shudder thundered through Sam's body, his heart ceasing its futile fight, and for the third time that day, the framer was dead.

Osiris stood over Sam's motionless body, waiting for a few moments before he bent down and placed his palm against the pommel of the protruding blade Osir, pushing it all the way into the young man's heart, the weapon melting into Sam's body. The great father's massive finger pushed on Osir, ensuring that the entirety of the weapon was inserted.

'Now rise, my son. Rise and be reborn,' Osiris boomed as he spoke, rising to his feet.

'Arise former mortal, Samuel Baker, rise and transcend. Arise my new god of the dead. Arise!' As the father creator spoke the last word, Sam's body convulsed with spasms, before becoming still.

The framer's chest once again rose and fell with breath and he opened his eyes. Steadily, he rose to his feet, his body feeling clean and refreshed, yet very different. All the new god's senses were alive, his soul bursting with exquisite beauty. His focus was crystal clear and his awareness all encompassing, yet he sensed death. He could feel that death was lingering inside of him, a part of his very being, and such delicious agony it was. The veil of life had been lifted and the underworld that he had triumphed over would become his new workplace – Horus, Thoth, Ammit and the maggots would be his colleagues. It was goodbye to picture framing and hello to oblivion.

Sam watched as Osiris came closer to inspect his new creation, 'You are magnificent, my child.' The father creator seemed well pleased, after all it was not every day that a new god was born, especially one forged from the soul of a mortal man. 'Perhaps my greatest failing was that my gods were created from the divine. Maybe I needed a god based on the mortal soul, so that he may feel as mortals do, to better understand human nature and just punishment. In time you must forge yourself a new body, but for now you will retain your spirit-form. Now, although you are to be my new god of the dead, we cannot call you Anubis. That name will always only belong to its original owner. No, you shall have a new name. My son, I shall name you after the catalyst that has wrought you anew. You shall be named: Osir.'

CHAPTER TWENTY·TWO
Shall We?

ANUBIS HAD TAKEN THE full impact of Jalel's blow, the strike sending the god and his host to the bitumen and into unconsciousness. It was Erica who came to first as she struggled to raise her head up from the road, her mouth sour with the iron-laced taste of blood, her chest burning raw from the demon's scratch, and her t-shirt damp and sticky with blood.

Anubis? There was no reply. She was alone – well not really alone, she had some rather unpleasant company in the thief, who was staring intently at her. The foul monster smiled at Erica, its busted mouth presenting the festered stump of its severed tongue, the offensive organ flicking about, simulating cunnilingus.

Repulsed, Erica stood to her feet. *Now what?* The thief did not know that Anubis was unconscious, perhaps she could attempt to fool the demon.

'Thief, you will not win this fight!' Erica called out, her voice as low and gruff as she could manage, as she attempted to impersonate the god. She widened her stance, bringing her fists up as she had seen Sam do as he prepared to fight.

The reporter had neither the physicality, nor the intention of fighting the demon alone, but she was damned if she was just going to stand there and become a victim to the monster. She only had to delay Jalel in the hopes that Anubis would wake soon, then once the thief was defeated, she could help Sam. Erica desperately shot a look over to where Sam was laying – he was still. *He must be just sleeping. He's just resting,* she reassured herself. Her hopes, although present, were somewhat shallow and she felt stricken with fear.

Movement stirred in Erica's periphery. It was Jalel moving toward her. *Anubis!* Erica trembled, her nerves prickled her gut and her heart sank with the lack of Anubis's presence and her inability to delay the thief any longer. Adrenalin suddenly pulsed through her core and her fight or flight response kicked in – she would stand and she would fight.

Erica backed away from Jalel as he charged at her. She was still a little disorientated from being knocked unconscious, but she managed to dodge to the side of the thief and turned quickly to face his back. She kicked out her leg, the heel of her foot making contact just above the demon's buttocks. The outcome was less than effective, the force of the impact forcing her to bounce away from the thief.

Erica looked up in time to see Jalel swing around, his clawed hand swiping wildly at her as she managed to dive to the side, rolling onto the road and finishing the move upon her hands and knees. She was still kneeling as Jalel turned to face her, he clasped his hands together, raising them high, before bringing them down heavily toward her head. In desperation Erica threw her hands up to shield the top of her head.

The blow would surely have caved the reporter's skull in had Anubis not awoken just in time to catch the demon's fists in his hands. The god took control of Erica's body, transforming into his bestial form as he rose to his feet, firmly clenching the thief's fists as he did so. Anubis savagely bit out at Jalel's face, taking a chew of demon flesh with him as he threw the monster backward off his feet. Anubis spat out the foul meat and saw that he had bitten off the thief's nose, and he then turned his attention to Osir. He had unfinished business with the thief and the sacred blade was the only way to defeat him.

But Osir wasn't on the ground. It was sticking out of Sam's chest. Had the thief stabbed Sam as he and Erica lay unconscious? Anubis grunted with anger, his comrade had fallen by the god's own hand and, as unintentional as his death had been, Anubis felt such guilt – he was not about to let Sam's death be in vain. Jalel had to be stopped. The god rushed over toward Sam's body, his hand reaching for Osir as he drew close to his fallen friend. Just as the blade was within his grasp, Anubis watched as Osir sank down into Sam's chest, disappearing below the flesh. 'No!' the god howled, incredulous. 'What sorcery is this?'

Such was the supernatural nature of Osir's disappearance, that Anubis immediately suspected the spirit of his brother Apep had somehow stolen the blade away from him.

Quickly, Anubis scanned the area for the tell-tale shimmer of Apep, but there was nothing, only the demon-thief, who was now rising from the bitumen, his face gushing blood from his missing nose. Jalel hissed loudly with pain and he stumbled about briefly before his vision focused and settled upon Anubis. Again, the demon charged and this time he was ready for any avoidance from him. As Anubis began to move to the side, the thief corrected his course and collided heavily with the god, sending him crashing to the road. The thief leaped on top of Anubis and proceeded to clamp his massive hands tight around Anubis's throat.

The crowd of onlookers erupted with screams, some directed at the demon, but most were cheers for Anubis – willing him to fight back, yet the god could not loosen the thief's grip, nor could he squirm free from under the demon.

'I can't breathe!' a panicked Erica screamed to Anubis, who was himself now struggling to draw breath, his strong muscular neck still resisting the increasing pressure of the demon's chokehold. *'I shall not give up, Erica, and I will get us out of this somehow.'* Somehow indeed, the god continued to thrash about, attempting to dislodge the thief, but with every burst of movement he grew weaker, his muscles and brain now straining for oxygen. Again, Erica spoke to the god, this time she had a strange sense of calmness about her, a sense of resignation, *'We're going to die. It's okay – we tried. At least we will see Sam again.'*

'No, Erica, I will not lose both of my friends this night.'

'Yes, yes, it's going to happen, you know what? It's okay. I don't want to live without my Sam, and I want to be wherever he is. I don't care if it's heaven or hell, I need him.'

'*Enough!*' the god growled to his host as he focused on Jalel's busted face. '*I shall not – I cannot lose this battle. I will not let the thief loose upon this world.*' With one final push of strength, Anubis threw his hands up, thrusting them up between the demon's arms and weakening the elbows enough to force the thief to fall forward. Anubis pushed his arms outward and managed to break the thief's chokehold, before throwing the monster off his body.

Air happily surged down into the god's lungs, but he was weakened and unable to sustain his bestial form any longer and as such, he succumbed to his lack of strength. Erica brought her consciousness forward and her feminine form followed. The reporter was still on her back as she slowly crawled away, her eyes fixed upon the thief, who was now back on his feet and walking toward her with murderous intent, his horrendous, now almost featureless, face flushed with rage.

Erica knew that neither herself, nor Anubis had the strength to stave off another of the demon's attacks. She desperately searched the crowd, hoping to elicit the assistance of the police, or anybody who would step forward to help, but to her dismay there was no help forthcoming. She had to try to get to her feet. Perhaps she could run, get some distance between her and Jalel to allow Anubis enough time to recover sufficiently to fight again.

Erica rolled onto her stomach and lurched to her feet. Yet, her legs would not hold her, and they buckled under her weight, just a few feet away from Sam's body. She decided that if she were about to die, she would die in the embrace of her love.

The reporter fell onto Sam's body, her eyes looking into his – which were still and lifeless. Tears rolled down her cheeks. Her Sam was gone. He had become her best friend, lover and totem of strength, and he had provided her with affection and humour. Now, as she looked through watery eyes, she felt safe, as if she were home, as if wherever he was, she wanted to join him. Erica lay her head down upon Sam's bloody chest, his t-shirt cold, wet and sticky – she didn't care, she was with him and soon they would be together again.

'Hey! Jalel!'

The voice sent a shock of adrenaline through Erica, for she knew that voice. She loved that voice. She raised her head, turning to look back in the direction from which it came.

Sam was standing a few metres behind the thief, who had turned to face him, the demon's maw aghast with surprise. Sam was not solid and he had no body. He was some type of spirit and he was radiant – glowing with brilliant violet-coloured energy.

'I have come for you, thief. I have come to end this!' Sam shouted at Jalel, his ethereal body standing on the road, as if he had a physical form. The power of Osir had given Sam substance – not physical solidity, but more of an energetic force. The crowd of frightened onlookers could also see him, in all his glowing glory. While the human soul gives off a pale blue glow when disembodied, indiscernible to the sight of all except those considered to be sensitive to such entities, Sam's glow was that of the gods, that of the divine and that of Osiris himself.

Anubis was also imbued with such a soul tint, and he instantly noticed as much. *'What … What is this?'* Anubis blubbered.

'Anubis, what are you talking about? It is Sam isn't it?' Erica asked frantically.

'I am unsure. I think so, but there is something wrong with him – something different.'

'Different how? I don't understand.'

'He should not glow that colour.'

'No shite! He should not glow at all. Is he ... is he dead? Is he a ghost?' Erica's question was laden with fear and sadness as she considered that Sam may not be staying with her.

'He is in spirit. His body is dead, yet he is not what you would consider a ghost. He is ... well to be honest, I am unsure what he is. His soul glows brightly of the gods, but the colour is wrong, it should be green. I only know of one thing that shines such a colour ... No, it is not possible.'

'So, my boyfriend is a god now?'

'No, I mean, he should not be. I mean ... I don't know what I mean!' Anubis replied, frustrated at not knowing the truth of the matter. *'Perhaps this is Apep's work. Perhaps he did steal Osir and maybe he is now disguised as Sam, but to what end? Revenge?'*

Anubis had no further time to dwell upon the situation, as Sam spoke again, 'Surrender your soul and those of your remaining victims to me, thief, or else I shall take them from you!'

Take them from me? Ha! You are nothing now! You are a ghost, a mere fart on the air! You cannot hurt me, boy!' Jalel snarled at Sam, *'I'm glad that you are here, boy! Now you may witness me stealing the lives of your friends. You may watch on helplessly as I tear them apart and devour their souls. You and your love will never be together, ever again!'*

'You know what, thief? You talk too much, and I'm glad that I took your tongue ... Now I will take the rest of you!' Sam replied telepathically as he shaped up to fight.

The thief did not have time to react as Sam came at him, his new god-speed catching the demon off guard. Sam delivered a front heel kick to the monster's chest and caught the demon's chin with a right hook. The blow was as real and dynamic as a physical attack, the strike dislodging his lower jaw from the socket, teeth spraying loose to the road.

Jalel stumbled backward, away from Sam, his eyes now wide with fright. The thief then discovered that he was unable to flee. Since the banishment of Apep's soul, the demon had lost the ability to phase shift away. The skill effect had been discharged the last time he had rendered himself invisible.

'You see ... I'm not a ghost. Now I am a god,' Sam spoke calmly as he walked toward the thief. *'I just don't have a body right now, but that is going to change soon,'* Sam said as he looked at the mangled meat of the demon body before him.

'Apep? Is it you?' Jalel asked tentatively, his fear rapidly welling up inside his chest.

'Apep? No, although he was of valuable assistance on my journey. I am Sam ... Well, I was Sam – now I have a new name – you may call me Osir.'

The revelation struck Anubis like a bolt of lightning. *'Osir? Of course!'* The explanation for the disappearing blade now had a resolution. The god realised that Sam must have somehow sought the assistance of Osiris, and the father god had, in his infinite wisdom, provided a powerful solution to the situation.

'Sam?' Erica called out to her love. 'What is happening?'

'Hey there, beautiful, I'll explain everything to you soon. First, I have to finish this,' Sam replied, before returning his attention to Jalel.

Osir could see inside the demon-form. He could see the soul of the thief's first victim and that of Jalel himself burning brightly there. Unfortunately, the soul of Kurt Banks was nowhere to be seen. His essence had been completely absorbed by the thief, and so Osir knew that once Jalel had been rendered from the flesh, the body would no longer be viable for sustaining life. *'It'd be a pity to waste such good flesh.'*

With a broad smile, Osir rushed at Jalel, his movement fast and fluid, and before the thief had time to react, the newly forged god was at his back. Osir drew his left hand down to his side, the same hand that he had not so long ago cut from his own body. He held the hand there as it was quickly charged with the life-taking force of the Osir blade, his hand flat, palm facing forward, and fingers formed together, pointing to the ground. The god pushed his hand up, toward the thief's back, the lethal palm penetrating effortlessly into the flesh. He grabbed the essence of the first and only remaining victim and pulled it swiftly out of the meat, a thick line of blood flung out with it, as the woman's soul was cast out of the demon. Osir lowered himself and struck up at the thief's head, grasping the soul of Jalel as it passed and exited through the front of the demon's face. The momentum of the strike carried the spirit of Sam up and forward, and he simply walked into the body of Kurt, like stepping into a sheer curtain, the flesh wrapping itself around Sam's soul.

With his ethereal hand still protruding from the head, and Jalel safely secured in his fist, the god Osir began to work the cells of the body, moulding the flesh and rearranging the skin and hair to take on a familiar form. Once again, the former mortal known as Sam stood in the middle of the street, his body once again living meat, his hand still outstretched, with the soul of the thief glowing through his fingers. Osir brought his clenched fist close to his lips, 'Oh, you're not going to escape this time, thief. I'm taking you to a very special place, an exquisitely terrifying place, a place where all your most intimate fears shall render you apart. Oh, the delicious agony that awaits you there.'

Erica was filled with joy and excitement at seeing her Sam made flesh again. She got to her feet and staggered over to him, and he turned in time to take her under his free arm, her head crashing heavily into his chest as she clamped her arms tight around him.

'Sam! Thank god you are okay. I thought I'd lost you,' Erica cried as she spoke, her Irish accent thick with relief and happiness.

'I wasn't about to leave you to fight the thief alone. Oh, you should have seen what I've seen, what I've been through. Well, that will have to wait for another time. I have to get this little bastard to hell,' Sam said with a smile, holding his fist up to Erica, the blue soul of Jalel shimmering between his fingers. He then turned his attention to his friend, 'Anubis, I need to take you with me. Your father wants you at his side, and there is much to discuss along the way.'

'Erica, I have to leave now, I must return home,' Anubis said softly to Erica.

Erica could sense Anubis's excitement at the opportunity to finally be free of his imprisonment. She could also sense his sorrow at having to leave his new-found friends. 'Is that a human emotion that I detect from you? Are you sad? I didn't think that gods could feel mortal feelings. Hey, don't feel sad, this is great – everything is going to be fine.'

'Of course, you are right that I do feel a little sad at having to go. Perhaps the gods should learn more from mortal souls. Maybe we need to feel a little more. I … I will miss you, Erica Murphy. Thank you for all that you have done. You are an amazing, brave young woman.'

'Well, thank you, Anubis, and for the record I shall miss you too.' With their goodbyes said, Erica nodded for Sam to take Anubis from her, presenting her lips to him and Sam gently brought his mouth to Erica's as she opened herself up.

Sensing his ride was here, Anubis withdrew his essence from Erica's being and Sam took the green glow of the Anubis soul into his mouth and breathed the old god in. 'You'll be much more comfortable riding up front with me,' the new god said to his predecessor.

'Thank you, Sam. I am so very grateful to you. I am ready to go home whenever you are,' Anubis said as he settled comfortably into his old host's body, like slipping into an old favourite jumper, warm, safe and familiar.

Sam turned to Erica, her battle-worn face gazing up at him, 'Erica, I better go take these two home.' He then looked into the crowd and spotted some paramedics who had gathered medical cases and were making their way through the crowd toward them.

'Okay, but you will come back?' Erica asked, with a slight look of concern.

'Yes, I will be back as soon as I can. There is much that has to be done back with Osiris, but don't worry. I'll be back before you know it. The paramedics are coming to help, and you should go with them to the hospital for a check-up. I'll meet you there,' the god said before he kissed her tenderly.

Erica was relieved to feel Sam's kiss and she knew for the first time that 'Osir' may be the new official title given to him, but he would always be her Sam, and she would address him accordingly. 'Okay, Sam, be back when you are ready. I will be waiting.'

Sam nodded before he turned his attention to the nervous crowd. 'People, hear me! I am Osir – I am Anubis reborn, the new god of the dead. I am here to help you, to guide humanity on behalf of our father god Osiris,' Sam spoke loudly as he addressed the onlookers, taking a few steps in their direction, before stopping several metres away. 'I will not harm you. I am here to teach you all about the ways of the soul. However, for those of you out there that like to commit harm against others …' With a shudder and several painful grunts, Sam shifted his body, taking on the canid form of his brother god, only this time it was not Anubis that was providing the blueprint to the cells, it was Sam. The result was a more streamlined version of Anubis, leaner and meaner in his appearance. His eyes glowed gold at first, before turning bright red. His body was muscular, yet slender at the same time, providing martial arts agility in place of the power-fuelled build of his former cast. Then, with sharp teeth bared, he calmly continued his speech to the awestruck crowd, the whole event being caught live on all manner of recording devices, 'I will come for you, for those evildoers out there. I will rip you apart and drag your soul to hell. There is a new god in town and humanity *will* get its act together.'

Osir turned to face the shocked police sergeant and addressed the man directly, 'Sergeant, kindly advise your superiors of my presence and warn them not to interfere in any matters pertaining to my divine purpose.' Then he returned to speak to all present, 'Gods exist, and I exist – as do you all. We are all on the continuing journey of the soul. I will leave you now, but I will return to live among you. There will be many lessons to learn, beginning with the first and most important lesson: be kind to each other and be kind to yourselves.'

Osir turned abruptly and murmured a spell under his breath. A small rip appeared in the air before the god – like a tear in a sheet of fabric – and placing his hands inside, he opened the air like a curtain and stepped through, disappearing from the view of mortal man. Once on the other side of the curtain, the fine fluorescent green tendrils of the stone arch doorway appeared once again. And as before, the mortal, formerly known as Sam, passed into the underworld.

Donovan Banks was a welcoming sight as Sam approached the Gate of Greeting, the god having transformed back to Sam-mode.

'Samuel, my boy! You made it!' Donovan said as he rushed to embrace the young god.

'Hello, Donovan, yes I did and there is much to tell you. All shall be revealed in time, but first, I have a few surprises for you.'

Sam placed his closed fist out in front of him and opened his hand. The soul of Jalel sprung free of Sam's hand, expanding rapidly like a released spring, taking on his original appearance before crashing hard to the maggot-covered ground. The frightened thief jerked his head about taking in the bizarre landscape about him, before staring wickedly at Sam and old man Donovan. After a moment, the thief discovered that he had a body and more importantly – he had his tongue back. He spoke, his voice trembling with rage, 'Damn you, boy! You have ruined me! And you – old man, I have devoured your son Kurt. He is demon shit now!'

Osir placed a reassuring hand upon Donovan's shoulder. 'It's okay, Donovan, the hell-spawn will extract Kurt from the thief.' Then turning, he spoke to Jalel, 'You have done horrible things, Jalel, and in turn, horrible things shall be done unto you. You have three choices here now. One: you can come with me directly to Durat and accept your internment there, or two: you could follow me and try your chances along the trials of the soul, or thirdly: you can go your own way, wandering eternity alone, trying to find a way out – a way which simply does not exist. The choice is yours.'

Jalel hissed loudly at Sam, 'You will not take me anywhere! I will find a way out of here and I shall have my revenge!' the thief shouted, before he sprung to his feet and sprinted away from Sam and the old man.

'Suit yourself, thief!' Sam called out after Jalel, then turning to Donovan, he continued, 'He'll be back, and he'll need my help. I could have simply destroyed him, you know, but who am I to interrupt the punishment of wicked souls – everyone deserves a chance at the trials.' Sam smiled as he spoke to Donovan, 'Oh, I have another surprise for you.'

Sam stepped away from Donovan and turned his face to the sky, opening his mouth wide. A green glow floated free from him and settled upon the floor, before taking the shape of Anubis.

'My lord!' Donovan exclaimed, dropping to his knees.

'Donovan Banks, my old friend and protector! Please arise from the maggots,' Anubis boomed as he stretched his limbs, happy to finally have his body to himself again. 'Oh, this is indeed a happy day. Finally, I can go home to my father once again.'

Anubis turned and embraced his former host, 'I know that your brethren name is Osir, but you will forever be Samuel Baker to me. Thank you for saving my life – thank you for everything.'

Sam returned Anubis's hug, 'You're very welcome, my friend. Now come, brother, we must guide Donovan along the trials and then we have an audience with our father Osiris.'

Anubis nodded happily and gestured for Donovan to follow him, with Sam bringing up the rear of the trio. Then, looking back over his shoulder Anubis smiled, 'Gentlemen, shall we?'

ABOUT THE AUTHOR

Scott R Lean was born in Mackay, Queensland, Australia in 1974. In addition to his writing, he is an artist and photographer.

Scott is married and father to three children. He enjoys travelling and has spent time with his extended family in Bolivia, exploring the ancient ruins of Puma Punku and Tiwanaku, along with Machu Picchu, Peru. He has also walked the Great Wall of China. Scott enjoys the arts and has appeared in several amateur musical productions, he enjoys singing and karaoke.

A natural-born storyteller, Scott has breathed life into his debut print novel - a story that has been over twenty years in the making.